AN
AMERICAN
DECADE

RICHARD ARONOWITZ

LONDON BOROUGH OF WANDSWORTH	
9030 00005 5258 2	
Askews & Holts	08-May-2017
AF	£7.99
	WW17000794

Published by Accent Press Ltd 2017

Paperback ISBN: 9781786150011
    eBook ISBN: 9781786150028
Printed in Great Britain by Clays Ltd, St Ives plc

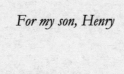

For my son, Henry

Who rides so late through the night so wild?
It is a father with his child.

Johann Wolfgang von Goethe,
Der Erlkönig 1782

PART I:
ARRIVAL

CHAPTER ONE

Wuppertal-Elberfeld, western Germany, October 1929

His new wife lay dying in her childhood bed. She was thirty years old and they had been married for only six months. Her family had brought Ida home from the hospital so that she could spend her final hours with them. Christoph sat by her side clutching her hand tightly, refusing to turn his gaze away from her still face which glistened with the lightest sheen of sweat. She was unconscious and had not spoken or opened her eyes in more than twenty-four hours. Her breathing was shallow and the rise and fall of her chest was barely perceptible now. The doctor, out in the hall with Ida's ashen-faced mother Perla, had told them that it would not be long. Her father, already an old man, was in the back of his tailoring shop, too inconsolable to speak.

Christoph was blaming himself; he was cursing himself bitterly, sitting there in silence, her hand clenched in his, for not having made her visit the doctor sooner. She had been complaining of pain in her abdomen for some days before she finally went to see her doctor across town. If only he had listened to her more carefully: if only he had told her in no uncertain terms to go to the surgery straight away, had taken her there himself, things might have been different. He was losing her and he could not bear it. He was pale with guilt and fear.

Ida Bernstein had been a beautiful bride. They had married in Wuppertal's main synagogue in March, although Christoph was not Jewish. He had had some religious instruction from the rabbi on Sunday afternoons and by the time of the wedding he was familiar enough with the ritual to know what he should say and do at each part of the ceremony. In truth, her brothers and sisters were almost completely assimilated and they thought of themselves as more German than Jewish, only going to synagogue with their parents on high and holy days at most. Ida had known little about the wedding ceremony herself.

Not one prone to unalloyed joy, Christoph had nevertheless been very happy that long spring day. His parents had been there, of course, and stood out in their expensive clothes. His younger sister, her husband and their little boy had also been in the congregation, shifting uncomfortably in their hard seats because of the unfamiliarity of the setting, the service and the mournful singing of the cantor. His parents had grown fond of Ida and were pleased with Christoph's choice of bride, despite the young couple's differences of religion and background. His parents both came from rather grand old families in the town.

Christoph had known the Bernsteins since childhood and knew Ida best of all. There were five Bernstein children – Ida was the oldest and closest in age to him. Abraham was the next eldest; then there were another two daughters, Miriam and Hedwig. The youngest boy, Isy, was just under twenty. The Bernsteins all had dark-brown hair and expressive eyebrows, and grew into young adults blessed with strong features and good looks. They were a close-knit and loving family and had

2

warmly welcomed Christoph.

It did not seem to interest them in the slightest that he had been raised in the Lutheran church. Although their parents had been religious Jews back in Poland, when they had come to Germany in 1910 all of that had fallen away. Isy had even been sent to the Protestant school closest to their house, although he did not have to attend the religion lessons there, and this younger generation of the Bernsteins were Germans beyond anything else. They had left school as soon as they could to work as apprentice tailors and seamstresses to help support the family.

The wedding party was held at the old-fashioned Hofgarten hotel in the upper part of the town, paid for by the groom's parents. There was no honeymoon as Christoph had a series of singing commitments in the south-west of the country straight after the wedding. When Christoph returned from his short singing tour, he and Ida settled peacefully into their new life together in his small apartment on Lothringerstrasse and they were happy for those brief summer months. As they had known each other for almost all of their lives, they understood each other's likes and dislikes. One knew almost instinctively what pleased or displeased the other.

They were still young and their lives shimmered with dreams and possibilities for their future. They had so much to experience together, so much to look forward to. They had only recently begun trying for a family when Ida became ill and Christoph was left a widower at just thirty.

CHAPTER TWO

October 1930

The great hulk of the ship juddered and vibrated with a low rumble like thunder as it came into port. Christoph had been on board the *Albert Ballin* for ten days as it sailed down from Hamburg to Cherbourg, then onwards to Southampton and New York, and he had spoken to no one. Sometimes, his fellow passengers had heard him singing in his cabin: *Lieder* by Schubert, perhaps, or other songs from the classical repertoire that they did not recognise. To those with an appreciation of music, he had a wonderful tenor voice, even through upholstered wooden walls. To the few others who noticed this ghost of a man, he had a closed-off, faraway look, with his hair slicked straight back from his forehead, as if he were framed in a promotional photograph of a film star they did not recognise.

The ship was docking in an outer quay. Its immense iron hull seemed to Christoph to be about to break apart as it slowed, groaning and echoing with guttural booms and creaks, its formidable weight working against itself. He could make out only dim shapes on the quayside through the maritime fog. He clutched his papers in his hand and could not begin to know what to expect. He was only thirty and had left everyone he loved behind in the Ruhr.

He knew no one in Manhattan except his childhood

friend, the composer Matthias Walter who had grown up in a villa on the same road in Wuppertal and had moved to New York five years earlier. He had not been able to establish, due to the carelessness of a cable operator on board ship, whether Matthias would be at the pier to meet him. He was not sure that he would recognise Matthias in the crowd after all this time. Christoph had attended English language classes at night-school in Wuppertal for almost nine months before he left – the first time that he had tried to master the language since finishing with it in disgust at fourteen at the gymnasium – but he was on unsteady ground away from his mother tongue and fatherland. He was not at all sure that the Americans spoke an English that he would readily recognise.

Amongst his papers, slightly dampened by the sea-salt spray of the passage, was the address that he would call home, written in Christoph's neat copperplate hand in blue ink: *233 East 89th Street, New York, New York*, a single room above Matthias's apartment. The address sounded almost mathematical, like some sort of equation; a world away from his family home on the Weinbergstrasse, where the name of the road told you where it went and what it was. Matthias had used the room for storage, he had written to Christoph, but would clear it out and furnish it with a bed in time for his arrival. Christoph knew that East Eighty-Ninth Street was on the Upper East Side, but had no idea what life was like there. He had come to New York to make something of his life, and to sing.

The mist had lifted by the time the ship came in to the pier. The ship's crew announced in German, and then in heavily accented English, that the passengers must disembark in an orderly fashion, one deck at a time. They started at the top, with the upper classes. It was almost one and a half hours before Christoph was stepping off the wide gangplank onto the quayside to join the long line of passengers waiting for their papers to be inspected by the Immigration Service officials. He took his final step off the ship that had been his home for almost two weeks and touched American soil for the very first time. He would have to find his shore legs again. At the end of the snaking line, the huddled would-be immigrants were either given permission to land or were denied entry and immediately sent back on board to wait for the boat's return crossing. An official, whose elastic accent surprised him, checked his visa and papers before stamping two identical forms with an unintelligible mutter and a theatrical flourish of his hand. Christoph had been granted entry to the United States without really knowing what was going on and clutched his copy of the form tightly in his hand.

It was damp and cold and the wet air crept through his winter clothing. He could see the Statue of Liberty a long way off across the water, floating in the mist that still lingered out to sea as mysteriously as an apparition in a dream.

Where was Matthias? There were still so many people standing around, alone or in groups on the pier, even though it had been almost two hours since the ship had come in. Christoph worried that it would be impossible to spot him. A light drizzle was falling now and he lifted the collar of his woollen overcoat to cover the back of his neck and brought the brim of his hat down lower on his forehead. There was a sudden hand on his shoulder. Christoph almost jumped out of his skin.

'Are you lost?' a man's voice said, then laughed a full-throated laugh. Christoph span round and there was Matthias, looking undoubtedly a little older and, he could not think of another word, somehow more *American*.

'*Du bist gekommen!*' Christoph said.

'*Aber klar*,' Matthias replied matter-of-factly. 'But now we must speak English, *mein Lieber*. You must practise your new language.'

'Yes,' Christoph replied. That was his first English word in this new land. 'Yes, I must practise,' he said.

'It's a long walk to the six-line train and cabs are too damn expensive. We'd better start and get you to East Eighty-Ninth. You must be tired.'

It was just after noon and the sun was still hiding behind cloud. Christoph's trunk was to follow by shipping agent, and all he had was one large leather valise that they took it in turns to carry through the streets of lower Manhattan towards the subway.

The buildings were all low-rise here. Christoph had thought that they would be skyscrapers.

'Where are the high buildings?' he asked.

'They're farther up the island; Midtown mostly. Here they're more like the houses and streets back home, but everything is straighter, more *rechtlinig*: built on a grid pattern.'

They walked east and then north, leaving the waterfront and the bustle of the docks behind them, all the while Christoph's eyes taking in the newness of his environment.

The valise was getting heavy by the time they reached the subway station near City Hall that served the number six line. Christoph had rarely disappeared underground before to take a train. He noticed the echoes and the musty air;

how every person waiting on the platform stood as if alone in the world. The train's wheels screeched as it came into the platform and electric sparks lit up the dark underside of the train for the briefest of moments.

Christoph could not believe he was actually in New York City, underground. None of it had sunk in yet. Seeing Matthias again was like seeing a ghost from a past life: they had not seen each other in at least half a decade, and even in Germany in their early twenties they had not been that close. Christoph had left Wuppertal to study at the conservatoire in Berlin and Matthias had gone to Munich to study composition at the academy there. They had only met up now and then for a drink or for a walk when they both found themselves back at their parents' homes at the same time.

The train seemed to stop and start northwards for an eternity. Christoph clamped the worn valise tightly between his knees, with Matthias seated to his left and a stranger to his right. Everyone was still wearing their hats or caps, even underground. The exact meaning of the word 'Depression' plastered on the front pages of newspapers that many passengers were reading at first eluded Christoph, although he soon guessed that it concerned the economy, the land and not its inhabitants' mental states as such. He knew before he left Wuppertal that he was an emigrant from one collapsed economy to another. He had set foot on American soil one year to the month since the Wall Street crash. One year to the month since Ida had died. Ida, his dearest dark-eyed Ida, whose memory he had betrayed, seeking comfort and solace with her younger sister Miriam when Ida had not been long in the ground. Miriam, with her fine seamstress's fingers and her beautiful nut-brown hair.

Miriam, with her gentle soul and her caressing touch. Ida, her dark eyes melting into nothingness, cold in the ground beneath the cypresses.

The shattering rattle and echo of the train's wheels formed a pulsing crescendo of noise in his head, yet thoughts of Ida would not be drowned out by any amount of sound. Why had he not realised that she was so seriously ill? He had turned to Miriam in his heartbreak for human warmth, for succour, for some flesh to drown his sorrow in, for his very survival. But all of that, he tried telling himself, was already so far away and so long ago.

Matthias was sitting beside him in silence, distractedly drumming out some arrangement with his fingertips on the seat between his legs.

'Is Depression the same as our *Weltwirtschaftskrise*?' Christoph asked him, forcing himself out of his dark thoughts.

'Yes,' Matthias answered. 'It's like our *deprimierend*. The Americans say 'depressing', and it's only going to get worse. I hope at least the Nazi Party will turn things round back home, if they can ever get into power. They were making a lot of noise and saying the right kinds of things when I was a student in Munich. They still seem to me to be the one party that could sort out the terrible mess in Germany.'

'But I really don't like what they stand for,' Christoph replied. 'They're far too, um, *aggressive* for me. I think it's because I don't come from a good worker family.'

'And I do?' Matthias asked, laughing. 'My father, the eminent professor, would take quite some issue with that idea. Anyway, let's not talk politics quite so soon.'

'I hope that people still want to hear singing here, despite the Depression,' Christoph said, concentrating as hard as he could on the language.

'How's the voice? As good as it always was?'

'I think the air of the sea made it more, ah, more *kräftig*.'

'More *powerful*,' Matthias guided him. 'It will need its full power to be heard over here.'

Christoph could not make out what the driver was saying over the loudspeaker system every time the train slowed into another of the curious subterranean worlds that were the subway stations, hot and half-lit, peopled by dark shapes like the anterooms to hell.

'He's just announcing the station names,' Matthias explained.

'How far are we going?'

'A couple more stops. Where we live, in Yorkville, is not far from Eighty-Sixth Street station.'

'I'm looking forward to arriving finally.'

'I was terribly sorry to hear about Ida. That must have been a really hard blow for you and the Bernsteins,' Matthias said over the din.

'It was an unbearable time: I just had to get away from there, Matthias, after losing her. I couldn't keep on living there with all those memories.'

'Anyone would understand,' Matthias replied. 'Did they give Ida her people's kind of burial?'

'Yes, she was buried in the Jewish cemetery up on the Weinberg and then there was the sitting of Shiva, when one remembers and prays for the deceased. How's Valentina?' Christoph asked tentatively, trying to change the subject. Matthias had written to him some months earlier that his wife's health was not good, and his tone had been serious and concerned.

'She's much better, thank God. It was what they call

11

over here "women's troubles"; she lost a baby early in her pregnancy,' was all that Matthias would say on the matter. 'You'll see Valentina yourself later.'

'I'm very sorry about the baby,' Christoph said. He felt that his accent was as thick as the fog that had enveloped the shore, and was amazed at how fluent Matthias seemed to be in his adopted tongue.

'I'm sure my loss was in no way as hard as yours, although Valentina took it very badly,' Matthias replied. 'To lose your wife so soon like that must have been unbearable. I didn't know what to say when I wrote back to you. I'm sorry if I didn't put it right.'

'It's been very hard for everyone, her family most of all. I just had to get away from Germany. I had to get away.'

'I feel bad that I've never written to the Bernsteins with my condolences.'

'You're a long way away from all of that over here, Matthias. I'm sure they knew they were in your thoughts. By the way, how do you say *stolpern* in English?' Christoph asked; he was keen to shift the conversation away from painful memories of home to the here-and-now.

'It's like "stumble" or "stutter" or something like that. Why do you ask?'

'Because I feel that my English is stumbling or stuttering,' Christoph said with a slightly forced laugh, trying to lighten the mood. 'Did you attend evening classes when you came here?'

'Can't you tell?' Matthias said with a warm smile. 'I have even begun writing some *libretti* in English. Let's show the Americans what we Germans can do!'

Christoph had only left his homeland twice before: once on

a tour of the beautiful churches of Holland with his communion class at the age of fourteen; the second time in 1916, when he turned seventeen and was sent to the Western Front. The subway train screeched and sparks exploded in the darkness of the tunnel. He preferred not to think of the Front. The deep shrapnel scar high up in his right thigh, itself shaped like a shell-burst or the clenched fist of a child, throbbed every time his thoughts strayed into those deep recesses of his mind where he had buried these painful memories. His voice refused to sing when these thoughts surfaced, threatening to envelop and paralyse him with the fear he had struggled to cast aside.

He was now the farthest he had ever been from home and he felt a little afraid.

CHAPTER THREE

The room contained nothing more than a single bed and a plain bedside table with a lamp sitting on it. Matthias warned him that the electricity supply to the building could sometimes be unreliable. Christoph left his clothes in the valise as he had nowhere else to put them. He was grateful to Matthias that he was only charging him a couple of dollars a week in rent. He had to use the block's communal lavatory and sink on the floor below. Matthias and Valentina had a tin bath leaning upright in one corner of their cramped apartment, which Matthias told Christoph they would fill for him when he wished to bathe.

The building was five storeys tall, built in a reddish-brown brick. Christoph judged that it could not be more than thirty years old. The narrow pavement outside the front door gave onto a quiet street that sloped very gently up to the avenues that cut across it, where all the omnibuses, taxis, horse-drawn delivery wagons, trucks and private cars he had seen while walking with Matthias across the Upper East Side seemed to converge and blast their horns at one another. The road itself was quiet and his room, like Matthias's apartment below it, was at the back of the building.

Christoph walked down the half-flight of stairs to the apartment and knocked gently. It was just after four o'clock in the evening and the light was fading fast outside. Earlier,

15

he had only stood in the apartment's kitchen for a few minutes to drink a glass of water after their long journey from the docks, while Matthias searched for the key to his locked room. Valentina was out buying food for supper somewhere nearby. Again, he had not seen her for at least half a decade. He and Valentina had been such close friends when they were children: she lived a little further away down the Weinberg from him than Matthias, but they had both gone to kindergarten together. Now she opened the door, and he was surprised by how well she looked. He had forgotten how beautiful she was: he had always had something of a soft spot for her. She and Matthias had been a couple since they were in their late teens.

'And how's our darling *Nachtigall*?' Valentina asked and smiled warmly at him, but there was a dark sadness in her eyes. She used to call him by this nickname, 'the nightingale', when he had first begun to show a talent for singing. As he kissed her once on each cheek, she added: 'I was so very sorry to hear your news last year, it was such a shock that I felt quite numb after reading your letter.'

Christoph nodded, not knowing how else to respond.

'You must be tired after your journey.'

'A little,' he replied. 'But I'm happy to be here.'

'How many years has it been?' she asked. Her accent was still quite heavy.

'At least five or six. I was in Berlin when you left for America.'

They fed him supper at the kitchen table: it was the first and last time that he sat down to a meal with them in their apartment. They had cooked cuts of beef that he did not recognise. They were delicious: large and fried so rare that the juices ran red. Matthias must be finding an income even in this bad situation.

'How's the family?' Matthias asked.

'Older,' Christoph replied. He had never been much of a conversationalist. He was more eloquent singing other people's words, other people's songs.

'And how are the Bernsteins coping since their loss of Ida?' Valentina asked. They had all known the Bernstein boys and girls since they were children, but Valentina and Matthias knew nothing about the cloud of guilt above Christoph: his affair with Miriam that began half a year before he left Germany and only months after Ida had died.

'They have not been able to get over dear Ida's death. She is much missed by everyone,' he said

'That's easy to understand,' Valentina said quietly. 'She was a lovely girl, as I remember her.'

'Will you sing for your supper?' Matthias asked, suddenly changing the subject, and seemed to mean what he was saying. Christoph wondered whether all of this emotional talk was making Matthias uncomfortable: he had always had rather a cool, dispassionate intellect.

'But my voice is cold. Let me have a glass of hot water and we will see what it can do.'

Once the pan had boiled and Valentina had poured the water into an earthenware mug, Christoph sipped slowly, blowing on it every now and then, and began after some minutes to hum to himself very quietly, going up and down the scales. His pitching was perfect and he held each note just long enough to let his vocal cords warm and stretch themselves to accommodate it, before a slight tightening of the throat on the way up the scale or a slight opening on the way down took him to the next note.

Christoph got up from his chair and walked to the

window that looked out onto the apartment building behind theirs. Lights had come on in that dark block, signs of lives played out not two hundred feet from them; lives no less meaningful or complex than their own. Christoph turned to face his hosts, still seated at the small table in their cramped kitchen, and a Liszt song suddenly came out of his mouth, bringing colour and warmth to the room on this cold evening. Matthias clearly recognised it at once and Valentina seemed soon to remember where she had last heard it. It was the song about the Lorelei, the siren of the rocks that lures sailors to their doom.

> *Ich weiß nicht, was soll es bedeuten,*
> *Daß ich so traurig bin,*
> *Ein Märchen aus uralten Zeiten*
> *Das kommt mir nicht aus dem Sinn …*

The beauty and subtle power of his voice was so out of place in that plain kitchen that Valentina could not look at him, but played her fingers around the rim of the empty glass on the table in front of her. Matthias, who had not heard Christoph sing for many years, could not understand why he had not achieved success as a singer back home. Matthias had always loved the story of the seductive Lorelei because it was such a powerful German myth; his country needed magical myths in these dark times. As a composer himself, he understood just how masterful Liszt's delicate conjuring trick of a composition was.

Christoph's voice rose and fell, telling the story of the siren and the sailors who met their fate on her cruel shores, fates likened by the poet to his failed love-affairs, and then silence fell on the apartment again. Valentina and Matthias

18

clapped enthusiastically and Matthias raised his water glass to Christoph. It had been too long since he had last had an audience for his singing. The months since his last public performance felt like a lifetime.

'You come with high praise indeed from Herr Walter,' Leo König said.

'That is kind of you to say, Mr König.'

Christoph had walked the thirty or so blocks down to East Fifty-Fifth Street to meet Matthias's agent. It had taken him more than an hour and his legs, unused to walking such long distances after the days on the ship, were throbbing with tiredness. König had not offered him a seat. He wanted Christoph to stand so that he could see what shape he made as a performer. He wanted Christoph to sing.

'When did you last perform in public?' König asked.

'Three or four months ago: it was a small concert with perhaps fifty persons in the town hall at Düsseldorf.' He thought back to his impromptu performance in the kitchen of Matthias's apartment a few nights earlier, and smiled.

'Something amusing you, Mr Rittersmann?' König asked, shifting his compact, pugnacious frame impatiently in the expansive leather armchair that made him look even smaller in stature.

'I was just thinking that I still cannot believe I am here, in New York. I was looking at all the high buildings when I walked from Herr Walter's apartment, where I'm staying. It all seems so impossible.'

'It's quite a city we've got here, I'll give you that,' König replied.

'Berlin is so much smaller, and Wuppertal where I come from is like a village when you compare.'

'I was born in Berlin,' König said. 'I came here with my parents in 1890 when I was ten. The Big Apple wasn't like this back then, I can tell you.'

'You are *German*?' Christoph asked, astonished. He had detected no trace of an accent.

'I *was* German. We all become something else once we're here,' König replied. 'You'll see. It'll happen to you as well. Herr Walter is becoming as American as apple pie, although he still seems to hanker after our Vaterland a little. I've always had the impression that it was his wife who wanted to come over here more than he did. Anyway, what'll you sing?' he added.

'Mostly what I sing are *Lieder*, light opera and *chansons*: so not too much *Sturm und Drang*, unless we're speaking about Schubert and Liszt.'

'Let me hear something,' König said abruptly.

Christoph did not much like his manner, although to look at him, chubby and short and equipped with round glasses that made his eyes seem huge, he gave the impression of a perfectly benign, myopic mole.

König had three or four tenors on his books, but none of Christoph's calibre. Christoph sang a Schubert *Lied*, 'The Winter's Journey', full of sadness and longing and the wintry isolation of the human heart. His voice made sounds and shapes and formed tones that only very few could create. He could hit a note like the best archers can hit a bull's-eye: spot-on, the arrow of his voice held there at the dead centre of the note, quivering with a controlled vibrato. König's tone had softened when the song was over.

'That's quite an instrument you've got there,' he said. '*Kompliment.*'

'*Danke,*' Christoph replied. 'I have worked hard on it.'

He took a sip of water from the glass that König had given him and did not know what to do but simply stand there.

'Here's what we'll do,' König said. 'I'll speak to some of the impresarios I do regular business with, and we'll see if I can get you some early slots in the music halls and cabarets. I take twenty per cent of whatever you earn. It's not exactly Carnegie Hall, but it's a start and it's where most lighter singers begin in this town. You haven't got the build for opera. Do you sing anything in English?'

'I can learn,' Christoph replied. 'What do people here want to listen to?'

'I'm sure Herr Walter can help you with an English repertoire. He has his ear to the ground.'

'The ground?'

'You know, what's new; what people *want* to hear singers sing,' König explained.

Leaving König's office, Christoph felt hope for the first time in months: hope for his singing career, which had inexplicably faltered in Germany, and hope that he would finally make something of his life. Despite König's dismissive manner, Christoph knew that he had recognised an ability in him that could not be learned. His was an innate gift.

Immense steel skeletons reached towards the heavens over Midtown. They punctuated the skyline and emitted a symphony of noise: the shearing shriek of girders being cut by acetylene torches; the timpani of bolts being rammed into place by hydraulic guns; the low thunder of earth-movers and jack-hammers. Christoph walked as if in a dream; the city loomed above and to either side of him – impossible, vertiginous and immense. Matthias had told him the Chrysler Building had only recently been completed and he could see it soaring above the lower blocks: the tallest building in the world. He looked up, pulling his coat tightly around himself to keep out the icy wind. He had heard that the Empire State Building was half built and would eventually dwarf the Chrysler. It seemed to him that the city was gripped by a mania for height. It seemed as if the Americans were trying to build themselves up and out of the Depression.

Money was constantly on Christoph's mind. His family were not poor, and his father had given him a thousand dollars before he left Wuppertal, as well as paying for his passage on board the *Albert Ballin*, but he had made it clear that his son should make his own way from then on. Christoph calculated that he could survive for about one-and-a-half years on the money his father had given him before it ran out; two years at the most if he really tightened his belt. He needed König to come through with some regular singing jobs. He wondered if anyone in Manhattan was in the mood for singing lessons and what the going rate per hour might be.

That night Christoph slept fitfully. The room was ice-cold and the small coal-burning stove in the corner had burnt itself out shortly after one. The bedclothes that Matthias and Valentina had given him were not sufficient to keep his body warm; he would have to buy a thick counterpane to help him sleep through the winter without freezing.

He lay there without knowing whether he was asleep or awake. At one point he thought he was fast asleep, his eyes tightly shut against the dark, at another he was sure that he had been lying under the sheets sleeplessly, only to wake with a start from the terrifying recurring dream in which mortar shells and rifle rounds screamed and whined overhead, him cowering as low as his body would allow in the dug-out. He was drenched in sweat, despite the coldness of the room.

He had not slept well since the Front. *The Front*: he had no idea how he had survived it. He had kept his head down, his nose clean, tried to be a good toy soldier. He was barely a man when he was called up; he had never even had sex. He sang to keep his comrades' spirits up when the machine-gun rounds whistled past and the shells exploded overhead. His voice had been untrained then, but brought a tear to many a fellow soldier's eye. It was the constant state of fear, like shit-scared prey, that made them so prone to emotion.

When they had to go over the top of the trenches he had run like a blind fury, his legs sinking into the clinging mud. His bunk-mate Hans, who had been running close beside him, had fallen dead on top of him. The searing metal from an exploding shell had taken one side of his head off and a small fragment of the shrapnel had hit Christoph in the groin, embedding itself deep in his flesh. As he was being stretchered away, having been pulled screaming from beneath his friend, he turned to see Hans lying there with the eye in the good half of his face open to the beautiful evening sky, before he passed out from the pain.

The shard of shrapnel had lodged very near an artery and the surgeon in the field hospital had to remove it with great care. The scar that the wound left was shaped like a large starburst inside his left thigh and Christoph was barely able to walk for two months. He was discharged from the army and went back home to the Weinberg to convalesce. He was only seventeen and cried in his mother's arms when he got home. He never spoke to her about what he had seen.

He put his uniform at the back of the wardrobe and did not look at it again. The local girls smiled at him and giggled coyly amongst themselves when they saw him, as if he was some kind of returning hero, but he was sure that they would not look at him so amorously if they saw his battle scar.

He did not have a girlfriend until he was twenty and studying at the conservatoire. Her name was Frieda and she was a barmaid at the local inn where he went for a drink with his singing friends. She had a little room up under the eaves and looked at his scar with gentle curiosity rather than distaste. She was five years older than him and taught him what sex was. She was a good teacher and, when he had left the conservatoire and they had long since gone their separate ways, he always remembered her fondly. None of the women he had ever been with had reacted in horror to the scar, despite his fears and his own disgust at the sight of it. It had faded to a shiny, pale pink over the years and dear Ida had called it his 'lucky star'.

He had felt terrible guilt – Hans had died and he had lived – but never talked about it to anyone, and over the years the guilt had faded away to be replaced by a strong revulsion towards violence and authority.

CHAPTER FOUR

If he was ever going to make anything happen with his singing career in New York, Christoph realised that he would have to make a major leap: he would have to go from being a small fish in the stagnant backwaters of west and south-west Germany to becoming a bigger fish in the glittering currents of New York's singing scene. But so far he had had no luck at all at the few auditions that he had taken, trudging for miles around Manhattan looking for out-of-the-way venues that advertised open auditions in *Variety* magazine.

The four or five auditions had been uniformly oversubscribed. Over fifty men and women, from opera singers to jazz vocalists, would turn up at each venue, to compete for just one slot, once or twice a week. Christoph knew that he could not do it alone: he needed the support of an industry insider, someone to give him advice and encouragement – and not least, contacts – as he tried to establish himself as a singer in New York. His confidence had been shot by the lack of opportunities, hence success, back home. Christoph knew, without a doubt, that he was talented, he just needed the opportunity to be *heard*. For the right ears to be listening for more than a minute or two's audition on a cramped stage, while thirty other people queued, coughing and shuffling, in the wings.

Weeks had passed since Christoph had seen Leo König

and he had still received no word that the man had got him any auditions or found him any work. As the winter tightened its grip ever more firmly on New York, Christoph spent his days wandering around the Upper East Side and across Central Park to the West Side. Occasionally he would find himself further still, in Mid- to Downtown Manhattan, getting to know the city and looking for singing work: for hotels that might need a lobby singer, for openings to offer private singing tuition, for *anything* singing-related that might earn him some money. By late November, in the early mornings the trees and grass of Central Park were covered in hoarfrost, which did not disappear until almost midday. The sun began to set not many hours afterwards, and the cycle would begin again.

Christoph's trunk had been delivered by the shipping agent and with it came the first pangs of homesickness. He sat at the table he had bought for his bedroom with the trunk open beside him and wrote a long letter to his parents. He had only sent them a short note when he had first arrived in America, to let them know that he was safe and well. He now wrote about his first few weeks in New York, and a little about Matthias and Valentina, who they would really only remember as children. He wrote another letter to his sister, Rosa, and his little nephew, and both of these messages home served only to intensify his feelings of homesickness and loneliness. In truth, he saw Matthias and Valentina less often than he had hoped and had taken to eating his suppers in a diner on First Avenue. Sitting at a window seat he watched the dark stream of workers and businessmen make their way home from the office buildings and shops of the Upper East Side. Only a few millimetres of glass separated him from the pedestrians going between their lives of work and home, but he felt like an observer looking in on their lives from an unbridgeable distance. He missed his parents, his sister and her little son more than he had imagined he would. He had thought that the newness of New York would distract him from old memories. Yet there remained a heavy, dragging sadness whenever he thought of Ida. He was not sure what to feel when he thought of Miriam with her gentle, fine hands and her soulful gaze. He tried not to think of her too often. Thinking of her and what they had done together threatened his pure, untarnished memories of Ida.

Matthias had changed since Christoph had known him in Munich. He had always been prone to voicing strong opinions, with little regard for his listener, and tended to dominate conversations, particularly on the subject of politics. But now he was dogmatic and much less nuanced in his views. He would enter Christoph's room un-announced a few times a week, or he would invite Christoph downstairs for a cup of coffee with Valentina. Sometimes, when the weather was good, he would invite Christoph out for a walk over towards the river or the park. Always there was an ardent tone to his voice and a dogmatic conviction in his own beliefs when they discussed the economic and political situation back home.

Matthias believed that what Germany needed was a strong leader, someone who could shape a new destiny for the country, who could give it back its pride. He said that leaving Germany, his distance from it, had made it easier for him to see what was needed there.

'Then perhaps we should go back home and you can

27

offer your services in Berlin! What are we still doing here?' Valentina said with a forced laugh one day, obviously tired of this familiar subject.

'Vally, this is no laughing matter. Look at what we were left with at the end of the war and how hard things have been for us since then. Our country needs to reconnect with its fighting spirit, its self-belief. We came here to make a better life for ourselves but I've never once abandoned my homeland or my love for it. New York isn't home, it's just where we live now. We'll go back to Germany when the time is right.'

'Do I have any say at all in the matter?' Valentina asked. Matthias did not answer her this time.

Unlike Matthias, and despite his loneliness, Christoph had no desire to go back home. He wanted to be in a place that held no memories for him, where his past cast no shadows, and the anonymity of New York City suited him perfectly.

At Christmas, Matthias took Valentina away for a short holiday in upstate New York, and Christoph found himself alone in his little room as the last days of 1930 came to an icy end. He stoked the stove and tried to concentrate on the German novels that Matthias had given to him as a Christmas present. Miraculously, the little diner nearby stayed open and Christoph had his first Christmas Eve supper in America there. Matthias had brought him some post before he left for his holiday. The small bundle included a Christmas letter from his parents, which must have crossed with his own as they made no mention of having received his: they seemed to be getting on with their lives as fully and actively as they had before his departure.

28

To his surprise, there was also a letter from Miriam. He opened it like a gift from his past on Christmas Day morning.

C. Rittersmann
233 East 89th Street
New York, New York

10th December 1930

Dearest Christoph,

    Have you reached America safely? For all that you have written you could be at the bottom of the ocean. I have some news that you will understand if you look back: new life grows inside me day by day. I can feel the baby quickening now as I write; it has a strong will. And you are gone.
    I am waiting for your letter; I have been waiting for your letter for three months. You will be a father by the spring and what will become your little family should be with you there.
    I hope that this has reached you, as I know no one in New York who can find you and tell me that you are all right and that you are waiting for me. I hope that you are not too cold. I have read that New York has very icy winters.

    Yours, as ever,
    Miriam

Christoph sat on the end of his bed nearest the stove and read and reread the letter. His hands were shaking slightly and he could feel a flush rising in his neck and cheeks. He had not seen Miriam since early October, a week or two before he set sail, and had slept with her a last time a month or so before that. She had never once mentioned noticing any change in herself over the summer or in the early autumn. He thought of her dark, shoulder-length hair, her soft lips and fine figure and would have given anything to have her in bed beside him.

Had he guessed that something had altered in her when they last saw each other? He would not allow himself to believe so. In truth, Miriam was the more beautiful of the two sisters, but after Ida's death he had turned to her for comfort, not love. He knew that she wanted more from him, but he had not been ready to give her so much that it might betray Ida's memory, or prevent him from escaping his past in Wuppertal. Miriam was younger than Christoph but had told him more than once that she wanted to start a family before too long. He should have been more careful. He tried to forget the promises that he had made to her when they said their goodbyes at the quayside in Hamburg.

He was going to be a father? He did not feel at all ready; he still felt like a child himself. He could not believe what he had just read, and went over Miriam's words, through each letter of her finely formed hand, as if the rereading would alter what she had written. It was a long time before he felt strong enough to get up from the bed. He walked down the flight of stone steps to the lavatory and closed the door behind him, shooting the bolt firmly into place. He knelt down before the toilet bowl and vomited over and over again, until there was nothing left to come out.

It snowed all of New Year's Eve and into New Year's Day. The construction sites were stilled for the holiday and soon covered in a purifying, uniform blanket of white. The roads and sidewalks of Manhattan became treacherous underfoot, where the snow settled and turned to ice overnight. Christoph took the sturdy walking-boots from his trunk and wandered through the city, singing quietly to himself. German folk legend, the collective memory of a race and a nation, formed the accompanying theme to his fugue-like tours of the city. He was a somnambulist in song.

It was not easy to get lost, as long as you knew where you were going; that is, you had a street address. It was a city of simple logic. If you could sight read a musical score, you could navigate Manhattan with your eyes only half open, leaving your mind free to turn inwards on itself, to thoughts of home, of those that you had left behind, of dear Ida, and of Miriam, and the child she was carrying. How could he not have known? In his darkest moments in the first hours and days of the New Year, Christoph threw accusations at himself that he must have guessed, that he had run away to New York like a coward.

When the winter sun broke through the cloud, sending the snow crystals into an ecstasy of light, he absolved himself of all guilt and laid the blame firmly at Miriam's feet. She should have told him. She had no right to let him go without knowing.

The Empire State Building's footprint took up three city blocks. Wooden hoardings protected the perimeter of the site, but the ghostly structure towered upwards into the low-lying mist, eerily silent and abandoned. The sheer volume of steel and stone occupying the aerial world that had previously only been the dominion of winged creatures, of seagulls, or flittering pipistrelle bats, filled Christoph with a sense of vertigo and dread. He could never imagine ascending in one of the building's lightning elevators once it was eventually completed and stepping out on top of the world. He marvelled at the skyscrapers, but preferred to inhabit a low-rise world.

When Matthias and Valentina returned from their holiday in the freezing upstate countryside, Christoph felt compelled to tell them about Miriam and what she had written in her letter, but he could never find the right moment or the right words.

Anger was soon supplanted by a remorse that swept through him like a winter flood, scouring away the fear that had gripped him from the moment he had first read Miriam's words. This surge of emotions left Christoph entirely unable to frame his thoughts about the child that would soon be his, or put into any coherent sequence of words what he felt about this news. In the end, he said nothing to anyone.

One evening he sat down at his table and wrote another long letter to his parents, telling them more about his life in New York, but mentioning nothing about the other news from home. How could he tell them that Miriam was expecting his child when they knew nothing about his relationship with her? They were getting old and more conservative and would only be appalled that he was not coming home at once to marry her. Another evening, he sat at the table for hours as the light faded into night with a blank sheet of writing-paper in front of him and the fountain pen in his left hand, but only managed to write Miriam's name and her home address of Lothringerstrasse 37, Wuppertal in the upper left-hand corner of the virgin page before he gave up and lay down on his bed to sleep. He lay there like an effigy, rigidly wide awake: he knew that he had to send Miriam a letter as soon as possible, but wanted to write something meaningful, an honest response that told her how he felt about this impossible news but did not commit him to having to return home to Wuppertal. He could not go back there, not yet: he had too much that he wanted to achieve in New York, a whole life to live there.

Christoph received a short note from König on the 10th of January. It had been almost four months since Christoph had sung at König's office and it was the first time that he had heard anything from him in all that time. The note, handwritten in an almost illegible scribble on the talent agency's headed, old-fashioned notepaper, brought some good news. König had finally secured an audition for Christoph at the Palace Theatre at the end of the month. He asked him to come down to his office to discuss the details.

As Christoph waited in the anteroom to König's office the next day, he could hear him shouting into the telephone. When his diatribe was eventually over, his secretary signalled to Christoph that he should knock on the door and go in. At first, squinting up from his desk through his glasses, König did not seem to recognise him, but then gave him a strange vulpine smile, baring a mouthful of American teeth.

'The Palace Theatre used to be quite something,' he said without any preamble. 'I've got good connections there. Sarah Bernhardt, Fanny Brice, Eddie Cantor, they've all performed there over the years, and that new guy Bob Hope has also played there, but it's been going through some tough times lately. Everyone wants to go to the movies nowadays.'

Christoph was only familiar with Sarah Bernhardt's name. He was flattered that a theatre that had once had her on the bill was keen to hear how he could sing.

'They need new blood,' König continued, 'even unheard-of performers with a talent that they can build on, market. They've got to find new ways to bring in audiences. They need people who look like movie stars, but who can sing or dance or act. You've got the looks and the voice.'

'Thank you, Herr König,' Christoph said. 'I don't know about my looks, but I believe in my voice. But something I don't understand: these stars, *die glänzenden Sterne*, don't they still want to sing at that theatre, or to dance or do whatever it is they do, if it's so famous?'

'The management's having big money worries and can't pay the stars what they want any more. They're looking around for cheaper – I mean less expensive – quality entertainment to get audiences in. It's hard times for everyone.'

'They won't find my demands too … um … too steep,' Christoph said and smiled sadly.

'Let me deal with that side of things,' König snapped back. 'You just get there by one o'clock next Wednesday and ask for Mrs Lipchitz. That's Martha Lipchitz, L-I-P-C-H-I-T-Z for zebra. Haven't you got a pen? Always carry a pen in this town.'

He scribbled Lipchitz's name and the theatre address down impatiently and passed them to Christoph on a scrap of paper picked seemingly at random from his desk.

'What are you going to sing?' he asked. 'Better make it something snappy. None of those *Lieder*: they're too downbeat.'

'I'll talk to Herr Walter,' Christoph replied. 'I'm sure he can help me choose something good.'

Later, when he looked at the crumpled half-sheet of yellowed paper back in his room, he saw that König's writing was entirely illegible. He would not forget the lady's name in any case, and would find the theatre even if it meant walking up and down Broadway all morning.

CHAPTER FIVE

The Palace Theatre was halfway up Broadway in Midtown and Mrs Lipchitz was a matronly casting director in her early forties. The building was shaped like an inverted T and was taller than it was wide; the exact opposite of Mrs Lipchitz herself. Christoph had chosen a song with Matthias that was very popular on the radio and gramophone: 'Who'll Mend My Broken Heart?' by Joe Liebermann and Eddy Spiegel. He had been troubled by some of the Vs and Ws in the lyrics, worrying that he might pronounce one consonant hard and the other soft when it should be the other way round, but Matthias reassured him after several run-throughs that he sounded almost American and that he sang the song beautifully.

Mrs Lipchitz sat on her own, right at the front of the vast auditorium, under a cloche hat with its brim turned up. Christoph sang straight at her, looking down from the front of the bare stage. His voice filled the cavernous space, even without the help of a microphone.

> *Who'll mend my broken heart,*
> *Now that night has stolen day*
> *And we are just two souls,*
> *Each playing out a tragic part?*

The song was familiar to Martha Lipchitz, who was suffering from the lack of heating in the theatre and shoes that were pinching her feet. She had bought them a half size too small, as they were the only ones near her size left in the store and she could not resist them. Martha listened to this glistening-haired, fine-featured German sing and liked what she heard. The man looked as if he had stepped straight out of the Berlin cabaret. The song she could take or leave, but his voice was something else.

'Very good, Mr Rittersmann,' she said when he had finished singing and was standing there somewhat awkwardly, wondering what to do next. 'I like your tone and your delivery. You look good as well. Leo thinks very highly of you.'

'Thank you, Mrs Lipchitz,' he replied. 'Shall I sing something else? I've prepared plenty more.' He liked the word 'plenty'; it had been a new one for him when Matthias had said it recently, and he was glad to have made use of it.

'No, no; that's enough to get a good impression,' she replied. 'We'll call you back to meet the artistic director soon.'

Christoph felt elated when he left the theatre. It was an impressive building, however unsteady its financial foundations might be, and the fact that Mrs Lipchitz had liked his voice gave him something real to hold on to for the first time since he had come to Manhattan, some hard evidence that he really could rekindle his singing career. It meant even more to him than König's approval had done, as he was all about the deal and less about the craft, the magic of the stage, the limelight. That was Mrs Lipchitz's world, and Christoph wanted more than anything to be a part of it.

*

Matthias had finished composing his first symphony by the beginning of March 1931. He had been working on it ever since he and Valentina had reached New York and, apparently in homage to his adopted home state, he had called it the *Empire Symphony*. It was to have its world premiere with the Chicago Symphony Orchestra in early June.

'The Yanks will just think it's about their good old US of A,' Matthias said with a laugh to Christoph one day. 'They won't guess for a moment that what my symphony is really about is the German empire. There's still time for one, you know.'

'The *German* empire?' Christoph replied, suppressing an astonished smile. 'I don't think we've been much good at building one of those over the years.'

'Nonsense: our nation was just too divided, too many principalities and kingdoms until the nineteenth century, and since then we've never had the right leadership for empire-building. That can, and will, change. Mark my words.'

'Didn't we learn our lessons after 1918? I know that I'd found out all I wanted to know about trying to expand the German realm during my time in the war.'

'Yes, you had a particularly hard time, no one denies that. My desk job was a little easier, I admit. I really did want to fight, you know. My lungs just weren't up to it. When I failed the medical I cried, you remember.'

'You composed some jolly good marching songs at your desk if I recall, Matti.' Christoph had not called him Matti since they were children. 'I never understood why you didn't send them to the top brass for the use of the troops.'

*

The autograph manuscript ran to a pile of pages more than an inch high. Matthias had found an amanuensis to help him write out the definitive score to give to the printer, but wanted Christoph to read through it before he gave his score to the copyist.

'You'll be my eyes and ears,' Matthias said to Christoph some days after their discussion of empire. Matthias had avoided coming up to see Christoph until he felt that he would be more receptive to his request. Much to Matthias's relief, he had readily agreed to go through the score. 'I've become blind and deaf to this beast after all these years.'

'What do you want me to look for exactly? Isn't it too late for making changes? I've never read through such a long musical manuscript before.'

'Any loose phrasing in the arrangement, passages that don't flow, sudden changes in tempo that seem incorrect, things in the manuscript that you cannot read ... you'll know what to look for,' Matthias replied. 'I wanted you to be the first to read the whole thing after Valentina.'

'That's kind, Matti. I'll enjoy reading it. Surely your notes won't be as difficult for me to stomach as your views are sometimes.'

'Perhaps they are difficult for you to hear, but I feel I should always speak directly to an old friend like you. What hope is there for friendship if one can't at least talk politics? In return for your going through the score, I'll compose a song for you. There'll be no hint of the marching band in it, I promise,' Matthias said.

'I could sing it as my first song at the Palace Theatre, if they hire me.'

'You'll be on Broadway and me in Chicago. It's all a

rather long way from that old inn in Wuppertal, isn't it? What was its name again – Zum something?'

'It's still there: Zum alten Bock. I always drank the Hefeweizen there and you, of course, the finest Riesling.'

'Back then when we were students I had no idea how hard it was to earn money, none at all. I haven't drunk Riesling in years,' Matthias said and laughed ruefully.

'I haven't drunk any alcohol since I arrived here. I don't think I'd much like the American beer,' Christoph replied.

'You'd have to know where to find it first,' Matthias replied. 'Officially, we're still under Prohibition. Shall I leave this with you then?' Matthias indicated his daunting manuscript stacked neatly on Christoph's small table.

'Yes, of course. I'll try and get through it within a week.'

'Can I just ask one thing, that you keep it in your room? This is the only fair copy that there is. Other than this, I just have my rough drafts and my notes.'

'It'll stay right here on the table,' Christoph replied.

It began with a slow movement, sweeping and richly romantic, then edged gently towards a quiet and graceful elegy. In these notes, Christoph could feel Matthias's looking back, his longing for the life that he had left behind in Germany. He spent more than a day going through the first movement and had very little to add and few alterations to suggest. It was hermetic and polished, almost perfect. He admired the technical precision, the virtuosity, but was hoping for more warmth, more drama, as the symphony progressed. There was something a little cold, a little Teutonic, about it and the last thing that Christoph wanted was to plough through a musical paean to those sides of the German psyche, the Germanic *Geist*, that he most despised.

The deep rumble of kettle drums heralded storm clouds gathering over vast landscapes in the second movement. The limitless and mysterious heartlands of a vast continent seemed to be everywhere: in the susurrating harp strings of a gentle stream, in the crashing drums of a falling boulder, in the searing staccato violin notes of an eagle or some other bird of prey. Was the drama of nature taking place in Matthias's new home, America, with its limitless plains and prairies, or in some imagined place back in the dark heart of Europe? Christoph could not be sure. Matthias had moved from bourgeois small-town German life to nature in its rawness of tooth and claw within two movements. Christoph was surprised that he could capture nature's power and drama so well, wherever its imagined spaces might be, as he had never once seen Matthias out in the countryside. Christoph could not deny that all of this was very powerful, he was just not sure that he liked it very much.

After five days of going through the manuscript stave by stave, Christoph had reached the end of the fourth and final movement, which was the synthesis of all that had gone before it. After the lush romanticism of the third movement, in which Christoph thought that he could detect Valentina's presence in the warm honey tones of the viola and the French horn parts, the fourth movement was at times plangent and soulful, at others bombastic and bold in its use of thudding percussion and insistent trombone, and at still others simply beatific and full of life's joys, with high strings and parts for oboe and clarinet.

Christoph had made annotations here and there in pencil in the margins of the manuscript, perhaps fewer than fifty in total, pointing out where a note could be held for one extra beat or where Matthias had neglected to resolve fully the arrangement of one instrument's part. He was surprised to find that the *Empire Symphony* was more traditional and backward-looking than he had expected. Matthias revealed himself to owe far more to Beethoven than he did to the pioneering work of Schoenberg or Bartók. Overall, the *Empire Symphony* had a certain stridency of tone running through it, one well hidden by the rich layering of voices and parts but nevertheless still there, and it was very ambitious as a debut of this ostentatious size. He was a little jealous that Matthias's composition was to receive such a distinguished first public airing, but Matthias had, after all, already made a name for himself with his shorter works in Germany and New York.

Christoph had received no news at all from König or from the Palace Theatre. As the days went by he wandered around Manhattan looking for auditions. Christoph could feel himself sliding into self-doubt again. Not having his family near him nor anyone else that he loved by his side, he had to face the path of finding work, of finding a livelihood, of finding fame and fortune entirely alone. Matthias was far too preoccupied with his work as a composer and with his strident brand of politics, and he and Valentina were too wrapped up in each other to give Christoph any meaningful support. He had not considered the extent of the isolation he would encounter before he left Wuppertal. He had been too caught up in his desire to get away, and with the idea of the opportunities that New York would offer, to think about what would happen if things did not come as easily as he had anticipated.

Christoph finally heard from the Palace Theatre through

König in the second week of March. Mr Perlman, the artistic director, wanted to meet him. It was almost six weeks since he had had his audition with Mrs Lipchitz and he had almost completely given up hope that it would lead anywhere. He walked back down to the theatre on the appointed day and stood once more on that vast bare stage that he wanted so badly to fill with his voice, to inhabit as a star at whatever hour on whatever day of the week they would let him sing. The artistic director sat much further back in the auditorium than Mrs Lipchitz had done. He was already seated when Christoph walked onto the stage and he shouted out a distant greeting that Christoph returned with an awkward nod of the head. He had seen other performers in street clothes hanging around backstage and in the foyer of the theatre and knew that he must be one of a whole line of artists that the man was auditioning that afternoon. He took off his cap and said his name.

This time there was a piano to accompany him, and Christoph had brought the sheet music with him so that the pianist could sight read the accompaniment to his song. Christoph's hair was slicked back with brilliantine and he wore a white shirt with sharp pointed collars, a jade-green tie and a grey dog-tooth jacket over dark flannel trousers. He looked the part and had chosen a jaunty Herbie Baxter number to sing this time.

> *Who's that gal walking down the street*
> *With her feet so dain'y and her waist petite?*
> *Tell me who's that gal that I'd like to meet,*
> *Tell me who's that gal, my sugar sweet!*

The tempo was a fast jazz one and Christoph snapped his fingers as he sang. He could see the artistic director tapping his knee to the rhythm of the song. It seemed that the song was getting into him, beguiling him with its tempo and sweet melodies. When Christoph had finished singing, the artistic director clapped generously and got up from his seat, walked down the aisle nearest him and stood right in front of the lip of the stage, almost at Christoph's feet.

'You've got quite a voice,' he said in a thick Brooklyn accent, which took Christoph by surprise.

'Thank you,' he replied, looking down at the man's moustachioed face.

'Tell you what we'll do: warm up on Tuesday nights. Tuesday night is "new singers night" you see,' the artistic director said, quoting the Palace Theatre's recent publicity intended to drum up an audience as the Depression's grip slowly strangled Broadway and the theatre's attendance fell week on week. 'You can sing from seven to seven-thirty before the main acts start at eight. Three dollars for the half-hour. Only new material. No old stuff.'

'I'm very pleased, Mr Perlman,' Christoph said. 'This is wonderful news. You'll tell Mr König?'

'I will,' he replied. 'Start the first Tuesday night in May. Bring the sheet music for the piano.'

Chapter Six

Matthias and Christoph went out on a walk one day in mid-March, the flowers coming into bloom in Central Park, when Matthias brought up the subject of the Nationalistic Society of Teutonia. Matthias told Christoph that he had first heard about Teutonia in 1928 from a German friend in Yorkville who had mentioned that he was a member. Matthias said that the unit met up socially for drinks and discussions at the Yorkville Casino and other such places on the Upper East Side. At first, the meetings were mostly social; a good deal of German beer was drunk and stories were swapped about the old country. Most of the men, for they were all men, were under forty and had come to America in the late 1910s or more recently. Christoph detected a strange mixture of urgency and awkwardness in Matthias's voice.

'You know, I've been meeting once or twice a week for the last couple of years with some decent German chaps over at the casino. You should join us sometime.'

'I had my dose of "decent German chaps" back in Wuppertal and Berlin. I came here to escape them,' Christoph replied.

'Nevertheless, you might find what we talk about in the meetings interesting. We discuss how things can be improved in Germany, and what we can do from here to help with that.'

'How things can be improved? Not ever allowing Hitler or the Nazi Party anywhere near the Reichstag will guarantee that things will improve in their own time. I imagine that you and your casino chums have other ideas.'

Matthias had told Christoph that he had once heard Hitler speak in a beer hall in Munich when Matthias was nearing the end of his student days. Matthias said that he could not forget Hitler's speech that evening. The man was a force of nature, an undiscovered element, his oration was as fluent as water and it spat fire. His logic was hard and cold like ice. He had never heard anything like it – the things Hitler said! They were outrageous, but made such sense when you went away and thought about them. Christoph thought that sense was a very long way from where Hitler stood and he was shocked when Matthias told him that he had joined the Party in 1929.

'If you just came along and met them, perhaps my friends in Teutonia could persuade you that their position, their view of things, is the right one.'

'Teutonia?' Christoph said with an exasperated laugh. 'What sort of name is Teutonia, for God's sake? It sounds unpleasantly pompous and reactionary, like the name of one of those fraternities in Heidelberg or Freiburg.'

'It's an old name for our race, our nation. You know full well what it means, Christoph.'

It seemed to Christoph that Matthias had been holding back from mentioning the organisation to him ever since Christoph had arrived in New York, given the recent loss of his Jewish wife.

'I know what it intends to mean and don't like the sound of it. Why on earth have you got yourself involved in this thing?'

'It's a well-ordered society with thousands of members, not a "thing" as you so eloquently put it.'

'Have you told Vally that you're mixed up in this?'

'I'm not "mixed up" in anything at all. I wanted to join Teutonia and did so with a clear head. Such a clear head, in fact, that they've made me the unit's treasurer.'

Christoph imagined just how much that would have flattered Matthias's slowly bloating ego.

'So Vally doesn't know?'

'She doesn't need to know,' Matthias replied angrily. 'It's none of her goddamned business whether or not I get together with some like-minded Germans to talk politics once in a while.'

'Well, you can be one hundred per cent certain that I'll never come along to any meeting of Teutonia and you should leave those bigots well alone if you have any sense left. We're never going to agree on politics and it's probably best we don't discuss the topic again.'

It was their first real argument since their childhood and that conversation in Central Park changed something fundamentally between them. Christoph no longer trusted Matthias, because he knew without having to be told what Teutonia stood for. Any movement in America that allied itself with the Nazi Party would be vehemently anti-Semitic and avowedly racist. Later, he did what he could to find out exactly what the Society was trying to achieve.

The Free Society of Teutonia was formed in Chicago in 1924 by the Gissibil brothers – German immigrants and Nazi Party members. It renamed itself the Nationalistic Society of Teutonia in 1926. The Society had quickly set up outreach units in other cities across the Midwest and on the

Eastern Seaboard. New York City and Newark in New Jersey both had small branches of this first organised group of Nazi Party supporters and fanatical Hitler devotees in America. It sought to show Americans that Nazism was the way forward, and could be the future of their country as well. Each outreach branch across America was raising money to support the Nazi Party back home, in the hope that this would help Hitler to gain power and pull Germany back from the brink of the abyss.

Teutonia's units had grown steadily, from Chicago to Milwaukee, from St Louis to Detroit, Cincinnati to New York City, in fact wherever there was a sufficiently strong ethnic German population, and by the time Christoph had arrived in America they had raised militias modelled on Hitler's *Sturmabteilung*. They were preparing for something, for some action, although what that was precisely, the Gissibil brothers back in Chicago, at the epicentre of the movement, had not yet made clear.

The New York City branch of Teutonia had become one of the most active units of the Society. Matthias was its treasurer, and had now also become responsible for helping to recruit new members. They were not going to have any impact in New York unless they could swell their numbers even further. There were rumours that the German consul to New York City was a supporter of what Teutonia were trying to achieve in America.

He could not believe that Matthias would ever join such a group. What the hell was he thinking? Strong opinions on politics were one thing, and he knew that Matthias had always been more on the right than on the left, but he had never thought even for a moment that he could become openly racist or a xenophobe. He had grown up with the

Bernstein children, for God's sake.

Christoph decided from now on he would carefully listen to what Matthias might tell him, he would glean snippets of information through word of mouth out on the streets of Yorkville, and read the newspapers whenever he had the chance.

He owed it to Ida and to Miriam and their family to work against the hate that such organisations spread. Christoph promised himself that he would find out, by whatever means he could, what Teutonia was up to in New York City. Yes: he owed that much to the Bernsteins at least, and to the sacrifice of his own youth that he had made for his country during the World War.

CHAPTER SEVEN

Apart from this unpleasant disagreement with Matthias, Christoph felt happier and more alive with possibilities than he had felt before in New York. Spring was on its way into the city and with it, finally, the opportunity to make something of his singing career. Yet he couldn't shake off an acute sense of longing for more, for someone to share his new life with. He knew hardly any women in New York apart from Valentina, and rarely had the chance to speak to them unless they were waitresses in diners or casting directors in out-of-the-way theatres.

A second letter from Miriam arrived at the end of March. Matthias brought it up to his room one morning with a cup of black tea. They had talked very little since their walk in Central Park ten days earlier, and Matthias only said a few words to him before shutting the door behind him and going back down the stairs. Christoph sat awkwardly on the edge of his bed as he read the letter.

C. Rittersmann
233 East 89th Street
New York, New York

10th March 1931

Dear Christoph,

You have a baby daughter. I have named her Eva after my grandmother. She is beautiful and looks like you.

It seems that you have abandoned us. I have been waiting for a letter from you for more than six months now. You owe me at least this much: to let me know how you are and what you feel about this news that you are a father to a beautiful girl.

My task ahead of bringing up our child on my own if you do not come back to me will be a hard one. But I have my brothers and my remaining sister near me and I expect that they will be there for me if you are not.

Yours, as ever,
Miriam

Christoph sat at the little table and read and reread her letter. The tea threatened to scald his throat, he drank it so quickly. He could not take in the enormity of what Miriam had written. His memory of her face had become a little more imprecise, a little more diffuse each day that he had been in New York and it was as if his ability to grasp her words had evaporated as irretrievably as the image of her in his mind's eye.

Again, he tried to reply to Miriam, staring blankly at the page after the first few lines. He hated himself for not knowing what to say, but until he had the right words he could not answer her. He had known the Bernstein children since he and Ida were six or seven years old and Miriam was just a baby and he was ashamed that this lifelong friendship, this enduring love for them and their family, had faltered into dumb silence on his part. He blamed his confusion, and his need for escape, on Ida's sudden death two years earlier. Her dying should not have precipitated his search for comfort, for solace, in Miriam's arms. He felt as if they had broken some unspoken taboo, and their daughter was the result. When he sailed from Hamburg on the *Albert Ballin*, he meant to leave Miriam and his old life behind, to start a completely new chapter in New York. Now, with the news of his daughter, Christoph's resolve faltered and he began to ask himself whether he should try to get them over to America. Then, remembering all that he still had to achieve in his new life, he pushed this thought to the back of his mind. But he struggled to ignore the question, so persistent was it.

Christoph needed to confide in someone, but had no one he could turn to in New York. He was afraid that if he told Matthias and Valentina, they would judge him harshly for turning his back on Miriam. Vally most of all would not understand why he had left Germany if she knew that he and Miriam had been lovers. Matthias had, it seemed to him, always put Valentina before his career as a composer and had only gone to America because she had wanted to start a new life, a family, with him here.

Ida's illness had come on very suddenly. She had been staying at her family home, not far away, for a few days while their apartment was being decorated. When he went to see her for breakfast with her family one morning that early October, the leaves on the trees that lined Lothringerstrasse just beginning to turn a golden brown, she said that she had woken in pain during the night and had been unable to get back to sleep. She looked pale but happy to see him. She said that it must be her time of the month that had come early.

The pain got worse over the next three days and no menses came. She went to bed but could not rest, did not eat and barely drank. Her grey-haired parents, ashen-faced, hovered around her bed. The whole family knew that the situation was serious. The doctor came to the house on the second day and raised some hope that it was dyspepsia, but when he came again the next day and saw that she was much worse, he ordered her straight to hospital. She arrived there on the Thursday evening, but was brought back home by private ambulance to die late the next day. She lived until the Sunday lunchtime. They had diagnosed a twisted bowel, the twisted section slowly dying inside her and poisoning her because of its own constriction. There was nothing that could be done to save her.

She said goodbye to Christoph the day before she died, squeezing his hand as tightly as she could, as she slipped into a coma on the Saturday night. She was in great pain. She told him their brief time together had made her very happy, but that he must now let her go and find someone else to love. It broke his heart to see her in such pain and he could not stop himself from crying. She tried to comfort him when it was she who needed comforting.

They buried Ida in the Jewish cemetery up on the Weinberg in the family plot shaded by tall cypress trees. They buried her with his surname and her nickname, lovingly inscribed: '*Iddy*' *Rittersmann* chiselled into her granite headstone. It was a beautifully sunny autumn day. Birds were singing in the trees all around the cemetery and Christoph could not comprehend all of this rich life continuing around him. Her family sat Shiva for three days afterwards and Christoph joined them in their quiet, dignified mourning.

Having accepted him as part of the family, the Bernsteins felt sorry most of all for Christoph. His wedding had been only months before and now he was a widower. Miriam was four years younger than Ida, almost twenty-six, and was there for him when he felt most raw. She was kind to him. Their romance was a surprise to both of them and he knew all along that it could not last.

At first, Christoph felt guilt, shame, for sleeping with Miriam. It happened in the apartment on Lothringerstrasse, with Ida's clothes still hanging in their wardrobe and her things laid out on the chest of drawers in the bedroom, her toothbrush still in its cup in the cramped bathroom. He felt that he was betraying Ida and talked about it with Miriam. She felt exactly the same, but neither of them could break off the affair. They needed the comfort of physical contact, of flesh on flesh. Sometimes, early on, Miriam cried in his arms.

Their relationship lasted for perhaps six months. Their families knew nothing about it: both of them felt it was better that way, with Ida's death being so recent and still so painful for everyone. Miriam was dark-haired, dark-eyed and sensitive. She was also very loving and gentle, but had a strength about her that was remarkable. As the months went by, Miriam seemed to recover her spirits and to accept her sister's death, or at least she learnt how to live with it. It was

Christoph who found it hard to comprehend and the sadness ground away at him. As Miriam grew closer to him, he pulled away because of what she reminded him of.

He had seen enough pointless death on the Front and could not bear the grief. That was when he decided to go to America. He wanted to live; he wanted life, not death.

His last months in Germany had been strange ones. He sang at some town halls and smaller concert venues, including one or two singing appearances in Wuppertal itself. He felt as if he was falling out of love with his homeland while the country was falling apart. The price of bread had rocketed, now costing as much as a wireless radio used to cost; there were unemployed men standing on the street corners of the town, hands stuffed into coat pockets, looking for work. His singing career, after the long years of trying, was hardly a cause to break open the champagne. And far, far worse than any of that, even than the trenches, was that his wife had died and his life seemed to have slipped out of his control somehow. He just wanted to get out of Germany.

When his papers for the United States came through, he was elated and felt free of everything for the first time in years. He had no real concept of what *his* life would be like in America. When he tried to imagine the average daily life of an American citizen, he was distracted again and again by childhood memories from ten-pfennig stories of gangsters, of hoodlums and cowboys and Indians. He could not imagine the ordinary, only the extraordinary.

His mother did not want him to go and his sister had tried to persuade him to stay. They did not understand his need to escape.

When he set foot on the main deck of the *Albert Ballin*

and once the great ship had got under way, he looked out to sea and not back at the harbour walls of Hamburg receding slowly into the distance, Miriam still standing there on the quayside waving after the stern of the ship with her white handkerchief, until they were only a shadow of a memory on the horizon.

CHAPTER EIGHT

Midway through April, Matthias left for Chicago to begin rehearsals with the orchestra for the premiere of the *Empire Symphony* which was due to take place at the end of May. Before he left, he came up to Christoph's room to say goodbye.

'You'll look after Valentina?' he asked.

'If she'll let me,' Christoph replied. 'I think that she can look after herself pretty well.'

'If she needs any help she knows where you are, after all.'

'Upstairs like an older brother. I'll keep my eye on her, Matti.'

'Then I'll see you in Chicago in six or seven weeks' time,' Matthias replied. 'You know that the main unit of Teutonia's there?'

'What of it?' Christoph replied curtly.

'I'm going to use my time outside of rehearsals in Chicago to build stronger relations with them.'

'Listen to me, Matti. I won't tell you again – stay away from that organisation. What they stand for, what they want just isn't right. Don't talk about Teutonia to me again.'

'I've never met the Gissibil brothers before,' Matthias replied, either choosing to ignore what Christoph had just said or lost in his own thoughts. He looked distractedly out of the little room's window onto the apartment block behind their own. 'And they're the ones who got this whole thing going in America. It's building up quite some momentum now, you'll see.'

'You're not listening to me, Matthias. From what you've told me, the Gissibil brothers are utter poison and their *Toytonia* – he pronounced the name with a sarcastic attempt at a German-American accent – is nothing less than a Nazi outreach organisation here in America.'

'Most of us might be members of the Nazi Party back home, but we're not a Nazi organisation. We just believe in the Fatherland and in doing right by it.'

'*Quatsch!*' Christoph replied angrily, 'That's utter rubbish and you know it.'

'No I don't. I'm telling you the truth,' Matthias replied, turning round to face Christoph and raising his hands as if defending himself from attack.

'I can't believe what's happened to you over the last seven years, Matthias. Why have you become like this? What changed?'

'I haven't changed. It's the world that has changed, Christoph. The world.'

Christoph was glad when Matthias left and relieved that they would not see each other for almost two months. He was beginning to think that he should find somewhere else to rent in the city. He could not go on living under the same roof as him.

He knew that he had to rehearse some new songs for his first half-hour at the Palace Theatre, but every time he stood in his room with the sheet music in his hand ready to begin, his mind strayed to thoughts of Wuppertal, to Ida, to Miriam and the daughter that he had never met. He felt nothing but guilt when he thought of home and anger when

62

he thought about Matthias. He stood silently in the middle of the room, sometimes for minutes at a time, without any perceptible movement other than the rising and falling of the breath in his chest.

He did not know what to do. He had always been a man who found it hard to make a decision. The Front had shattered his nerves in his late teenage years; the painful memories that he suppressed – the trenches, mortar rounds, machine-gun fire, hunger, death – had left him traumatised. Coming to New York was one resolution that he had made and stuck with. He did not want to go home, not yet. He had so much to achieve, having a daughter had not been part of the plan.

Just as suddenly as the dark cloud of guilt and memory had descended upon him, on the morning of his first performance at the Palace Theatre, Christoph woke to find it gone. He got up at first light in anticipation of his performance that evening, and could not believe his luck that he would finally be singing at the Palace that night. After months of uncertainty and endless waiting, his chance had come at last. That night, way down the bill but up on stage, which was what mattered most to him, he soared through the four songs he had chosen and his singing drowned out the sound of the mortar shells exploding in his mind. His voice was his talisman to keep him safe, to ward off the memory of what had happened to him and his friends in the war. More than three-quarters of his platoon had gone into the mud, that sucking devourer of corpses and men. That figure never left him; it was imprinted in every part of his body. More than three-quarters of his platoon dead.

*

As Matthias's work as a composer still brought in very little money, Valentina worked as a cloakroom attendant at a movie theatre Midtown, so she was out of their apartment for long hours most of the week and some weekends. She left Christoph a key in case he wanted to take a bath. It took patience and effort to fill the tin tub even a quarter full with water boiled in a large pan on the kitchen range.

He was sitting in the tub one morning, the lukewarm water lapping at his ankles and cramped buttocks, running the hard bar of soap over his shoulders and lower back, when he heard a key in the lock. He levered himself out of the bath as fast as he could, reaching for his towel and wrapping it around his waist as he stepped onto the bare floorboards.

'*Ach, lieber Herr Rittersmann*,' Valentina said with a playful tone in her voice, 'don't hurry your bath on my account.'

'I … I was finished,' he replied, blushing deeply and gathering up his clothes from the sideboard with the hand that was not clutching the towel at his waist.

'The projector broke and they sent us home. No work until it's fixed,' she said, smiling.

'I'll empty the bath down the sluice when I'm dressed,' Christoph said, backing towards the door, still flushed and perspiring slightly beneath the film of water that covered his skin.

'Shall I put some coffee on the stove?' she asked.

'That'd be very nice,' he replied.

Christoph never failed to fall a little for Valentina's beautiful face. He feared being seen naked because of the ugly scar on his right thigh. It had taken him a long time before he had allowed Frieda or Ida or Miriam to see him naked in daylight. It had been a near-miss with Valentina just then. Valentina was not his to be seen naked by, and confusion and shame had made him embarrassed and tongue-tied.

When Christoph returned, Valentina had laid out coffee and cakes on the kitchen table; *Kaffee und Kuchen* to remind them perhaps of home. Feelings of homesickness rose in him again, a surge of longing and emotion that he quickly suppressed. His fear of the responsibilities that lay in wait for him should he return home eclipsed his nostalgia for the bosom of his family, and the familiar surroundings of Wuppertal.

'Would you like some walnut cake?' Valentina asked.

'Thank you, that would be nice. Sorry about earlier – I mean still being here when you came back. I hope I didn't alarm you?'

'*Alarm* me?' Valentina said and laughed loudly. 'No, you didn't alarm me. You just made me smile because you were in such a hurry.'

'I didn't want to embarrass you, I wasn't dressed. It's a long time since we were children,' Christoph replied.

'Can't adults see each other without clothes on?' Valentina asked and giggled like a little girl. Christoph sensed that she was playfully flirting with him. He blushed for the second time that morning, although this time less deeply.

'It's what nature's given us,' he said. 'But I think that Matthias would not be happy if he knew I was standing in your apartment talking to you with only a towel around me.'

'Matthias is a long way away,' Valentina answered slightly sourly.

'But still …' Christoph began then let the sentence peter out as he took another bite of the delicious cake.

*

The following Sunday morning, there was a knock on Christoph's door. The projector had been mended, Valentina said, and she had worked all day on Saturday. She wanted to get out of Yorkville and the Upper East Side for a change of scene and suggested that they go to Coney Island for the day.

'How far is it?' Christoph asked.

'It's not too difficult to get there,' Valentina said. 'We can take the subway down to Brooklyn then the El train on to Coney Island. You can walk along the beach and see the sea. When was the last time you went to the seaside?'

'I've no idea, perhaps when I was about nineteen. Probably the time I went on holiday to the Baltic with some friends from the gymnasium.'

'You haven't seen the sea for more than *ten* years? How can that be? I love the water.'

'Well, of course I *crossed* the sea to get here, but I haven't *been* to the seaside for years: the waves don't seem to respond to my singing,' Christoph joked. 'I prefer cities and towns where I at least have the possibility of an audience.'

'All the same, singing and performing aren't everything,' Valentina replied. 'What about nature? What about this world of ours? What about love?'

'I like nature when I'm in it, and I like the idea of love. But in practice, so far, it seems to have caused me nothing but problems.'

'Why? Are you talking about darling Ida – surely what her death caused you was *great sadness* rather than "problems" – or do you mean someone else?'

'Someone else, of course: but that's a story for later,' is all that Christoph would reply.

'Isn't it a little too soon for someone else?' Valentina asked, looking sideways at him, but then added: 'Unless it's the right person and someone who would make you happy again, of course.' He did not answer her.

The El train rattled through a suburban sprawl of newly built homes cheek-by-jowl with run-down slums. Christoph and Valentina sat beside each other on the wooden seats, and when the train swayed her body touched his. It was the closest that he had been to anyone in almost nine months.

The train stopped at the terminus at Coney Island, a station supported by giant steel girders bolted together into a rigid geometry that held the rails high above the street that ran beneath it. The gentle April sun was at its zenith by the time they had walked down the station steps to the street below and made their way to the promenade. On the skyline the giant 'Wonder Wheel' flashed its red lights invitingly, and the dizzying 'Cyclone', the wooden roller coaster, stood enticingly nearby. The Sunday crowds thronged the front, children ate candyfloss on sticks and apples dipped in toffee. It was as if the whole world was there and everyone had unfurled themselves after the long winter under the benign sun, which cheerfully watched the gaiety and diversion below.

Christoph had never seen anything quite like it, even in Berlin. They dipped into a tent where a woman was wrestling with an albino python. The small crowd gawped and the atmosphere was eerily silent in the half-light. The snake's tongue flickered as it tasted the air. The woman looked like someone out of a Greek myth, but whoever had carved her had given her the wrong head, one that was somehow almost mannish and slightly too big for her delicate shoulders.

'*Eine Göttin ohne Schönheit*', Christoph said, a goddess without beauty.

'Indeed,' Valentina replied as they left the tent, and laughed her lovely laugh. 'D'you want to go on the roller coaster?' she asked when they were once more walking along the boardwalk next to the sparkling stretch of sand that divided the island from the sea.

'Is it dangerous?' he asked.

'No, not dangerous,' she replied. 'It's thrilling, it's exciting. It was the talk of New York when it was opened. If we're going to do it, we'd better do it *before* we have some lunch.'

The man operating the gates was a gruff, muscular native of Brooklyn, judging by his accent. He seemed to have trouble understanding Christoph when he asked for two tickets for the ride. Once they were locked into their sleek wooden car, Christoph began to worry that the serpentine, twisting track ahead, behind and to each side of him could only lead to vertigo or a terrible accident. He could hardly believe that the car would stay on the track when it rode the steeper inclines and curves, but the warmth from Valentina's body pressed close to his gave him some comfort. She had, after all, been on the roller coaster more than once and survived to ride it again with him. A klaxon sounded and the chain of cars bumped and clattered away.

Christoph felt the need to loosen his tie and undo the top button of his shirt as the cars rode up the first giant incline. He put his hat in his lap for fear that it would fly off. The car seemed to stop momentarily at the top of the climb where the track levelled out for a stretch of ten or fifteen yards, before apparently disappearing in front of them into an empty abyss of air. Before he could do anything about it, Christoph was falling into this abyss, or rather shooting and sliding into it in this wooden car at such a speed, the fastest he had ever travelled in his life, faster than any train, that he thought he would have to swallow his stomach again if he ever wanted to eat another meal. Valentina screamed with delight next to him and clutched his arm. Before he knew where he was, Christoph was shooting upwards, only to plummet once more to an even greater depth, then ricocheting skywards and running downhill again at great speed. The tears were streaming down his face.

When they finally came to a standstill near the burly gate operator, Valentina turned her head towards Christoph and gave him a kiss of sheer joy on his cheek.

'That was *incredible*!' she said. 'I'd forgotten quite how good the Cyclone was.'

'I ... I don't know what to say,' Christoph replied, looking pale. He was not sure that he would be able to stand up when they got out of the car. 'I have never experienced anything like that in my life.'

After they had eaten some late lunch in the middle of the afternoon, Valentina said she wanted a ride on the merry-go-round near the waterfront. Almost all of the other riders on the garlanded wooden horses were children, but Valentina sat there beaming out at Christoph as she came round the carousel again and again. As the horse rode up and down on its pole and Valentina rode the gentle swell with it, Christoph felt the first deep stirrings of lust that he had felt in a very long time.

That same night Christoph was in bed reading, the room cold despite it having been a beautiful spring day, when he heard gentle knocking on the door. He got out of bed, pulled his thick woollen dressing-gown over his pyjamas and opened it. Valentina was standing there in her nightgown with her dark hair falling around her shoulders, crying.

'What's wrong?' he said, and cuddled her to him. They had known each other since they were so young. She said nothing, but sobbed in his arms as he held her. He gently closed the door and led her into the room, and sat down next to her on the bed.

'Matthias hasn't written since he left,' she said, still sobbing and sniffing after some minutes of sitting on the bed, her head on his shoulder and his arm around her.

'I'm sure he's very busy with rehearsals,' was all that Christoph could think of saying to comfort her. He found it unforgivable that Matthias had not been in touch. Valentina was so beautiful. She was obviously fragile after what had happened with the stillborn baby last year. He realised for the first time that he had started to despise Matthias.

'Are you lonely here?' she asked suddenly. 'I'm very lonely.'

'Yes, I am,' he said. 'But I don't want to, I cannot, go home. Not yet.'

Apparently without any conscious decision passing through their minds, and without another word being spoken between them, they found themselves kissing. Valentina's mouth was delicious and she sought out Christoph's mouth again and again. Christoph was surprised that she was such a passionate kisser; she was certainly the one taking the lead. Her lips were soft, so soft. Their nightclothes fell, tangling with the bedclothes, and if either of them felt any guilt they were not aware of it then. Valentina caressed his scar and showed no revulsion.

70

She lay back and pulled Christoph towards her. Her body shone in the lamplight. It was soft and warm and he seemed to have known it forever. He closed his eyes and saw her riding up and down on the merry-go-round and smiling her beautiful smile. She smelled of lemons and sex and he pushed inside her over and over until he came.

CHAPTER NINE

The auditorium of the Palace Theatre was half full on this humid evening in early May. The ladies in the front row were fanning themselves. Christoph felt a tremor run through his legs as he walked to the front of the stage, up to the microphone on a stand that stood waiting for him there. Tonight he was the second act in the new singers' hour that took place between seven and eight every Tuesday, and he had not been impressed by the first singer, a man named Toots Waller who sang as if he had swallowed a bluebottle.

The compère's words were still echoing in Christoph's ears as he grasped the microphone stand to stop himself from swaying: "Now, *lay*-dees and *gen*'lmen, I'd like to introduce a great talent fresh to New York. He's famous in Germany and now hoping to make a name for himself in the Big Apple; he put the 'R' for Romance in the Rhine, it's Rittersmann the Romantic.'

The crowd fell silent as Christoph nodded to his accompanist and the lights came down on the house. He could just make out Valentina in the third row of the audience, off to the right. The pianist played the sprightly opening bars of 'It's My Way or the Highway' by Lou Gantz and Christoph smiled as he sang, not because of a beneficent cast of mind towards the audience, but because he could not have picked a song more at odds with the saccharine stage name that the compère had just bestowed upon him. Its wry humorous take on love's disharmonies rang out across the auditorium.

> *It's my way or the highway, darling,*
> *It's take me as you find me, dearest,*
> *Or leave me on my own: oh leave me on my own.*

> *It's my way or the highway, darling,*
> *It's leave me as you found me, dearest.*
> *Or take me as I am. Oh please take me as I am …*

His voice was the one thing that he could not live without, his only gift, his closest friend. It soared up to the rafters and down to the denouement of the lovers' tale in the song. The audience was silent, not even a cough escaped, Christoph held them in the palm of his hands. The applause fell on Christoph like summer rain, kind and much needed after a long drought.

Christoph filled the rest of the half-hour with other popular songs: 'I Remember Venice' by Ernie Strand, which certainly did provide some of the romantic nostalgia that his moniker had promised; 'Fizz-Bomb Bang' by Rogers & Strang, a comedy number about a little girl who plays with fireworks and sets her doll's house alight; and 'Lonely, Lonely Me' by William West, another lushly romantic swoon-song that had the audience sighing and swaying.

Christoph cut a dashing figure with his hair slicked back from his strong forehead and his dark-grey suit cut in the latest fashion. He was becoming increasingly concerned about the amount of money remaining in his bank account after paying for his new suit, but felt that he must look the part now that he was higher up the bill at the Palace Theatre. Valentina had chosen the cloth with him at a tailor's on Madison Avenue weeks earlier, and the tailor's apprentice had delivered the suit to him only two days ago.

They had not discussed what happened between them just a few nights earlier and nothing had happened again. It was as if Valentina had become his almost-sister once more over the last few days. She was not at all awkward or embarrassed when she was with him, and held his arm when they were out walking through the streets and avenues of Manhattan, but she had not visited his room again. She had still heard nothing from Matthias.

After the third singer had performed, the three of them made their way from the limelight, and the hubbub of the audience released from their uncomfortable seats, into the dark recesses of the theatre.

The green room was down a set of bare concrete steps and sparsely furnished. Valentina joined Christoph and, sitting on one of the wooden chairs wondering whether anyone would come backstage to ask for his autograph, he realised that she was the only person in the whole of New York City who had come to support him because she cared about him and not to hear what he could do. Leo König, his agent, had watched him from high up in the stalls, to hear how his voice travelled in the theatre, but had sneaked out to get back to his family supper before the soprano Janice Rodriguez came on and had not congratulated Christoph, other than with a wave and a full-toothed smile from the other side of the theatre before he left.

Christoph could hear one of the two main acts of the evening singing. He was an opera singer, a baritone, and had a fine timbre to his voice, with a rich mellifluous tone and good depth. Christoph knew that, given the chance, he could also become a main act, a draw, a crowd-pleaser, and lift the roof off the theatre. He wondered why the baritone had decided to go solo and was not part of an opera company. Christoph was not used to fraternising with other performers and sat with Valentina on one side of the green room, sharing a glass of cheap red wine with her, while Janice Rodriguez and Toots Waller chatted amicably to each other. It was difficult not to see them as competition. No one came to ask for an autograph.

Christoph was given three dollars and a friendly smile for his half-hour by the artistic director, Mr Perlman. It was the first money that he had earned since arriving in New York. The applause with which the audience had rewarded him after the last sweet notes of 'Lonely, Lonely Me' meant more to him than any amount of dollar bills ever could.

Christoph could not sleep. He still had the applause of the audience in his ears, the gentle swell of their murmurs of appreciation. It was a little like trying to sleep beside the sea when a storm tide was coming in. His scar was throbbing inexplicably. He wondered whether it was because of all the excitement, the heightened circulation of blood in his veins, or whether it was God punishing him for being happy. He could not decide what to do about Miriam or about his daughter. He did not know what to think about the other night with Valentina. What he did know was that he felt profoundly uncomfortable with what had happened. He turned and turned in his bed until the sheets and covers were all twisted and damp with perspiration, and until he could not lie there sleeplessly any longer.

Yorkville was silent at 2 a.m. The occasional night-delivery truck rumbled down Second Avenue on its way downtown, witnessed by the few people still out walking through the neighbourhood on their way to night shifts or back home late from work, from illicit drinking or gambling dens. From what he had heard, Prohibition had failed in the United States long before he had arrived, particularly in the big cities, and Christoph knew from Matthias that home-brewed liquor was sold on almost every block.

He headed over towards the East River and then walked south several blocks down York Avenue, passing no one at all as he strode along humming quietly beneath his breath. He seemed to have the city entirely to himself. Welfare Island and its hospital-asylum loomed eerily between the buildings that lined the side of York Avenue nearest the river and Christoph wondered what went on in that dark ghost of a building, and how you ended up there.

He did not know where he was going; he just walked. He covered many miles that May night, the long hours after his first full performance at the Palace Theatre filled with footstep after footstep, block after block of asphalt, concrete and stone. He felt a curious mixture of exultation and despair. The applause of his footsteps in these empty, echoing streets a celebration of what he had achieved that night, the true launching of his singing career in the United States. But always at the back of his mind Eva, his daughter he did not know, teased him, flitting in and out just beyond his reach, and Miriam, whom he had left behind. And why had he got involved with Valentina? Christoph shook his head trying to empty his thoughts, and then stopped. It was hard to separate what had happened with Valentina and his feelings towards her from his anger and agitation at Matthias and his increasing involvement in far-right politics.

He did not wake up until after noon the next day. He had gone to sleep at first light, having walked down Manhattan as far as the Brooklyn Bridge, then back up to East Eighty-Ninth Street again. He had collapsed into bed and woke up groggy and disorientated. For a second he thought that he was back in Wuppertal, in his old room and familiar bed. When he realised where he was, he felt a sharp pang of loneliness and fear. He had no one at all with whom to confide his dark thoughts that gave him no peace; no one with whom to wake up and share the bright excitement of last night at the Palace Theatre. Valentina was the only person in New York whom he wanted to talk to and she would now be at work at the movie theatre. He could not tell her about Miriam or about his daughter and Valentina was at the root of this unease that he felt, so he had no one to talk to.

At the close of the working day, Christoph was at König's office to talk about the performance of the night before and to give him twenty per cent of his three-dollar fee. König was, as usual, on the telephone when he arrived and Christoph had to sit in the anteroom on a chair in front of the secretary's desk and wait for him to finish the call. He could hear unwelcome snatches of phrase that made him wonder whether the call was actually about him: '… should've paid it to *me* to pay him out …' and '… the contract is with *me* … yeah, next time.'

König was all smiles when Christoph entered his office; there was no evidence in his eager grin that anything was wrong. He even stood up and came out from behind his desk to shake Christoph by the hand.

'So, we have a potential star in the making?' he said.

'You think so?' Christoph replied, secretly very relieved and delighted but trying not to let it show on his face.

'I know so. I just spoke to Mr Perlman and you're the only one they're keeping on from last night's new singers. The other two are gone. He might even give you a little longer sometime soon. He says your voice gives him gooseflesh and it's nothing to do with the theatre's terrible heating.' He chuckled deeply and retreated back behind his desk.

'As you know, I have been waiting for this chance for a long time, Mr König. I won't let it go to waste. I think I can get stronger every week.'

'I'm sure you will, I'm sure you will.' König smiled again, like a wolf smiles before it devours its kill.

'I wanted to give you the sixty cents that I owe you,' Christoph said as he put the money down on König's desk.

'Nice doing business with you, Mr Rittersmann,' König said and shook his hand. 'Just let the Palace pay *me* next week, and I'll give you your share,' he added, as Christoph was gathering up his coat from the spare chair and turning to leave.

That night, shortly before eleven, there was a knock on Christoph's door again. When he opened it, Valentina was standing there as if she had just come in from the street, her light summer coat buttoned up and a hat on her head.

'I had to be there for the last screening tonight,' she said. 'It's been a long day. I don't think I could sleep if I went to bed now.'

'Vally, come in – or we could go for a walk,' he said, bending forward to give her a kiss on the cheek. She smelled of fresh air and a perfume that he could not name. 'It's a nice night. Up to Central Park and back again?'

'It would be good to get some air,' she replied. 'I've been inside all day.'

The night was mild and they walked arm-in-arm up the gentle slope of East Eighty-Ninth Street and over the avenues that bisected it, wide like rivers, until they reached the edge of the park. Valentina's closeness to him, her warm body pressed right up against his as they walked, made Christoph want her, want sex itself, more than ever, but he knew that the first time they had slept together would be the last. He did not so much care about hurting Matthias: it was more that he could not do it to himself. Things were still far too complicated and unresolved back home. It was better to be outside with Valentina than in his room. They hardly exchanged a word as they walked, but they were comfortable with one another and happy to walk in near-silence.

An ornate carriage, pulled by two immaculate white horses, glided down Park Avenue like an apparition. The horses trotted in perfect synchrony, and the clatter of their hard hoofs echoed and bounced off the high buildings that lined the avenue. The coachman tipped his top hat at Christoph and Valentina, and must have taken them to be two lovers out on a night stroll. The visitors to the city, who sat huddled together in the open-topped carriage, waved as they passed and then turned their heads to look into the dark interior of the park.

They got back to the door of their building just after midnight and Christoph was suddenly exhausted. Staying awake until dawn that day had caught up with him and he was half asleep on his feet. He tried to say goodnight to Valentina at her apartment door, but before he could say anything she had climbed the half-flight of stairs ahead of him to his room.

'I don't want to be alone tonight,' she said, pushing open his unlocked door.

'I'm really dog-tired, Vally. I couldn't sleep at all last night after the performance.'

'Perhaps you'll sleep better with me in your arms,' she said softly.

'No, we need to sleep alone in our own beds. We can't do what we did before, Vally,' he replied quietly, looking down at the floor and not at her as he said the words. 'It wasn't right. I can't be with you in that way.'

'I think you deserve a treat for your success the other night at the theatre,' she said, moving gently towards him and touching his arm.

'We've been friends nearly all our lives, you and I,' Christoph said, now turning to look her in the face. 'It was a mistake what we did, however much I liked it.'

'But Matthias hasn't written. I don't want to be alone. I don't think he loves me since what happened last year.'

'He does very much, I'm sure of that. And it was wrong what we did,' Christoph said. 'He needs you and you need him.'

'What do *you* need?' she asked, suddenly bitter, her mood darkening and her beautiful mouth forming an ugly sneer as they stood in his room together. 'I thought you needed warmth, sex. You seemed to want me.'

'I do,' he said. 'And I do want those things, but I can't have them from you. Matthias would never forgive you and I don't want to break up your marriage.'

'But you've already bitten from the apple, my Adam – I've already let you taste its flesh,' she said with a sarcastic

81

laugh, and slammed the door behind her as she left his room.

That night Christoph's sleep was wracked by nightmares of the Front, of exploding shells and searing shrapnel entering his flesh, painlessly and soundlessly.

CHAPTER TEN

The black locomotive belched clouds of steam up into the cavernous space beneath the roof of Grand Central Station. It was the end of the second week of May and the air was thick with heat. Christoph stood under the arch at the entrance to the platform with the small leather valise that he had purchased second-hand especially for the trip, waiting for Valentina who was coming straight from the movie theatre. The train to Chicago departed at three o'clock.

He loosened his tie and collar and let the sweat evaporate from the lower part of his neck. He draped his jacket over his arm and waited. He was very early; over-punctuality was something that he had learned while serving in the army. There, you were not allowed to be late, even for your own death. There were still more than forty-five minutes to go until the train left, and he had their tickets in his hand.

There was still an awkwardness and a distance between them, that was for sure. It had been more than a fortnight since she had left his room in her fit of pique and they had not spoken for several days after that. Only when Valentina had received a long letter from Matthias and an expensive-looking invitation card to the premiere, a week before the event itself, did her mood improve and she forgave Christoph for rejecting her. At least, he assumed she had forgiven him, as she slipped a note under his door, begging him to come with her to Chicago and to try to forget what had happened between them. He did not really want to go, but was curious to see what Matthias had been up to there.

The passengers had almost finished embarking by the time Valentina reached the platform. She was out of breath but smiling. A porter was helping her with her case.

'Sorry I took so long,' she said, as they climbed into the carriage. 'The subway was very slow. Are you excited? I can't wait to see Matthias and Chicago.'

'I'm looking forward to hearing how the conductor and the orchestra have interpreted the symphony,' Christoph carefully replied as they walked along the corridor, trying to find their compartment. 'I read it through from the first note to the last, and feel that I know it a little. I haven't been to a big concert since Berlin. It'll be vunderful to see such a famous orchestra play.'

When he was tired or anxious like he was now, Christoph forgot to soften the initial 'w' of certain words and pronounced it hard, with a dragging 'vun–' springing from his lips, which made Valentina smile even more broadly as Christoph walked down the carriage ahead of her, carrying both of their cases.

'I can't tell you how proud I'll be of Matti,' she said. 'I've forgiven him for not writing for more than a month. He described how hard they've been working – twelve-hour days or longer. I didn't realise. Then Stock, the music director, wanted him to make some final changes to the score.'

They found their sleeping compartment, which despite being in second class was smartly furnished with a bunk bed and a banquette. Christoph opened the window vent to get some fresh air to circulate as the train's whistle gave a shrill shriek and the great beast of iron and steel woke from its sleep and roared out of Grand Central Station.

They were travelling overnight and would arrive in Chicago in time for morning coffee. Christoph wanted to ask Valentina how she really felt about seeing Matthias again, or rather how she felt about herself after what had happened between them, but did not know where to begin.

'Shall I take the top bunk?' he asked, as he dumped his case on it.

'I'll have less far to climb,' she replied. 'And there'll be no danger of me falling out,' she added with a laugh.

'The top one has this rail: you'd really have to want to fall out to come to any harm.'

It took over twenty hours to get to Chicago, because the train slowed in the early hours of the morning to allow its passengers a full night's sleep. Christoph thought that this was a long time to spend in a small compartment with your childhood friend with whom you had recently, deliciously, slept behind her husband's back; the more so because he would readily do it again if it was not for how he would feel afterwards. He was terribly anxious about Chicago because he was not certain that Valentina would hold her tongue and he was in no hurry to see Matthias.

'Will everything be all right with you and Matthias?' he had asked as the train rattled through New Jersey.

'Why shouldn't it be?' she had replied nonchalantly.

'Because of, you know, *us*,' Christoph said. 'Because of what we did.'

'Don't forget that Matti's an artist: he's got more of a free spirit than you might remember. What happened with us was just lust, almost like a child's game,' Valentina had winked at him and half smiled with her lovely mouth, apparently trying to find humour amidst the awkwardness.

'If he ever found out, I think he'd understand that I was lonely while he was away from me.'

'I'm not so sure at all, Vally. I think you're being deliberately naïve …' Christoph began, his sentence petering out as he looked into her dark eyes. From the barely perceptible undertone to her voice, he could tell that she was anxious. He worried again that she would not hold her nerve and would tell him.

Christoph had always been closer to Valentina when they were younger, perhaps simply because he preferred female company, and would be relieved more than anything else if he and Matthias never had to see each other again. He did not want a relationship with Valentina, but did not want to lose her friendship either.

The great train hammered on across flat landscapes and the sun was still above the horizon as they ate supper in the dining car. Christoph would have to sing on fifteen Tuesday evenings at the Palace Theatre to cover the cost of his train ticket, and that cost did not include the meal. They both had roast lamb, well done, and the dark gravy ran over the fine white china plates. Christoph could pay his rent and something towards the electricity from what he earned each Tuesday night, as well as food, but he was never going to be a rich man working so little. He had gone far into the reserve of money that his father had given him. He needed König to find him other places to sing. He had not signed an exclusivity contract with the Palace.

'Where are you?' Valentina said suddenly. 'You're miles away, somewhere across that landscape.'

'I was just thinking about money, I'm never going to earn enough to keep a wife and a child singing at the Palace Theatre once a week. I need to find more work.'

'Who's talking about a wife and child?' Valentina asked and laughed, the light sound filling the subdued dining car.

'In the future, I mean, when I've made something of my life.'

'Haven't you already, with your singing and what's happening with it? Everyone who hears you says your voice is something special.'

'I have a very long way to go before l feel that I've done anything worthwhile,' he said.

After they had had one or two more drinks of soda water in the dining car following their meal, it was late and they were both tired from the journey. Christoph sat on the lower bunk while Valentina washed herself at the small sink in the cramped lavatory next to their compartment. He caught the curve of her breast in the mirror as she raised her arms to slip into her nightdress back in their compartment and he felt that familiar surge of desire again. When they had climbed into their separate beds and said goodnight, he lay there like an impotent child, forced to sleep in the bunk above her as she slept right below him under the surprisingly soft sheets in her negligee.

The train came into LaSalle Street Station just before eleven in the morning, after they had breakfasted in the dining car on toast, kippers and the finest coffee that Christoph had tasted in America. Valentina had slept like a baby, she said, while he had tossed and turned all night because of the intermittent trackside lights flickering through the blinds, the noise of the engine up ahead and because he wanted to be in bed with Valentina, not marooned up above like a sexless castaway. Now that she was not interested in him in that way and knew that Matthias was waiting for her, he had suddenly become ever keener to sleep with her again.

Manhattan had not immediately been what Christoph had expected, the high-rises and skyscrapers nowhere to be seen when he had disembarked, the cityscape rising above him in its vertiginous, phallic beauty only later that first day in America. But Chicago took his breath away as soon as he stepped out of the station. It was as if Babel had come to the Midwest. They took a taxicab straight to Orchestra Hall: it was the premiere that evening, and Valentina wanted to see Matthias as soon as possible to wish him good luck before the greatest night of his life. Christoph sat beside her on the hard seat of the car and his heart beat harder and faster the closer they got to the venue. They sped past the bases of endless skyscrapers and he even forgot to crane his neck to admire their heights. It was as though he were in any other low-rise city sitting in that taxi, he was suddenly anxious about what might happen while they were in Chicago. He had not thought clearly enough before he set off from New York about what he might be getting himself into coming here seeing Matthias again, after what had happened between him and Valentina. She, on the other hand, seemed not even to be giving it a second thought.

The building's rusty-brown and imposing façade gave little indication of what went on behind, apart from the 'Theodore Thomas Orchestra Hall' inscription above the doors, and did not prepare Christoph for the beautiful interior, the great curving balconies and vast concert platform. They certainly did things bigger and better in this country.

When Valentina enquired, the front-of-house staff said that the orchestra was going to begin its final rehearsal in an hour or so and that Herr Walter was off somewhere deep in the bowels of the building, resting before the suspense and exhilaration of the afternoon and evening ahead. She said she did not want to disturb him, but would wait to see him when he came out for the rehearsal. Christoph told Valentina that he would go for a walk and explore the city, but was sure to be back in time to wish Matthias good luck. In truth, he wanted to escape as soon as possible so as to minimise the chances of having to make small talk with Matthias.

He walked down to the waterfront and strolled along the shore of Lake Michigan, humming to himself the songs that he was learning for his next performance. The lake was a sea without waves and the city crept right up to its edge. The late morning was hot, with the sun shining down through a cloudless sky. He took off his jacket and draped it over his arm. He had left his case and coat with the cloakroom attendants at Orchestra Hall. He felt alone but not lonely and greeted the other walkers along the shore as they passed him with a friendly nod and a rise in the volume of the sweet sounds coming from his throat.

The thoughts went round and round even while he distracted himself with song. It was clear that he would have to find somewhere else to live. He could not go on being Matthias's lodger, even if he never found out about what had happened. Matthias's politics aside, how could he go on living in the same building, pass him on the stairs, accept cups of tea or coffee, be brought his post by him, even use his bath, when all the while at the back of his mind crept the thought that he had slept with Valentina? It was up to Valentina to decide what she should do about her part in all of this. He wished that he had not come to Chicago.

The city gleamed in the light. The glass of the

skyscrapers refracted and reflected the sunshine, passing it from one sharp corner to another like a message. Christoph was hungry and wandered through these steel, stone and glass canyons looking for somewhere to eat lunch. He found a diner that looked plain and simple and sat down at a corner table, ordering steak and potatoes with a glass of milk. He still had a few hours to kill before the concert began at seven-thirty.

The waitress smiled at him and asked, 'From out of town are you?' after she had taken his order.

'I live in New York, but I come from Germany,' he replied, wondering how she knew.

'You speak good English,' she said.

'I did classes at night-school before I came to America and before that at normal school when I was younger. I've been here for nine months now,' Christoph said, enjoying her company and suddenly feeling talkative.

'Well, enjoy your meal.'

'What's your name?' he asked, not wanting to let her go. She was pretty and friendly and he wanted someone to talk to.

'My name's Anne,' she said. 'What's yours?'

'Christoph, Christoph Rittersmann,' he said as she went to clear away the two tables that the only other diners in the restaurant had just vacated.

He ordered coffee and dessert and chatted some more with Anne as she lingered by his table. He was now the only person left in the diner, all of the other customers having finished their fifty-cent lunches. She was originally from Ohio, she said, but had come to Chicago for work. She was only twenty-two and her parents were both immigrants from Germany. She explained that she read German fluently and still spoke it at home with her folks sometimes, but that she was too shy to speak it with Christoph right now because she pronounced it with a strong American accent. She had bright blue eyes, dark brown hair and he thought she was very sweet. Anne told him that her ambition was to go to New York later in the year to see the city for the first time and to find work. Before he left the diner, Christoph wrote down his name and address on a paper napkin for her, as well as that of Leo König in case he moved apartment in the meantime.

Christoph did not get back to Orchestra Hall until a quarter to seven. It was a beautiful evening and the audience was beginning to congregate in the foyer and outside the main doors, savouring the last of the summer light. The lobby bar did not serve alcohol, and Christoph asked the bartender for a glass of their very finest Chicago tap water. He was confident enough in his English now to make this little joke. He stood sipping the water quietly on his own outside and tried to imagine how Matthias must be feeling. Very nervous and very excited in equal measure, he imagined. He could not see Valentina anywhere, but the front-of-house staff had been given his name and knew to let him into the performance, as there was a seat reserved for him somewhere towards the back of the auditorium. Matthias and Valentina had to sit right up in the front row alongside Stock, the Chicago Symphony Orchestra's music director; the city's mayor; and the great and the good of Chicago society. Christoph wondered what they would think if they knew about Matthias's involvement with Teutonia, and what that odious organisation stood for.

The announcement came that the concert would begin

in fifteen minutes and the throng of the audience funnelled slowly through the doors into the auditorium as if it was a single, pulsating organism, only to fragment once inside into individual audience members in eager search of their seats, their genteel conversations and high-spirited laughter echoing back at them from the distant ceilings of the hall.

Christoph saw Matthias and Valentina enter the hall, but he was trapped in his row of seats by six or seven people sitting immediately to his left nearer to the aisle. It would have been impossible to get out of his seat and reach them, even if he had wanted to, without causing annoyance to his fellow audience members only five minutes before the concert was due to start. In any case, the couple were surrounded by a small group of dignitaries as they made their way down the central aisle to the front row, and it would have been awkward to try to catch their attention in such exalted company.

Christoph found it amusing to think that Valentina still had to work in the cloakroom of a movie theatre to make ends meet when watching this glittering scene unfold around her husband, and he could not begin to imagine what the mayor and the other dignitaries would think if they knew what the *Empire Symphony* was really about. He had to hand it to Matthias: he had managed to pull the wool over a lot of people's eyes to be standing here in America tonight just before the world premiere of his *Meisterstück,* whose stirring music yearned for the aggressive expansion of the German realm.

The conductor strode up to the podium, his dark hair falling flamboyantly over his shoulders, and the elegiac first movement that Christoph remembered so well began. The orchestra played it ineffably. It was note-perfect, with not a bow-scrape or sigh of the French horn out of place.

The audience's appreciation after the first movement was enthusiastic, if restrained. American audiences did not seem to applaud quite so freely as German ones; there seemed to be something concerted, something synchronised about the way that they clapped, as if they were doing so to the rhythm of an unheard, regular drumbeat. As the symphony unfolded in all of its dark grandeur and mysterious nature-drama, so the audience's approbation grew ever freer and more ecstatic, until the hushed reverence with which they greeted the fourth and final 'Empire' movement erupted into a release of joyous, delighted cries when the conductor's baton came to rest for the final time.

As they stood to leave the auditorium, Valentina and Matthias were crowded by eager members of the audience wishing to offer Herr Walter their congratulations and surrounded by the dignitaries who had sat through the concert with them. Christoph did not want to push his way through the fray to offer his words of praise, but went out to the foyer and waited there. It was almost half-past-nine and it had grown dark.

The audience poured out of the auditorium into the foyer and onto the street, but it was not until ten o'clock that Christoph saw Matthias and Valentina coming out towards him, still surrounded by a group of people; the conductor, what looked like one or two musicians from the orchestra, and an older man who Christoph took to be Stock, the orchestra's music director.

'Did you enjoy it?' Valentina asked, smiling with a certain tension behind her eyes. Matthias was talking animatedly to the group of men, who were all carrying their hats in their hands and had not thought to put them on, even though they were about to go out into the night air.

'It was wonderful,' Christoph replied. 'Sorry that I did not see you earlier.'

'There were so many people who wanted to talk to us before the concert,' Valentina said. Christoph noticed the 'us' and the unity that it implied, and was surprised that she had made the mistake of thinking that it was her that the dignitaries and hangers-on wanted to get close to.

'Hallo,' Matthias said, his cheeks flushed with pride and the heat of the auditorium, and shook his hand enthusiastically. '*Grüß dich!*' He obviously did not sense that anything was wrong between them.

The group went for dinner at a nearby restaurant and chatted into the early hours about the concert and the great success of the *Empire Symphony*. Valentina sat close by Matthias, and Christoph, down the far end of the table, had no opportunity to speak to her alone. Matthias was jubilant and expansive, buying everyone supper even though he had little money. His gesture of gratitude for the group of musicians, orchestra staff and friends around him caused Valentina to look at him in concern.

Matthias clapped an arm round Christoph's shoulders as they finally got up from the table after more than three hours in the restaurant. When he leant in close to Christoph to talk to him, his breath smelled of whisky from the small bottle that Christoph could see bulging in Matthias's jacket pocket.

'So, you think it was a success?' he asked.

'You saw it for yourself, Matthias. The audience went wild with applause at the end.'

'And you? What did you think of it, my friend?'

'I liked the sound that the notes made, but not the

meaning that they carry for you.'

'A diplomatic way of putting it,' Matthias laughed loudly, turning his head back towards the rest of the group behind them, who were gathering up their coats and hats. 'You always had something of the diplomat or the civic functionary about you, my dear Christoph.'

'It seems you are the one with a functionary's role in that organisation of yours, if what you say is true. Two such artistic people with the hearts of bureaucrats: who'd have thought it?' It was Christoph's turn to laugh, although his tone had turned sour now. He wanted to shake off Mathias's arm from his shoulders.

'Talking of Teutonia, I've met up with my friends from the unit here while I've been in Chicago. It's a lot bigger and more organised than my group in New York. Their militia's very well trained, it seems.'

'I don't want to hear another word about any of this *Scheiße*. Didn't I make myself clear the last time that we talked about it?' Christoph said loudly and angrily, moving away from Matthias towards the door of the restaurant. Valentina glanced over at them in alarm, while the rest of the group looked on in bemusement at this disagreement between two old friends.

'But it was you who brought up Teutonia in the first place,' Matthias replied, raising his arms and shrugging his shoulders as if Christoph had completely lost his head. He went over to collect his coat from Valentina, planting a drunken kiss on her lips as Stock handed him his hat.

At nearly two o'clock in the morning, Christoph made his way to the cheap hotel where he was staying. The rest of the group, fractured by the note of disharmony between Matthias and Christoph, headed home in various directions across town. Valentina and Matthias went off by taxicab to the apartment that the Chicago Symphony Orchestra had lent to Matthias for the duration of his stay.

The next afternoon Christoph boarded the train heading east, back to New York City, alone.

PART II: YORKVILLE

CHAPTER ELEVEN

January 1932

Snow was falling on New York. Christoph had moved to a two-room apartment in Yorkville at 141 East Eightieth Street in June, shortly after Valentina and Matthias had returned from Chicago. It seemed that she had, after all, held her nerve and not told Matthias about their night together, but she had come up to Christoph's room nonetheless one stiflingly humid evening to ask him to leave.

'I'm sorry, but I think it would be much better if you found somewhere else to live now. I want things to work out for me and Matthias,' she said.

'Believe me, Vally, I'd already made the decision to move out while I was in Chicago,' Christoph replied. 'I'm sorry to say this, but Matthias has changed for the worse since we were in Germany and I don't like how he is now. Surely you can see that the things he believes in, his politics, aren't acceptable? Not here. He's going to make a lot of enemies if he carries on the way he has been.'

'Matthias and I don't talk about those things very much. He's my husband and I'll always stand by him,' was all that Valentina had to say.

He had not seen them since he'd moved out and not a day went by when he did not regret what had happened between him and Valentina. He often wondered how she was and whether she was happy with Matthias. Perhaps the trauma of losing her baby had weakened Valentina, diminished her, somehow. Before he had come to New York, Christoph had always believed, right back to when they were children, that she had such strength of character, such backbone, yet she seemed completely blind to Matthias's failings, to his moral corruption.

His portion of the weekly three dollars that he earned for his Tuesday evening performance at the Palace Theatre allowed Christoph to buy food and to pay his landlord, a Latvian who had come to New York twenty years earlier and had apparently made his fortune in imported herring. It left nothing spare, however, and the money from his father had now all but gone. He was anxious to know when he would cease being a 'new' singer and be given a more lucrative Friday or Saturday night hour to himself, with his name on the bill and up in lights. Now that König was getting his weekly cut, he seemed to have lost interest in further promoting Christoph's career.

Anne, the pretty waitress from Chicago, had written a note to him, care of König, telling him that her letter to his East Eighty-Ninth Street address had been returned to her unopened and that she would not be leaving for New York until the New Year. Christoph had written back to her immediately; he was half expecting her to announce herself to the building superintendent any day now. He had begun fraternising occasionally with the other performers at the Palace Theatre, but spent long periods of time on his own and could do with some company. Anne had seemed a nice girl when he had spoken to her in the diner and it was, after all, only gentlemanly to take her under his wing when she arrived in New York.

Christoph was on his way to New York Public Library, a letter from Miriam in his coat pocket. The air bit into the exposed areas of his face and hands as he was trudging through the snow. He had never known it as cold as this back in Germany, and now understood why all the rich women he saw walking down Park Avenue or getting out of their chauffeur-driven cars wore thick furs. He pitied the doormen of the Upper East Side more than anything else. They stood still as statues in this cold, huddled in their greatcoats, for hours each day. He needed to buy some thermal vests and long johns. He was worried that the weather might get to his chest: if it did, he could not sing and if he could not sing, he could not pay his rent or eat. He had nothing else to rely on but his voice.

Miriam's latest letter had been forwarded to his new address, arriving already four months ago. Neither Matthias nor Valentina had sent an accompanying note. While they had taken the trouble to send Miriam's on to him, they had chosen to return Anne's letter. He now understood that they must have done it for Miriam and the Bernsteins, not for him.

C. Rittersmann
233 East 89th Street
New York, New York

25th August 1931

Dear Christoph,

She has learnt to sit up on her own and smiles at me whenever I bend to feed her. She has the sweetest smile.

Eva has begun to crawl across the floors of the apartment at some speed and I must always be on my guard, lest she escapes my sight and comes to some harm or mischief. I wish that you could see her. I wish that she could see you.

I take it from your silence that you have chosen to leave us behind. I could accept that, but only if you could find the courage to write and tell me so.

Yours, as ever,
Miriam

He needed to write back to her. He needed to write back to her, he repeated to himself, if only to tell her that he had moved address. He struggled to formulate the right sentences in his cramped apartment so he had decided to try the New York Public Library on Fifth Avenue, in the hope that this great building made of words would somehow inspire him.

He took a seat at an old oak table in the Rose Main Reading Room, overwhelming because of its vast scale and the infinite knowledge held in the reference works on the shelves that lined its walls. He noticed that every other visitor ordered books from one of the librarians then waited patiently until they were brought to their place at one of the tables. Most of the readers looked like men or women you would see on the street, perfectly normal types that you could spot at any time of day walking around Midtown or the Upper East Side. They did not look like university professors. One or two even seemed a little dishevelled and down-at-heel, as if the Depression had evicted them from their homes in the harsh winter and driven them into the warmth and peace of the library.

Christoph was the only one there who did not order a book. He was there to write, not read.

141 East 80th Street
New York, New York

Lothringerstrasse 37
Wuppertal-Elberfeld
Germany

15th January 1932

Dear Miriam,

I am sorry that it has taken me so long to respond to your letters. ~~For a long time I did not know what to write.~~ It has taken me much longer than I expected to establish myself here in this new city and new country. ~~I can only apologise.~~ I am sorry for my silence.

~~The news of our daughter was a complete and utter shock, I must admit.~~ The news of our daughter was too wonderful to

describe, but surprised me greatly. ~~I did not know that you were expecting a child, and do not know what to say~~. All that I can promise is that I will return to Germany one day to meet her and to see you again. ~~Of course, I trust you that she is mine and will provide for her as best I can~~. I will send you money when I can.

Life here is strange and hard, but I am making some progress with my singing. ~~I hope that, one day, you will be proud of me~~. I hope that, one day, I will achieve what I came here for and make Eva proud that I am her father.

Yours, as ever,
C

P.S. Please note my new address above, as I am no longer living in Matthias and Valentina's apartment building.

The letter to Miriam was much harder to write than the one to Anne had been. He struggled to find the words to express himself, to tell Miriam how he felt about the news of his daughter, to know what to say to her after all of these months of silence on his part. He had to force the words out and hoped that they did not come across too awkwardly. He carefully wrote out a fair copy of his letter, folded it neatly into the envelope that he had brought with him and put it back into his pocket, ready to take to the post office that afternoon. The number of readers in the great room had thinned out towards lunchtime and Christoph wandered out onto the street to look for somewhere to eat. He was singing that night and needed to keep his strength up.

'I heard there's gonna be some sort a trouble over there

soon,' the postmaster said when he saw the destination of Christoph's letter.

'What do you mean? What sort of trouble?' Christoph replied, completely nonplussed that this man in a post office on the Upper East Side should have news about his homeland that he had not heard himself.

'I read something about the National Socialists pushin'' for power. They're somewhere right of Attila the Hun, apparently.'

'Oh, that party. They're no more than a joke: that little man's good at talking and was talking even before I left Germany in 1930. They won't get anywhere,' Christoph said.

'Well, I guess we'll see,' the postmaster replied.

That night when he was singing on the stage of the Palace Theatre in front of an audience that was fuller than usual, he could not keep his mind off what the postmaster had said. Once or twice he almost forgot the words to the songs that he had rehearsed so thoroughly. For a split second he was out with his timing of the first note of the first verse of 'Manhattan Misses', his last song that evening, after the accompanist had so deftly played the jaunty opening bars.

> *Manhattan misses they are divine*
> *In their mink and fox and fine ermine*
> *Genevieve, Annabel and Catherine,*
> *None of those Manhattan misses are mine.*
>
> *Oh, Manhattan misses so divine,*
> *Will one of you be my Valentine?*
> *From Park Avenue to East Seventy-Nine,*
> *I've been searching for my Valentine …*

The crowd did not seem to notice his slip and applauded loudly and long after his final number. Christoph had never had a Tuesday night when the crowd, whatever its size, had not responded enthusiastically to his singing. Mr Perlman, the artistic director, had recently been hinting that Christoph would soon be promoted up the ranks of his roster of performers to a Saturday evening slot, at six dollars for the forty-five minutes, but had yet to deliver on his word.

Anne arrived in New York in the third week of January after the snows had passed, staying with her paternal uncle and aunt in their tenement apartment on the Lower East Side. She announced herself to the building superintendent of Christoph's apartment the next day, and caught Christoph at home.

She was even better looking than he remembered and he was proud to walk down Third Avenue with her that afternoon, however cheaply made and plain her clothes might look to the well-heeled passer-by. She was far from being one of the primped and pristine Manhattan misses that he had sung about in that song, but she had a fine sense of humour and a natural, easy grace that most of those girls probably did not have. She said that she had a job lined up as a waitress in a hotel restaurant in Midtown, so a step up from the diner in Chicago. The pay was low but the prospects were good, even in this climate, and she had somewhere free to stay for as long as she needed it.

'So, I'm going to be around for quite a while. You'll have to get used to me,' she said with a laugh.

'Good, then we'll have plenty of time for me to show you around this wonderful city,' Christoph replied. 'I know it pretty well after almost a year and a half.'

'I hardly know anyone here, apart from Aunt Susan and Uncle Thomas and they're always so busy. I hope you'll be happy to be my own handsome tour guide,' she said.

'I'll do my best. I'm not so sure about the "handsome" part though.'

'Oh! Most definitely.' She laughed her sweet laugh again. 'You can be my German knight in shining armour in this unfamiliar city. Isn't that what the "Ritter" in your surname means?'

'Yes, that part means "knight". I'll try to live up to it. I hope I won't disappoint you.'

'I'm sure you'll do just fine,' she said.

CHAPTER TWELVE

Anne visited Christoph before or after her shift at the hotel restaurant almost every other day. He was grateful for the company and they went for long walks in the icy weather, through Central Park or around the Upper East Side and down to the river.

'You'll get sick of me before too long,' she said one day as they were walking down Madison Avenue. 'You shouldn't have given me your address.'

'Oh, there's no danger of that,' he said. 'I've been kind of lonely for a long time now. It's very nice to have some company.'

'Have you always lived on your own, since you've been in New York?'

'I was living with two friends from Germany, but it became a little difficult with them – we were all too on top of one another – and I moved out last summer. I've been entirely on my own since then and what I do for a living means that I spend a lot of time alone.'

Later, on another of their walks Anne said, intrigued 'You haven't ever told me what you do for a living, although you made it sound a little lonely. Are you a writer or a poet or something?'

'A *poet*?' he laughed loudly. 'I wish that I was. No, I'm a singer, a tenor, and I sing at the Palace Theatre down on Broadway. You should come: I sing each Tuesday night at the moment.'

'I would love to hear you sing,' she said, turning to him with an eager smile.

Anne had never been to a city quite like New York before. She was wide-eyed about everything and her eyes sparkled in the winter light; Christoph showed her around proudly, as if he were a native of Manhattan. He took her to the recently opened Empire State Building at Fifth Avenue and West Thirty-Fourth Street and they both craned their necks to look up at the soaring glass and steel, although neither wanted to pay good money to go up to the observation terrace on the eighty-sixth floor. The sunlight, broken and refracted by the glass, made their eyes weep as they looked up, as if they were overcome by the monolithic immensity of the building.

'Gosh, it makes our skyscrapers in Chicago look rather small in comparison,' Anne said, wincing against the sunlight. 'And that's no mean feat. You kind of feel you want to fall backwards when you're looking up, it's so high.'

'I've never really understood the Americans' urge to go upwards,' he said. 'If it's all about space, you Americans have so much more of it than us Europeans do.'

'Oh, I think it's just us Americans wanting to show off, to show the world what we can do,' she replied.

Anne was almost a decade younger than Christoph, but he soon realised that she had a wise head on her shoulders; she looked at the world around her with a clear-sighted maturity and gentle humour. She was always talking as they went on their walks through the city, telling him about her childhood in Columbus and her time in Chicago. He was happy just to listen to her stories, to watch the life of Manhattan go by around them and not to talk too much himself. He found hers an easy, relaxing presence and in her company he felt a comfort he hadn't thought he would find in his new homeland.

'When I was a child, I had this little kitty called Orinoco,' she said one day. 'I've never had a cat since. I was heartbroken when she died, I was about twelve. The problem with living in rented accommodation or with family as I do here is that I can't have a cat. I'd so much like another one.'

'Perhaps one day you – and your husband – will be able to afford your own place in Manhattan and then have a cat again.'

'My *husband*?' she let out a long, sunny laugh. 'I don't have a man in my life, let alone a husband.'

'I mean when you do, one day,' he said, hinting at something. What it was, he could not exactly say.

'Who says that I'll ever get married?'

'All pretty girls get married, don't they?' he replied. 'Marriage, a home, children, that's just what happens, isn't it?'

'I guess I'll have to wait and see,' she said.

He had the feeling that she was both teasing him a little and testing him, waiting to see whether he might declare an interest himself. He did nothing for the time being, although he wanted to. He had fallen for her, but found it difficult to tell her. They went on seeing each other as before, every couple of days, for their walks and visits around town.

On one of their walks, towards the end of February, Anne reached for Christoph and he held her warm, gloved little hand in his as they walked along a snowy footpath in Central Park. He knew then that she thought of him as more than just a new-found friend in a strange city, and this realisation made his attraction to her ever stronger over the following weeks.

Christoph, while wanting Anne in his life, was only too aware that he risked entangling a young and beautiful girl in the complicated private life that he had left behind in Wuppertal. If they entered a relationship and it became serious, something that required a meaningful commitment, then it deserved complete honesty from the start. There had already been one or two days where things were less harmonious between them, when she said next to nothing during their walks, expecting him to express himself finally, to come out with it and tell her how he felt, but still he held back. His reticence, the reasons for his need to tread carefully, to take his time and consider how to play things so as not to cause her – them – problems later on, frustrated him and made him tense and prone to an irritability that was most unlike him. For fear of saying something out of turn or something that might upset her, he, too, said nothing of importance on those days and they walked side by side, arm in arm, in near silence. It could not go on like this.

He told her that he had to go away for a singing commitment to the Midwest for a week, but stayed in Manhattan. He bought himself some time to think. He was too preoccupied with Anne even to be able to focus properly on his singing practice, even though he had quite a few new numbers to try out for the Palace Theatre. He paced up and down his small apartment for some of the morning, then when he could take that no longer he went out to walk around the city.

A new relationship might need complete honesty for its foundations to be secure, but he could not tell her about

Eva, not yet. He could not tell her about his affair with Miriam now. That was for certain. It would kill any hope of a relationship even before it had really begun. But he had to tell her about Ida, he had to tell her that he had lost his wife. That was the very least that he should do, Christoph told himself.

On the day before he was due to be back from his supposed trip to the Midwest, he sat down at the small table in his apartment and wrote Anne a letter. It flowed so much more easily than the letter he had written to Miriam and he felt bad that he had struggled to know what to write to Miriam, what to say to someone whom he had loved since they were children.

141 East 80th Street
New York, New York

Miss Anne Tietsch
c/o Mr & Mrs Thomas Tietsch
Apt. #53, 152 E. 26th Street
New York, New York

10th March 1932

Dear Anne,

You have my heart, but I think you have guessed that already. Even though we have only known each other for a short time, I must confess that I have completely fallen for you. I am yours if you will have me. I am sorry that my words are not more romantic. I am better at singing other people's words of romance than at writing them myself.

113

Before you decide on how you would like things to go on from here, and before we see each other again, I must tell you that I was married before I left Germany. My dear wife died in 1929, at only twenty-nine, of a sudden illness, and I have been something of a lost soul since then.

I am not looking for someone to replace her, for she is irreplaceable, but I am looking for someone to fill some of the emptiness that has been inside me since she left. If you feel that you are willing to have me as I am, and with the past that is mine, then I am yours.

I will wait for the apartment doorbell to ring, if it does again, with your three rings.

Your C

He took the six-line down to Twenty-Third Street and walked up and over to East Twenty-Sixth Street through the midweek crowds. The cold winter wind had given way to a warmer front over the last week and spring was finally coming into the city. Heavy buds and pale green leaves hung from the trees that lined the streets off Lexington and Third Avenue.

Christoph rang the bell for the superintendent at Anne's apartment building and asked to be let in, knowing that she would be out waitressing all day at the hotel and that there was no risk of bumping into her, and left the letter in her uncle and aunt's letterbox down in the lobby.

The very next day the doorbell rang with Anne's three short rings, which had become something of a secret code between them. As soon as Christoph opened his apartment door after waiting for her to climb the four steep flights of uncarpeted stairs, hearing the echo of the scuff of her footsteps in the stairwell, she threw herself into his arms.

'I'm so glad you're back! I'm so sorry for what happened to you … of course I'm yours, more than you can know,' she said between sobs. She looked lovelier than ever and Christoph could not have been happier.

By late April, Anne had moved into his apartment. Although she was much younger than him, it was clear to both of them that they understood each other very well and would make a happy couple. He had proposed to her on Easter Day and had already known for some weeks that he wanted to marry her.

Anne would always be surprised at how quickly they had fallen in love, but had said yes without hesitation and was only anxious that she would make a good wife. Her uncle and aunt had readily given them their blessing: secretly, they were relieved to have one less mouth to feed. They were impressed by Christoph's apparent sophistication, his obvious kindness and his artist's sensitivity. He seemed to wear his heart on his sleeve and they could see that he doted on Anne. The wedding day was set for a Saturday in late May.

Christoph still had not told Anne about Miriam or his daughter. After much soul-searching he had resolved that it would remain his one secret from her, harboured and tended like the smallest and weakest of flames. How would Anne ever learn about them? He kept Miriam's letters in a small wooden box pushed up through the hatch into the darkness of the loft space above the double bed that he had bought as an early wedding present. He would have to make sure to keep the only key to the apartment's postbox in the lobby safe on his key fob at all times, so that if another letter from Miriam arrived he could collect it without Anne seeing it.

A note came from Leo König in early May. He had some good news and needed to speak with Christoph at his office. Christoph went to a public telephone booth one block away from his apartment and called König's secretary to make an appointment for the next morning. The noise from the traffic and the passers-by made it difficult for him to hear what she was saying. At one point in their short conversation, he thought that he caught the words 'You seem to have taken a step up, Mr Rittersmann,' although he was not quite sure that he had understood her meaning properly. They arranged for him to see König at ten o'clock.

Anne had to make him a cup of cocoa that night as he could not get to sleep. He lay wide awake in their bed all night wondering what the news would be, finally falling asleep at dawn. He woke with a start just after eight o'clock, feeling as though he had just snatched some brief moments of sleep from the iron grip of the night sky in the dugout in the winter of 1917.

König was drinking a black coffee from a chipped white china cup when Christoph went into his office. König's first words immediately caught him off guard and he felt himself blush.

'Herr Walter told me that you haven't spoken for almost a year. It's a crying shame you've lost touch. Happens all too often in this city. Did you know they're thinking of going back to Germany?' König said, looking at Christoph across his large desk in an almost avuncular way.

'Are you sure? I can't believe it,' Christoph cleared his throat. 'I thought his career was going so well here. Why would they want to do that?' He was appalled but not at all

116

surprised to hear this news.

'Herr Walter's excited about the future there, it seems. I can't imagine anything worse than living in the same country as that shit Hitler. But I guess you and Herr Walter aren't Jews. Hitler's not a friend of the Jews ...' König trailed off. 'Herr Walter seems to think Hitler is Germany's future. He's not even in *power*.'

Christoph could not bring himself to say that he knew all too well where Matthias's politics lay. He wanted to tell König why he had not seen Matthias for all that time; he wanted to tell him that his late wife and last girlfriend were from a Jewish family and that he had a daughter who was Jewish, but he could not tell him these things. He was sure that König would not be impressed that he had produced a child out of wedlock and left her behind. More importantly, he knew that König might one day meet Anne.

'On a different note, I asked you to come here because Mr Perlman called me,' König continued. He did not usually discuss matters that did not relate to work, to music and the theatre, and Christoph was grateful to be back on the safer terrain of business. 'The Palace is offering you a Saturday evening: seven to seven forty-five. It's a little early, but not too bad. The going rate is six dollars, but I'm seeing if I can push them up a little, because you've waited patiently for quite a while.'

'Thank you, Mr König, that's exactly what I've been hoping for. Thank you for negotiating with Mr Perlman for me. I'm very pleased.'

'Negotiating for *us*, Mr Rittersmann, negotiating for *us* ... *mazeltov* on your leap forward: you'll have to rehearse plenty of new material.'

Anne had started her new job as a waitress at Hannigan's Hotel on East Forty-Third Street in March, and between Christoph's weekly fee from the Palace Theatre and her poor pay but good tips from the restaurant, the couple survived comfortably while the Depression sucked the lives out of others less fortunate in that great city. They were even able to put a little money aside, and now that Christoph's parting gift from his father had all but gone, he was glad that they could save at least a very modest amount of money each week.

While Anne was out at work, Christoph spent his days rehearsing songs in their apartment, which was very quiet on weekdays as most other residents in the block were exhaled by the building each morning, off to work or to school or to look for work. Christoph subscribed to music publishers' lists and was always on the lookout for new songs that might please his audience, who favoured light numbers, witty or romantic throwaways, over anything too heavy.

The sound of his rich tenor voice echoed along the empty corridors of his floor of the apartment block. Christoph wondered sometimes whether anyone was listening from behind closed doors and, if so, whether they could hear the words that he sang. He wondered how strong his accent sounded when he was singing, as he could not hear it at all any more. He felt like a canary in a cage whose owners had left it all alone to sing to itself and wished that he had made more friends in the city. Apart from the occasional letter from his parents, who seemed to be getting on with their late middle age quite well without him, he rarely heard from his family now, much less than he had when he first arrived. He was waiting to learn how they had taken the news that he was going to get married.

CHAPTER THIRTEEN

Ever since the trenches Christoph had lost any belief that he might have had in God, but Anne was a Lutheran and wanted a church wedding. He had been baptised and confirmed and seen the inside of a church every Sunday until he was fourteen, and had no reason not to go along with her wishes, but still he found it unsettling to have to profess to a faith that he no longer held.

'Surely you'd like God's blessing on our marriage,' she said, 'rather than us simply getting married at the town hall or someplace like that?'

'I suppose so,' he replied, 'although I didn't see any evidence of God on the Western Front. After all of that, I rather stopped believing in Him.'

'Perhaps when our own child comes along you'll see something of God's presence in the world again.'

'I hope so but I'm not so sure about that. The things that I saw made me doubt that He exists at all. Not that you shouldn't believe in God, of course, or teach our children to believe in Him. We can bring them up in whatever church you like when we have them.'

Twice a week they went to Zion Lutheran Church on East Eighty-Fourth Street to meet with the priest. Pastor Schmidt must have been in his early sixties and had a nose that reminded Christoph of the inside of a succulent pomegranate, all fleshy, inflamed corpuscles and capillaries.

He had obviously been quite a drinker at some point in his life. Perhaps he still was, although Christoph never caught any hint of whisky, wine or any other liquor on his breath when the three of them bent together to look at passages from the Bible. He was sure that Pastor Schmidt would know where the right place was to buy alcohol if he could not help himself and had to have a drink.

Pastor Schmidt seemed impressed by Anne's knowledge of the Bible, and much less so by Christoph's careless confusion of Old and New Testament stories and events. He paid Anne frequent compliments during their half-hour discussions and, from his questions, appeared to be suspicious about whether Christoph was in fact telling the truth when he said that he had been confirmed in the Lutheran church. Christoph assured him that he had, in 1913, in Wuppertal. In the end, however, Pastor Schmidt seemed happy enough to marry them later in May.

Christoph had taken to opening the postbox for their apartment only when Anne was out at work at the hotel. Anne had received no post yet at her new home, but she was a keen letter-writer and Christoph was sure that her family would be posting lots of letters from Ohio before too long. He dreaded her asking him for the key to the postbox, and when she did he told her that the lock was stiff, but that he had learned how to open it by pushing and twisting the key just so, until the lock gave way.

A letter from Miriam arrived in the second week of May and Christoph felt guilty even opening the envelope.

C. Rittersmann
141 East 80th Street
New York, New York

25th April 1932

Dear Christoph,

I was overjoyed to receive your letter: a sign of life at last. I read it to our daughter and, although she is too young to understand the words, she saw by my face and heard by my voice that it made me happy, and smiled as I read it to her.

Eva has my two brothers to dote on her, but she needs a father. I had hoped it would be you, as you are *her father. Perhaps when you feel that you have achieved what you went to America to achieve, you will come home to us.*

Yours, as ever,
Miriam

After reading the letter sitting on his and Anne's conjugal bed, making him feel that he was cheating on her just by reading Miriam's words, Christoph climbed up onto the bed and pushed open the hatch, groping blindly with his fingertips for the wooden box and pulling it towards the aperture and down to him. He inhaled fine particles of dust from the rafters as he did so. He flicked the small brass clasp of the box open, lifted the lid and added Miriam's latest letter to the small bundle. He considered, not for the first time, destroying the letters, setting fire to them in the empty grate or tearing them up and scattering them on the East River like confetti, but that would mean destroying the words of someone he had once held dear and the written evidence of his daughter. He could not bring himself to do that.

The last Saturday in May brought beautiful weather with it. New York lay under a cloudless blue sky and the temperature was rising by the hour. Anne's parents had travelled all the way from Columbus – she had no brothers or sisters – and her uncle and aunt were standing outside the pale façade of the Zion Lutheran Church, dressed up in their Sunday best and waiting for the bride and groom. Mr Perlman had switched the performance schedule at the Palace to allow Christoph the night off. He had sung the evening before instead with his name third on the bill, and it had gone well.

König had excused himself, saying that he would feel awkward in a church, and the only guests on Christoph's side were a couple of his fellow performers from the Palace.

The bride arrived by taxicab with her parents, wearing a white cotton two-piece suit, the skirt cut at mid-calf and the jacket decorated with a small corsage of two white roses on her left breast. The assembled guests, seven in total, gushed at how beautiful she looked in her modern and elegant dress and the simple white cloche hat that hid her hair.

Christoph wore the better of his two suits, the one he wore for the Palace, and walked the few blocks up from their apartment to the church. He wished that his family was not half a world away and could see him now on his second wedding day, more than three years since that wonderful day he had shared with his dear Ida.

Pastor Schmidt was standing on a low step in front of the plain altar, which was partly covered by a white cloth and decorated with a single lit candle held by a wooden candlestick. Christoph went from the bright sunshine into the gloom of the church and took his place in front of him. He knew that he was making the right decision, but nevertheless his palms were sweating and he had a fluttering in the pit of his stomach as he stood by the altar with his head turned towards the door, waiting for Anne to walk up the aisle on the arm of her father. He had met the baritone Henry Cliff and Laurie O'Riordan at the Palace and they had quickly become Christoph's fellow soldiers of the stage if not close friends. The first notes of the organ sounded out and Anne and her father came in through the door, silhouetted against the light. She looked radiant in her white dress, so beautiful and young. She stood beside Christoph at the altar, the back of her delicate hand brushing against his as they turned to face the priest, and in low tones barely audible to the guests they swore their enduring love to one another.

When they came out of the church into the bright sunshine after the short service, Christoph and Anne stood blinking into the sun as a photographer took a picture of them with their guests ranged either side in front of the Gothic revival façade of the church. Christoph stood with his arm around the slim waist of his new wife and knew that something fundamental had changed, that Anne would bring only positive things to his life, and that his world would never be the same again. She represented a break with Miriam and his past and, deep in his heart, he was sorry for that caesura, for that rupture with his old life, but knew that it was the only choice for him now.

They had a small reception in a separate room at the back of Die Lorelei, a favourite restaurant of the Germans in Yorkville, and Christoph sang two or three of the Schubert *Lieder* that he most loved for his guests.

When he went to the men's restroom between courses, he rummaged through the newspapers and magazines and found a clipped-together selection of newspaper cuttings on Teutonia and various other news reports on the progress of the Nazi Party in Germany. One recent clipping on Teutonia from the *New York Post* even mentioned Matthias by name, and this sudden reminder of all that darkness threatened to spoil his evening. He would have to ask the management the next time he came to the restaurant why on earth they saw fit to keep such *dreck* on the premises. Now was not the time to chastise them on the matter, but it left a sour taste in his mouth.

'You make my daughter happy,' Anne's father said to him when they were a long way into the night, clasping him around the shoulders after one too many glasses of the chilled Riesling that he had sought out for his beloved daughter's wedding on the black market back in Ohio, bringing the case all the way with him by train. The management of Die Lorelei had turned a blind eye and even provided ice buckets. Christoph thought at first that he was making a statement rather than a command, until he understood the tone in his father-in-law's voice.

'I will. I will do everything in my power,' Christoph replied emphatically. 'You have my word.'

Christoph was true to his promise and he and Anne settled comfortably into their married lives together. By the autumn of that year, she was pregnant with their first child.

CHAPTER FOURTEEN

May 1933

In October 1932 the Nationalistic Society of Teutonia had changed its name once again, this time to 'Friends of the Hitler Movement'. The Society was disbanded in March 1933 and by May it had re-emerged with a new name but the same old beliefs – the Friends of New Germany. Hitler's election to Chancellor of Germany in January that year had given the organisation a real shot in the arm, and its numbers had swelled.

The New York newspapers were reporting that Rudolf Hess, the Deputy Führer of Germany, had authorised Heinz Spanknoebel, a German immigrant living in New York, to form the Friends of New Germany in support of the Nazi regime. Christoph wondered whether Matthias was still involved, or whether he had already gone back to Germany to support the regime in whatever way he could.

Christoph was back in the Rose Main Reading Room of New York Public Library one morning in late May, trying to write another letter to Miriam. While flicking through some newspapers that were lying on a table he came across a recent article titled *HEINZ SPANKNOEBEL NO DESPERADO, ONLY RIDICULOUS GERMAN*. The article was written by a Jewish journalist named Philip

Slomowitz and it made for a damning profile on the leader of the Friends of New Germany:

> *As the first Jewish newspaperman to have met and interviewed Heinz Spanknoebel, Hitler's spokesman in this country, I can't suppress a feeling of amusement when I read statements glorifying this fellow and dignifying him with powers which he does not possess.*
>
> *I am particularly amused when I read in the* American Hebrew *that he is "a desperado capable of any act to attain his end." What remarkable powers are given this young man who has learned almost verbatim to repeat statements and views fathered by Hitler.*
>
> *What sort of fellow is this Spanknoebel? Simple, without logical power of persuasion, except by repetition and constant emphasis on the views of his "fuehrer", he makes no impression at all. He is tall and has the Hitler close-cropped moustache, but aside from that it would be ridiculous to credit him with the powers he is said to possess.*

Christoph found this portrait of the young leader of the Friends of New Germany, surely one of Matthias's peers, reassuring, as it made him out to be nothing more than an arrant fool. He knew, however, that things changed very quickly in such organisations – leaders came and went; the organisations themselves formed and then dissolved only to re-emerge in a new guise under a different name – and it would only take the right leader with enough charisma and vitriol to make a real impact in America, not just in New York but in other cities across the United States.

So far as he could tell, the Nationalistic Society of Teutonia and now the Friends of New Germany were not being widely discussed in the circles in which he moved. True, there had been steadily more frequent reports in the newspapers about Nazi organisations over the last couple of years and what they represented had been roundly condemned by the press, but the public seemed to know little about their leaders or how large the groups were.

Christoph knew that it was not a time for complacency. Having seen the belligerent zeal in Matthias's eyes whenever he had talked about Teutonia, he understood better than most that the men in these groups were dangerous and not to be underestimated. All that it would take was someone with the right oratorical skills, with the right amount of venom and rhetoric, to ignite something that would be hard to extinguish.

What were the Friends of New Germany trying to achieve in New York and in other major centres across the Midwest and the north-east of the country? They were aiming for nothing less than to change the political landscape in America. They were trying to promulgate a positive image of Adolf Hitler and the Nazi regime, whilst spreading a campaign of hatred, of boycotts and bigotry, of protests and denunciations, against Jews in the United States and against all those who they felt were counter to the National Socialist ideal.

The Friends of New Germany had begun spreading rumours that Jews were behind organised crime in the United States and this newly formed version of an older organisation was now printing large quantities of literature, of pamphlets and booklets, promoting Nazism. Its divisional leaders under Spanknoebel were busy setting up youth indoctrination camps modelled on the *Hitler-Jugend* back home. Christoph read all that he could on such developments in newspapers and magazines. Without Matthias's updates he now knew nobody who was directly involved in what was brewing.

Christoph knew that if he wanted to find out what the Friends of New Germany were up to before news made it to the press, the answer, at least with the New York City unit, lay right where he and Anne lived in Yorkville. He would have to try harder to find out where and when their meetings took place, whether still at the Yorkville Casino or somewhere else, to ascertain who the main figures were in the organisation in Manhattan. Spanknoebel seemed to have an overarching role, but Christoph was determined to find his local henchmen.

His painful thoughts of Miriam and his daughter and piercing memories of Ida were impelling him to find the truth, to challenge the reprehensible movement that threatened the very freedom of thought, the very freedom of expression, and that wanted to divide people and to explode the world into war again. It was for them that he had to make a stand against what Teutonia stood for and what the Friends of New Germany were now trying to achieve.

He knew that he had an advantage. However many members of the Friends of New Germany there were, and however many other Nazi organisations in America might spring up, the majority of right-thinking German-Americans were like him. They abhorred the Gissibil brothers, Heinz Spanknoebel and their ilk, and the bad name that they were giving Germans in America. These men and their followers were *Pöbel*, they were uneducated rabble, and needed to be treated as such.

Chapter Fifteen

Summer 1934

Baby Leo was already one year old and crawling vigorously across the wooden floors of their small apartment. He was aptly named, Christoph and Anne always told each other, because he had the heart of a lion. He was fearless and bold and they constantly watched over their little lion cub who had no sense of danger himself. Only recently, he had managed to crawl through the open door of their apartment, which Anne had left ajar after coming back home weighed down with bags of groceries, and had made it all the way to the elevators down the far end of the corridor before she became aware that anything was wrong.

Anne was proud of Christoph's relationship with their son. He was the model of a kind father; loving, playful and solicitous of Leo's every need. The thought of how it would have been to bring up a baby daughter was often on Christoph's mind as he looked after and played with his son and his awareness of his failure with Eva drove him to be as good a father as he could to Leo. She would be three and a half now, a proper little girl with plaits or a pigtail. The twinges of guilt he felt at keeping his secret life from Anne stabbed at him. Leo's eyes had become the deepest blue. They were pools of limpid water in which his father lost himself, plunging into their soothing depths where everything was pure, peaceful and simple.

Money had become tighter with Anne not working, but Christoph was still singing at the Palace every Saturday night and that just about covered their expenses. He had found work as a private tutor for five or six hours each week, teaching the young society ladies of Manhattan how to breathe correctly when singing and how to form sounds from their stomach and diaphragm, not from their nose. All but one of his tutees showed no promise at all, singing as if the sounds were being wrung from their throats. He went to their grand apartments or to houses lining the park or the smartest avenues and streets of the Upper East Side where tutor and student were watched over by proud, elderly parents, who discreetly placed dollar bills in Christoph's hands as he left for home.

If his career was not exactly stellar, then Christoph was at least making a name for himself in Manhattan. Part of the Palace Theatre audience came each Saturday specifically to hear him sing and he received the occasional letter through the box office from fans. It was always women who wrote, telling him how much they admired him, the brave journey that he had made from Europe to New York to find fame and fortune, and how beautiful his voice was. They viewed him as the compère had once described him: as Rittersmann the Romantic. He saw the hollowness of this lie, but was glad that his voice gave them pleasure. He did not hide the letters from Anne and she was tickled to read what others thought of him, as he changed a diaper or scrubbed out the tin bath after washing himself in front of the fire.

After he was injured at the Front, Christoph had often wondered whether he would be able to have children: the wound had been perilously close to his groin, although there had been no obvious damage to his *Eier*, his 'eggs' as they were colloquially known back home. The doctors had said that he would simply have to wait and see. Eighteen years later and he found himself a father of two, although Anne knew only half the truth. She said that the scar was his lucky charm.

'*Schätzchen*,' she said: that was her pet name for him, little treasure, 'would you like another baby one day?'

'Let's try to do the best job we can first with our little man, and then we'll see,' he replied.

'I missed out on brothers and sisters and would've liked to have had them,' Anne said. 'I want Leo to have someone to play with, someone to teach his cheeky ways to when he's older.'

'I hardly ever hear from my sister any more,' Christoph replied. 'I often wonder how she and my young nephew are doing.'

'You're rather a long way from them. Out of sight but not out of mind, I'm sure. She's probably just too busy living her family life back home to write very often.'

'I guess so,' he said. 'She wasn't happy that I left.'

'Why? Because she was going to miss you?' Anne asked.

'Yes, because I'd always been there for her, to protect her when we were little. She seemed to think that I was breaking up the family by leaving.'

Christoph always spoke German to Leo when they were at home and English to his wife and son when they were out in public. He had been naïve to think that Hitler would never win power and now he had become ashamed of what was happening in his homeland and what organisations such as the Friends of New Germany were doing in America.

Although a large population of Germans and German-Americans lived in Yorkville, he did not want to draw attention to himself when out and about in the city, for fear of encountering anti-German sentiment from New Yorkers. From what they saw of Hitler on this side of the Atlantic, Germany was becoming a laughing stock to the Americans.

Anne had never been to Germany, the country of her parents' birth, and had only the vaguest of notions what it was like. Christoph told her how beautiful parts of it were, about how exciting his time in Berlin had been. He explained that he feared Hitler was hell bent on destroying Germany's standing in the world when he claimed to be trying to save it from the Depression, which itself had come over from America, and the collective humiliation its people felt after losing the World War. Anne said Hitler sounded like an angry child who had been picked on by his entire class at school, perhaps because of some innate mental weakness or some physical deficiency.

Anne had begun reading one or two of the German books that Christoph had brought with him from Wuppertal and sometimes, after a glass or two of wine, she would speak to him in German. She certainly did not *sound* like a German, but Christoph was surprised to find that the fundamentals of her grammar were almost perfect. Christoph had seen this before in people who had learned a foreign language by rote from books or from parents from another country who had insisted on that old-fashioned punctiliousness of speech and language.

Anne was amused that Leo's first word was 'Mama'. Long before he was two years old he gushed a fount of seemingly random English words like 'worm', 'brick', 'shoe', 'cat' which entertained and delighted his proud parents. He was a bright little boy and Anne called him the Big Apple of Christoph's eye. Christoph told her that her puns, while they made him love her even more, were rather weak.

One day when Christoph was bathing Leo in the tub by the fire, he reached up towards his father's face as he was rubbing his back gently with the flannel and said 'Papa' for the first time. It was a moment that Christoph would never forget, yet echoes of Eva's imagined face clouded the moment for him as he closed his eyes and bent down to kiss his son's forehead.

He loved his son more than life itself, but could not let go of his past. In his next letter to Miriam he would ask for a photograph of Eva, so that he could picture her when he thought of her, and not have these anchorless impressions of his daughter floating in his mind getting in the way of the here and now. He wanted visual proof that she existed. It suddenly became very important to him.

In August 1934, almost four years after he had first set foot in New York, Christoph got top Saturday-night billing at the Palace Theatre for the first time. Christoph knew that he had not been the management's first choice for its top-of-the-bill singer. They had had to change the posters at the last minute on the Friday morning, as they had just learned that their two main stars for the Saturday night were unavailable at the last moment: Verity Lopez because she had come down with a raging sore throat and could not sing a note, and Erich Romero because he had unexpectedly left town for Las Vegas with his fiancée to get married. They suspected that the soon-to-be Mrs Romero was pregnant.

Anne had asked her aunt to mind Leo for the evening and sat in the front row of the theatre. She looked up at her husband in his smart, double-breasted grey suit as he sang about love and other women, but she was not jealous: he had committed himself to her and she knew that. He still had an accent when he sang, but that only made his singing more endearing, more uniquely *him*. She had only seen him sing twice before at the Palace and was immensely proud. Each song that he chose became his own, almost as if he had written them and deeply felt each word. She doubted that he would ever become a household name, that was the stuff of movies and silver-screen idols, but he earned a reasonable wage from the theatre and being up there on stage seemed to make him happier than just about anything else, apart from his family. She could tell that his time in the war and other events in his past that he did not like to talk about had made him unhappy before they met.

Christoph's song choices had become lighter, partly on the direction of Mr Perlman and partly because he had learned that it was to the sentimental, the witty and the gay that the audience most responded. He tried to add one *Lied* into his performance each week and sang it in his native tongue, hoping that at least a small part of the audience would understand. His heart lay in these classical songs, but his audience mostly wanted new songs that spoke to them about their lives: songs of the city, songs of urban love and incident.

> *Alice, oh Alice, alas Alice,*
> *You've got me on the brink,*
> *You've got me on a precipice:*
> *There's no lower I could sink.*

You've found another love
When your love you did promise,
Yes you were my turtle dove.
Alice, oh Alice, alas Alice …

The song was saved from schmaltz by the tipsy piano
accompaniment and the grieving naivety of the persona that
Christoph had adopted for it. He sang with an exaggerated
German accent and placed the emphasis on the wrong part
of each line to make the rhythm off-kilter and the song
stutter like the complaint of a feckless Heidelberg student
on his first visit to the big city. The result was entirely comic
and had the audience laughing.

Anne much preferred the serious songs and saw that her
husband did not need to play the comic to win his audience
over, yet she laughed because the song in all its silliness was
simply funny. It was no bad thing for him to mix comedy
into his repertoire, which some members of the audience
might otherwise find a little high-minded. It did not upset
her at all that Christoph sang of other women: they were
simply figments of the songwriters' imaginations. When he
had sung the last song, his immaculate tenor voice singing
out into the silence of the auditorium, the audience stood as
one to applaud him.

CHAPTER SIXTEEN

The autumn of 1934 marked the end of Christoph's fourth year in New York. He was beginning to feel more American, now that he had an American wife and an American-born son, his homeland coming back to him only as a distant dream. But the newspaper reports of Hitler's extraordinary hubris and outlandish propaganda kept his mind on Wuppertal, on little Eva and Miriam. He could not let go of them, not yet. He did not think that Hitler's Germany was what he had fought for in the war.

In November, Anne went by train back to Ohio for the two weeks leading up to Thanksgiving, so that Leo could spend some time with his grandparents. It was the first occasion that they had left Christoph on his own, but with his commitments to the Palace Theatre and to his singing students, he could not accompany them. He had not left New York, not even crossed the water that surrounded Manhattan, since his journey to Chicago. He was beginning to feel the need to escape the confines of the city, the maze of asphalt, concrete, glass and stone, and see some open countryside again.

'You'll be all right on your own?' Anne asked him as they stood on the station concourse. 'You'll remember to eat properly?'

'I promise not to spend every evening at the diner,' he said.

'Doing some cooking will keep your mind off us. It'll be good for our little cub to see his grandma and grandpa. We'll be back before you know it.'

'Our apartment, New York, will be empty without you. Promise to return to me safely,' he said as they boarded the train.

There were tears from Leo and tears from Anne as he waved them off from the platform, Leo because he had never been away from his Papa before and Anne because she was unsure how Christoph would do while they were away from him. She could not picture her husband on his own, although he had been alone in New York until she came into his life.

Christoph left the platform wishing that he was on the train with them. What was a thirty-five-year-old man with few friends in the city supposed to do in Manhattan without his family for company? Perhaps he could look up Henry Cliff and Laurie O'Riordan from the Palace, who had been his only wedding guests and who were the closest thing to friends that he had in New York, and go out for dinner with them two or three times over the next fortnight. He could spend the days practising new songs for the Palace, looking for more singing students and chasing König again to find another theatre or music hall that was auditioning for singers of his type. A regular midweek evening performance would be ideal.

Whatever efforts he made to fill the hours and the days, Christoph knew that he would have too much empty time on his hands and that he would spend most of the next two weeks on his own, either walking through the city, singing, or sleeping in the bolt-hole of their apartment. His mind would go back again and again to Germany, to little Eva and to dark-eyed Miriam, to what was happening in his homeland, and he would not know what to do with these thoughts.

He had not written to Miriam for more than six months, since late last winter, and at best wrote to her twice a year. Miriam sent him two letters to every one of his and there was now a small bundle in the box hidden from view above their marital bed in a tiny corner of the loft. The day after Anne and Leo had left he sat down at their dining table and told himself that he would not get up again until he had written to Miriam.

141 East 80th Street
New York, New York

Lothringerstrasse 37
Wuppertal-Elberfeld
Germany

15th November 1934

Dear Miriam,

I am sorry for my silence. I hope that this finds you and little Eva well.

~~You must be wondering what has become of me.~~ You must be anxious for a response to your letter of June. ~~All that I can give you as an excuse for my not writing sooner is that time seems to slip unnoticed through my hands.~~ All that I can give you as an explanation for my slowness in responding is that life is very busy here.

I am sending you $20 and ~~it is all that I can afford at the~~

~~moment, as I have a wife and young child to support over here~~ *~~in New York~~ I hope that this will help you to buy sufficient winter clothes for Eva to see her through to the spring or summer. I will send more money when I can.*

~~I would like to ask you a favour:~~ I have a small request: I would be most grateful if you could send me a photograph of Eva, so that I have something to know her by.

Yours, as ever,
C

Christoph wrote out a neater copy of the letter and took it to the post office, where the same postmaster who had commented about Hitler and the National Socialists was still working behind the counter. This time the man just stared at Christoph with a questioning arch of his eyebrows when he saw the name on the envelope and the destination of the letter. Somehow, his silence was worse than his words had been and Christoph left the post office feeling more unsettled than ever about the situation.

Winter weather was descending once again on New York. The months and seasons seemed to be coming round ever more quickly as the years went by. It felt like only a few moments since 1933 had become 1934 and the old year had given way to the new, already the circle was about to be repeated. A light snow fell on the 18th November. Christoph stoked the fire at night and sang wrapped in his coat during the day. He missed little Leo's sweet voice, his laugh that held nothing back. He missed Anne's touch, her warmth, her conversation. The apartment echoed with silence when he walked across its bare floors, and his voice came back to him when he sang.

*

There was no telephone in the apartment and Christoph had to walk over to Bloomington's Hotel on the corner of East Seventy-Ninth Street and First Avenue to ask the reception staff whether he could pay to use the hotel's telephone, so that he could call Anne's parents to make sure that they had arrived safely. No one answered the first time the operator put him through to their number in Columbus, the girl on the hotel desk hovering at a discreet distance as he waited on the line, but on his second attempt, two days after they had left New York, he got through. Anne's voice, usually so bright, sounded subdued across the crackling line. Leo had a head cold and they were both missing their songbird in Manhattan, although they were happy to see her parents and she was happy to see her childhood home again.

Speaking to Anne, hearing her voice made the silence of the apartment even more oppressive. Christoph pulled down the box of Miriam's letters and read each one slowly, sitting on the bed's soft counterpane with only the sounds of the street two storeys below for company. He still could not countenance destroying the letters or finding a safe place for them somewhere outside the apartment, such as a bank vault or a safe deposit box. He wanted them close to him so that they would compel him to *act* one day, to *do* something. He could not yet define to himself what this something, this action was. He read the last of Miriam's letters and his hands trembled almost imperceptibly.

Christoph had an audition at Jackson's Music Hall down on the Lower West Side the first Friday after Anne and Leo had left for Ohio. König had sent him a short note some days earlier, summoning him over to his office in order to

141

discuss what was on offer at the music hall before Christoph went for the audition. He was, as usual, on the telephone when Christoph got there.

'Mr Rittersmann, it's been a while,' he said when his call was eventually over and Christoph sat down on the chair in front of his desk. It looked as if König had had something done to his teeth: they looked whiter than usual and even more evident in his mouth. Christoph thought of sugar lumps.

'It's the first audition I've had in a long while,' he replied. 'It's not easy money-wise with my wife not working.'

'The movies are taking over,' König replied. 'So much so that I've been thinking of becoming a *movie* agent. There's so little work out there for live performers, for old-fashioned artists of the stage.'

'I don't really think of myself as old-fashioned,' Christoph said.

'Well, you're a craftsman in song, someone who's got traditional stage presence, who can hold the spotlight. But the movies are all about the face, the pose, the look. They can turn anyone who looks right into a star.'

'I like watching movies,' Christoph replied, 'but I don't think acting would be for me. I like being myself.'

'Jackson's Music Hall's smaller fry than the Palace,' König said, changing tack abruptly, 'but it's got a very good reputation for the quality of its performers and the pay's not bad.'

'And they want me midweek?'

'Tuesday or Wednesday evening, your choice, as long as you pass your audition. And let's face it, you're hardly going to fail.'

'It depends on what sort of singer they're looking for,'

142

Christoph replied.

'They're looking for a classically trained tenor who doesn't mind turning his hand to lighter numbers and popular songs. Can you see anyone else in Manhattan who'd fit the bill better?' König asked with an expansive sweep of his hands, his teeth glittering in Christoph's direction.

'And, don't forget,' König added, 'let me do the negotiating when it comes to the money.'

A few days later, as Christoph stood in the sunshine on that freezing morning with his back to the yellow façade of Jackson's Music Hall on West Twenty-Second Street, his breath pluming out of his nostrils into the air, he knew that the audition had gone as well as he could have hoped. The stage had been small, only half the size of the Palace Theatre, but the artistic director seemed to know what he was doing, talking of broadening the repertoire and the range of what they offered at the music hall to attract new audiences, and obviously liked what he had heard. He had offered Christoph the midweek performance slot of his choice after just one song. Christoph would have good news for Anne and little Leo when they came home.

Christoph had a celebratory meal the next evening at Die Lorelei with Henry Cliff and Laurie O'Riordan. They had been his guests there at the wedding, this time they wanted to buy him supper to congratulate him on his news. Christoph had not been back since his wedding night, when he had found those cuttings on Teutonia in the men's room. He was not at all keen to visit the restaurant again but he did not want to seem ungrateful to Henry and Laurie. He arrived half an hour early, his friends had probably not even left home yet. He wanted to find the owner, or at least the manager, and ask him why they had kept such cuttings on the premises. Had they been left there by one of the staff, or by the restaurant's patrons?

The only members of staff on duty were two young waitresses and an Argentine chef in the kitchen cooking the solid German fare that the restaurant was known for. They seemed not to understand what Christoph was talking about, and looked at him uncomprehendingly when he tried to explain. He was not going to get anywhere with them. Perhaps the articles had, after all, just been left there by a visitor and finding them did not mean that the restaurant somehow supported Nazism. Perhaps he would never know. He had misgivings about Die Lorelei: it seemed a little too proud of its German heritage and exuded a deeply ingrained nationalist confidence that raised the hairs on the back of his neck.

Henry and Laurie told him as they sat down to eat that they were also trying to find more venues where they could sing. They were pleased to hear that it was still possible to find work as performers in music halls other than the Palace. They ate fried wursts that still sizzled on the plates as they were served, and a large helping of potato salad. Henry and Laurie were both the children of Irish immigrants and neither of them lived in Yorkville. They were not used to being surrounded by so many German voices, but seemed to like the simple food and the German beer.

'When was the last time you were home?' Henry asked.

'September 1930,' Christoph replied. 'It's been a while.'

'D'you miss it?' Laurie said. 'You don't seem to talk about it much.'

'There's not so much to tell. You read the newspapers. I'm embarrassed by what's happening over there. Most Germans here would probably feel the same way if you asked them. It's only the ones who never left Germany who don't seem to see what's going on under their noses, or those who have come over here but appear to have been brainwashed before they left.'

'Anyway, your good health,' Henry said, raising his beer glass. 'I hope that things in Germany get better. It's hardly been a bed of roses in Ireland.'

'Anne will be pleased at your news, won't she?' Laurie asked.

'She'll be relieved that a little more money will be coming in,' Christoph replied. 'It's not easy supporting a wife and child on what the Palace pays.'

'Tell us about it,' Henry said.

'You don't have a child,' Laurie laughed and winked at Christoph.

'Well, me and the missus will do soon, I hope,' Henry replied, looking very slightly peeved.

Anne and Leo returned home on the icy night before Thanksgiving and it was the sweetest homecoming. Christoph met them at the train platform with a small bouquet of roses wrapped in brown paper for his wife and a new wooden toy truck for his son. There were tears again, but this time tears of happiness at their reuniting. The Thanksgiving meal that Anne prepared the next day seemed to be the perfect celebration of their coming together again as a little family.

CHAPTER SEVENTEEN

February 1935

The winter still held its grip on New York. Traffic and pedestrians moved slowly on the icy roads and a dense fog settled overnight on the city, not lifting until late in the morning each day. Christoph took Leo to play in the snow in Central Park, father and son both wrapped up in thick winter coats. Leo had never seen snow before; he skipped and played in it in wonder and innocence, curious at the white blanket that covered the city. He gathered up great armfuls of the ice-laden snow and scattered it around him, laughing with delight. His cheeks were red with cold and good health.

Christoph had never had a weak chest, but developed a head cold that turned into a cough in late February so he could not sing at the Palace Theatre or at Jackson's Music Hall for almost two weeks. He didn't get paid when he missed a performance, and Anne had to manage the household finances very carefully for weeks afterwards to make sure they had enough money to put food on the table, and to pay their bills. She had to turn to her parents for help for the first time since she and Christoph had been married. Christoph sat glumly in an armchair, with a woollen scarf wrapped tightly around his neck, and realised more clearly than ever before that his life in the United States had severed his old life, his family and their possible support in times of difficulty clean away. He blamed the weakness in his own being, his refusal to deal with the realities of his life head-on, as one of the chief causes of his illness now. His fear and essential weakness had battled his conscience and won, time and time again, over the past four years. He had been unable to tell anyone, including Anne, about his daughter in Wuppertal. His harbouring of secrets had drained his mental and physical reserves and laid him open to infections such as this.

He realised, when he could not sing, how much he depended on singing, how in love he was with his craft, his voice. His speaking voice did not mean much to him and what he had to say he deemed of very little consequence, but when he sang he knew that he was doing what he was born to do. As he sat in his armchair day after day, confined to the apartment and unable to sing a single note, he suffered from withdrawal symptoms and became irritable, even with Leo with whom he spent a large part of those two weeks playing as if he himself were again at kindergarten.

Anne did her best to cheer him up, as well as running the home and making sure that Leo was up, washed, dressed and fed each morning in good time. This process was reversed each evening so that she and Christoph could spend their evenings together, with Leo snug in his bed.

Christoph started singing very gently towards the end of the second week of March when the last traces of his cough had gone, only going up and down the scales and repeating short passages and phrases from songs that he knew well. His voice was in better shape than he had feared and by the following Wednesday he was confident enough in its recovery to sing at Jackson's Music Hall. He had missed the lights and the audience and was happy to be back in the world where he felt most at ease. The crowd at Jackson's Music Hall were rowdier than the patrons of the Palace Theatre and, if anything, showed their appreciation for his singing even more, shouting out and clapping loudly at the end of each performance.

Christoph's worries about money had eased a little by the spring of 1935, and he and Anne were able to put a small sum of money aside again each month. Leo was almost two years old and was outgrowing his clothes at a rate of knots. He was going to be a big child, a strong boy. He stuck by his Papa's side whenever his father was home, which was most of the day, and they formed an unbreakable bond, a jolly little unit that made Anne smile with unadulterated happiness whenever she saw them together. In their company Christoph felt almost complete, up in their apartment away from the hubbub and din of New York.

A letter from Miriam arrived one Monday morning in early April. Christoph waited until Anne had gone out to buy groceries for the week before he opened it. From the thickness of the envelope, he could tell that the letter held something enclosed within it. He took it to the dining table and sat down to the late breakfast that he had just started on. He had interrupted his breakfast to go down to the lobby to see Anne and Leo off and had opened the postbox with his key on the way back up to the apartment. He had somehow guessed what might be there and had no idea how this instinct, this foresight, could possibly connect with the physical movement of a letter across the world. It was entirely impossible that he could have known, yet he had somehow.

C. Rittersmann
141 East 80th Street
New York, New York

15th March 1935

Dear Christoph,

You asked me for a photograph of our daughter. I am
enclosing one that was taken of Eva in a photographic studio
in Wuppertal to celebrate her first day of kindergarten two
weeks ago, just after her fourth birthday. You will see that she
is wearing her hair in pigtails. They are one of her favourite
things at the moment; pigtails and her new little satchel that
she carries everywhere.

I am still working as a seamstress in the shop on
Neviandtstrasse, but the proprietor is in grave financial trouble
because Gentiles will not come to the shop to have clothes made
or alterations done and much of his business has fallen away. I
do not know how much longer he can keep me on. Please send
some more money for Eva if you can. We were very grateful for
what you sent before. My brothers are helping as much as they
can, but they are also facing difficulties and Abraham is soon
going to have a family of his own to support.

I hope that your life in America is what you expected and
wanted.

Yours, as ever,
Miriam

Christoph had held the photograph hidden behind the letter
as he read Miriam's latest news, and had forced himself to

read each word of the letter carefully before he would allow himself to look at the image of Eva. And now here she was: smiling out at him, standing side-on to the camera with her satchel on her back, her head turned towards him. He could see that she had dark hair like her mother and her eyes were soulful, overarched by expressive eyebrows. Her smile radiated out at him; she was a very beautiful little girl. He had to admit that he could see something of himself in her, although she had her mother's dark looks. His heart gave a jolt as if it had stopped momentarily. He could not eat another mouthful of his breakfast. She was only two and a half years older than Leo and she was already a proper little girl with a strong sense of herself, judging by the way she looked into the camera's lens with such confidence and openness. She did not even know that he existed.

That first image of Eva imprinted itself on Christoph's eyes, implanted itself into his mind with such force that it was as if he saw the world through a translucent, ghostly version of her face for weeks afterwards. Each time that he reached into the loft to retrieve the photograph from the box, Eva's face was imprinted again in his mind. Christoph went through that spring and summer thinking of very little else. He found the guilt almost unbearable and did not know whom he felt guiltier towards: Miriam; Eva; Anne; or Leo.

Anne might have noticed Christoph withdraw into himself at home, only putting on a brighter version of himself for the stage, but he could tell that she knew that prying into the reasons for his withdrawal would only be met with silence or excuses and that it was best to let her husband tell her what was on his mind when he was ready to do so. Christoph's silence on what was troubling him continued into the high summer, although his mood and enthusiasm for life, for Anne and for their little lion cub, showed a slow but steady improvement until he was almost back to his old self again by late July.

They even managed a week-long trip upstate that month to the Catskill Mountains. They stayed just outside the town of New Paltz in a small cottage on a farmstead. They were brought breakfast and supper each day by the farmer's wife, and it was the first vacation that they had ever taken as a family. The Catskills area was very popular with immigrants from across Eastern Europe, and it was busy with holidaymakers in the heat of the summer, escaping the even denser heat of the city. Mrs McCardle, the farmer's wife, had rosy cheeks and told them that her folks had come from Scotland, just like her husband's, in the middle of the nineteenth century.

'Mine came from Germany about thirty years ago,' Anne said. 'I was born in Columbus. My husband is actually from there. Germany, I mean.'

'Is that so?' Mrs McCardle replied. 'I've always wanted to go to Germany. I'm something of an amateur historian of northern Europe's cathedrals, and your country has some particularly fine examples,' she said, turning to Christoph.

'I guess you're right, though I've never really been to many of them, except for Köln,' he answered. 'Although I did have to go on a communion tour of Holland and some of its churches when I was fourteen ...' he trailed off as Leo let out a wail, wanting food or attention from his mother.

They spent the week going on walks through the woods and hills, Christoph carrying his son in a rucksack on his back. He had adapted it by cutting holes for his legs in the lower two corners of the voluminous canvas bag, leaving

Leo's head, arms and upper body sticking out the top. New Paltz itself had little to offer the tourist, although they ate lunch at some of its restaurants and wandered around its few shops after walking into town on a couple of the cooler mornings of that week. The weather was generally blissfully warm and Anne seemed happy that her husband's spirits had lifted again.

'What's been making you so down since Easter?' she asked him out of the blue on one of their walks. Leo was chattering to himself in the rucksack just behind Christoph's head.

'I haven't been down. I've just had things on my mind,' he replied.

'You're not unhappy with your little family, I hope?' she asked.

'Unhappy? No, I love you with all my heart.'

'Then what's troubling you?'

'Sometimes I worry that I'm not a good father.'

'You dote on Leo. When he remembers his childhood, he'll remember that above all else, I promise you.'

Christoph wanted to tell her the truth, to correct her understanding of what he had just said, but felt that old fear crawling into his throat so the words wouldn't come out. He could not bear to ruin their holiday, what they had together. It was the nearest that he had come to telling Anne about what he had left behind in Wuppertal without even knowing that he was leaving it behind. He bit his tongue and they carried on with their walk.

Back in New York, refreshed by the break from the city, his head cleared by the mountain air, Christoph resolved to put Eva to the back of his mind and to dedicate himself to his family and his career with renewed enthusiasm and energy. He began to teach Leo some German nursery rhymes and bought him a little wooden tricycle that he pedalled up and down the corridors of their apartment block with surprising speed, once he had learned to use the pedals rather than scoot the tricycle along with his feet. He tried to imagine his son as a man one day and what he might be like, but one look at those beautiful, clear eyes and the thought of Leo as anything other than a little boy became almost impossible.

Christoph could not delay answering Miriam's last letter for too much longer and was secretly putting aside some money each week from the Palace Theatre and Jackson's Music Hall so that he could send her another small contribution for Eva. After reading her letter for perhaps the tenth time, he suspected that it would not be too many months before she lost her income as a seamstress if the tailor for whom she worked was doing so badly.

He knew by then that the National Socialists' obsessive hatred of the Jews would not diminish, but still he could not understand why the party's supporters cared whether their suits were cut or their dresses taken in by a Jew or a Gentile. The fingers of one were as nimble as those of the other; their eyesight was no better or worse for being or not being a Jew. How could it possibly matter who sewed your clothes?

CHAPTER EIGHTEEN

October 1935

By the autumn of 1935, Christoph had been in America for half a decade. He had almost forgotten what it was like to feel German. His homeland was half a world away and getting more distant by the day. The latest news that he read in the newspapers particularly upset him. A new set of laws had been laid out at the Nazi Party rally in Nuremberg in September that defined a Jew in terms of bloodline, and it was quickly becoming clear that rights were taken away from you if you were categorised as a Jew in the Third Reich. People were losing their jobs, being excluded from their professions, and to leave the country you had to pay exorbitant exit taxes.

If Miriam lost her job as a seamstress, a job that was itself already very badly paid, how would she support herself and Eva? She would have to rely entirely on her two brothers for money. Her parents were both in their seventies and far too old to help. One of her brothers was a tailor and the other ran a greengrocery with his wife. He had not forgotten how Ida's and Miriam's brothers had struggled even when he was first married to make ends meet, and that was before Abraham was married. If they lost their jobs as well, who would help Miriam and Eva?

Christoph went to see König to ask him to look for

more work for him. His voice could take at least four or five performances a week, and as he was home during the daytime most days he would not be neglecting his family duties. He had not heard from König for a while and had learned that only the most successful performers did not have to chase their agents to look out for them.

'I signed up some movie actors since you were last here,' König said. 'They're even more sensitive than you singers. They *kvetch* about the way they're lit, the behaviour of their directors, their fees … if it wasn't such a growth industry, I think I'd stick with singers and performers.'

'Our world is a lot simpler, I guess,' Christoph replied. 'Give us a stage and an audience and we're happy.'

'There's tradition with you lot, hundreds of years of history, a repertoire. With the movies there isn't anything, it's all too new. No one knows where the limits are, no one really knows how it all began.'

'Have you heard of any new auditions for my kind of singer?' It was Christoph's turn to change tack abruptly; a tactic that he'd noticed formed a regular part of König's way of speaking. 'I'm looking to work another two or three evenings a week. Life's becoming a whole lot more expensive.'

'It's been a bit quiet lately on the audition front, I've got to say.'

'Well, if you hear of anything, anything at all that's at least halfway decent, please put me forward for an audition. I want to work. I need the money.'

'Another child on the way?' König smiled at him, but glanced down at a pile of papers on his desk and did not seem to be waiting for an answer.

'Not exactly,' Christoph replied.

*

Christoph sent Miriam fifty dollars that month, almost half of his and Anne's savings from their joint account. He vowed to himself to put the money back into the account just as soon as König had helped him to find another singing job.

He did not know how he would explain the absence of half of their savings if Anne found out about it, but would have to invent an unexpected cost or outlay. Perhaps he could say that König had told him that he owed him fifty dollars in unpaid fees, or that he had to pay out that amount in annual royalties to the writers and composers of the songs that he sang. Anything that sounded plausible would do. He hated lying to Anne, but could not let Miriam and Eva go hungry. If Anne ever found out the real reason the money was missing from their account, he imagined that their marriage would be over. Perhaps he was wrong, as Anne had always shown remarkable understanding for her fellow man and it was hardly as if he had been unfaithful to her, but he could not take that risk. He was afraid of losing everything he had. But not telling her was eating him up inside, consuming his conscience as he lay in bed beside her on sleepless nights. He would have to find a way to confess his past to her sometime, somehow.

Christoph was gaining quite a following at the Palace Theatre and drawing a growing audience at Jackson's Music Hall. Both venues now used the epithet 'Rittersmann the Romantic' to advertise him among their main attractions each week, a sobriquet that he found acutely embarrassing. This image of him was so far off the mark that it entered the realm of the absurd, but then the stage was a game and he

157

had no choice but to play along. Just because his brilliantine-sleeked hair glistened in the lights, his face possessed a certain satisfying harmony of shape and his eyes sometimes betrayed the misty sadness of a man far removed from his homeland, it did not mean that he subscribed to feelings of empty sentimentality. His appearance was just that – a trick of the light, a gift of his birth.

He meant every word of the songs that he sang; even the songs that were lighter and that seemed more frivolous held within them truths about life, about humanity, that spoke to him. Then there were the serious songs, his classical repertoire: the *Lieder*, Schubert, Schumann, Liszt, that meant far more to him than any of the others. Their melancholy, their beauty, the way they captured the depth of human emotion touched his heart in ways that he simply could not describe.

When he was at the conservatoire in Berlin he had been a model student, studying not just the theory and practice of singing, but immersing himself in learning about the history of *chansons*, *Lieder*, opera, the story of song going as far back as Gregorian plainchant, right up to modern-day show tunes and contemporary jazz numbers. It was his way of forgetting about the Front. When he sang, he could not think about anything else; when he thought about song, he did not think about the War.

He had never been much of a pianist and rarely accompanied himself on the piano as a student, but at the conservatoire everyone learned to play at least one instrument and he used to practise his scales with gentle fingers up and down his girlfriend Frieda's flawless back. His fine, tapered fingers traced out the gentlest arpeggios of desire along her spine, the softest glissandos as she lay there sleeping with the covers thrown off in the heat of the summer up under the eaves. Looking back at that time, when Ida and Miriam had been only childhood friends and nothing more, Christoph saw how simple it had all been. The pain of leaving Frieda behind when he returned to Wuppertal, the uncertainty about what he would do with his life had seemed to him to be insurmountable things. If only he had known how much harder and more complicated life would become.

CHAPTER NINETEEN

January 1936

A bitterly cold wind was blowing up Madison Avenue. Christoph was out with his son, looking for picture books, while Anne rested in their apartment. Leo's gloved little hand was warm in his. He was soon to be three years old and could only walk short distances before he needed to be carried on his father's shoulders.

'Papa,' he said. 'Why's Mummy sleepy?'

'Because she does so much for us and needs to rest sometimes. You're going to have a little brother or sister all for yourself.'

Leo was quiet for a moment and then asked to go on his father's shoulders. The sidewalk ahead of them was a sea of faces and of hats hurrying around them. Leo gripped his father's ears beneath his trilby so as to get a better hold.

'But Leo likes it just Mama, Papa, Leo,' he said in a quiet, timid voice from up behind his father.

'Well, I'm sure you'll love your baby brother or sister when he or she is here,' Christoph replied.

Leo said nothing more until his father had deposited him in the doorway of the first bookstore, and then simply said, 'Leo help Mama more.' His sweet nature, his innocent and unalloyed kindness almost broke his father's heart.

It was the greatest of pleasures looking at picture books

with Leo, telling him the names of animals and letting him repeat them before he turned the page; watching him look at images of giraffes, zebras, lions for the first time. Leo was spellbound as they sat on a low wooden bench together on the ground floor of the second bookshop that they entered on a cross-street just off Madison Avenue.

'Leo means lion,' Christoph said.

'Leo's a lion!' Leo said, letting out an attempt at a roar, which was more like the loud purring of a cat.

'You'll grow up to be big and strong like one, I'm sure,' his father said.

'Big and brave! Like Papa!' Leo exclaimed, grabbing his father's arm and pulling him down closer in to him, looking around, as if watching out for danger, with his father covering him to defend him against some unseen enemy. Christoph laughed, but it was not a laugh filled entirely with happiness.

Christoph had assumed that, aside from those few friends of Matthias, most of the Germans amongst whom he lived in Yorkville were as opposed to Hitler and the National Socialist regime as he was. But he was hearing ever more frequent rumours that this was not true. He had kept on trying to believe, perfectly blindly as he now saw, that the great majority of German immigrants or children of immigrants who had come to Yorkville would abhor the Führer and his dogma, his hysteria. He had hoped against hope that there were only a small minority of people who were as zealous in their adulation of Hitler and what he stood for as Matthias.

He heard of meetings in several German bars and pubs in Yorkville where there was now open and vocal support for the Führer. One of the performers at the Palace

Theatre – Otto Griebenbach, the *basso profondo* whom he did not know so well – told him that he had been in one of these bars, having a quiet drink with a few friends, when he saw such a meeting going on. He had asked the barman what was happening and had been told that it was a meeting of the Friends of New Germany.

'American Nazis,' the barman had called them, with a dry laugh by way of an explanation, Otto reported to Christoph in a confiding tone. He told Christoph that he was fairly certain he had spotted Matthias Walter there. He recognised him at once from a newspaper article. If Otto was not mistaken, then Matthias had not yet gone home, or at least not for long. Christoph was not surprised to hear that Matthias had been at such a gathering. He hoped that Otto was telling the truth when he said that he himself had just happened to be having a drink in the bar. You never knew whom you could trust amongst the Germans of Yorkville these days.

American Nazis! That phrase still sounded to Christoph like an absurd pairing of words, one that defied logic. How could anyone, of their own free will, support what the National Socialists stood for? Perhaps these supporters of the regime in Yorkville were people who had no family or friends back in Germany any more? People who simply looked at the old country from the freedom of America in a kind of abstract, detached way, believing that Hitler was doing good for Germany after the Depression without seeing all of the abysmal darkness of the man and his party. Christoph resolved ever more firmly that he would try to counter these voices of approval for Hitler.

He told Anne about this resolution to speak out against the Nazi regime, using his slowly growing reputation as a singer to help broadcast his message, and she was proud of him. All she saw was a principled man who was strong and brave enough to stand up for what he believed in.

Another letter came from Miriam at the end of February. She had now sent three letters since Christoph had last sent one in reply, and when he saw her handwriting on the familiar eggshell-blue airmail envelope, he cursed himself for not having written to her for so long.

C. Rittersmann
141 East 80th Street
New York, New York

25th January 1936

Dear Christoph,

Why have you not answered my last letters? I hope that nothing is wrong with you over there. If I receive no reply to this letter, I will assume that you do not want to hear from us any more and I will not write to you again.

Eva has to attend the Jewish kindergarten now and next year she will have to go to Jewish school because the National Socialists will not permit Jewish children to share their education with Gentiles. It is impossible to understand what harm Jewish children could be to their Gentile neighbours and classmates. Aren't we all God's creatures, after all?

Abraham is hoping to emigrate with Chanah to Australia. They can make a happy life away from all this madness. Their daughter, Judith, is already seven months old. Her coming into the world has given our family some light in these dark times. Eva has a little cousin to visit only a few streets away and to

164

dote on in the place of a younger brother or sister. Seeing how careful she is with Judith fills my heart with happiness.

One of our neighbours' children called Eva 'Jew' the other day on the street and laughed at her. She did not know what the word meant and came running to me in tears. I tried to explain as best I could.

You would find your country much changed if you came back here.

Yours, as ever,
Miriam

Anne had taken Leo out for a walk in Central Park and Christoph was supposed to be rehearsing some new songs. He had told Anne to be careful on the icy sidewalks, in case she slipped and fell. He paced up and down the living room of their apartment with the sheets of music and lyrics in his hand, but each time he tried to focus on the words they seemed so frivolous compared to Miriam's letter. Despite the cold, Christoph felt a light sweat break out all over his skin. Miriam was quite right to be angry with him. The only excuse he had for himself was that he had an entirely different life now, and keeping up with his old life meant jeopardising his new one. He hid her letter in the box, alongside all the others in the loft, and sat down at the table to write back.

141 East 80th Street
New York, New York

Lothringerstrasse 37
Wuppertal-Elberfeld
Germany

8th February 1936

Dear Miriam,

I hope that this reaches you safely and in good time for Eva's fifth birthday. There is nothing I can say in my defence for not having written to you sooner. I have wanted to write, but have not written. When there has been silence, it has not meant that I was not thinking of you and little Eva. You are both very often in my thoughts. I carry the image of Eva everywhere, if not in the form of the physical photograph that you sent to me, then in the unforgettable image of it in my head. She is a beautiful girl.

I have to tell you that I have a wife and child now in New York, a boy called Leo who will soon be three years old, and I am not sure that you would recognise anything of my life as it was back home. I hardly recognise myself.

Yours, as ever,
C

P.S. I am sending you a little money and I will try to send some more before too long.

Christoph folded his letter around three ten-dollar bills and wrote out the envelope in his careful hand. He put it in his jacket pocket to send later that day. He had written the letter in one draft but did not know what good this sudden fluency would do. He could imagine Miriam being deeply hurt by the news, despite not having seen him in almost six years. Perhaps she was still holding out the faintest of hopes that he might come back to Wuppertal one day, if not for her then for the sake of their daughter. Hope dies when you have no reason to hope and she would have none after she had read his letter.

'Have you been rehearsing?' Anne asked when she and Leo came back in. 'How's the voice today?'

'Oh, it's soaring like a bird in flight and the songs are the air. You know how it is with me,' Christoph joked.

'You mean you've been pacing around the apartment *not* practising a note?' Anne smiled.

'You know me too well,' he said and laughed. 'I was *meaning* to practise, but kept having other things on my mind that I needed to do.'

'What other things?'

'Oh, just some correspondence I had to deal with and one or two administrative things. Nothing to worry about,' he replied.

'Well, perhaps you can practise now that Leo and I are back. It's always nice to hear you sing when it's just us. It doesn't seem like *you* when you're up on stage.'

'Since we met, I've only ever been singing for you up there,' Christoph replied and gave her a tender kiss on the lips.

*

167

The Palace Theatre gave Christoph top Saturday night billing for the first time in April. Anne brought Leo along to the show, dressed in a sailor suit and looking the very picture of a perfect little American boy. Christoph had rehearsed an entirely new sequence of songs for the evening, including 'The Stars are in Your Eyes' by Frank Dean and Higham D. Green.

> *The stars are in your eyes, darling –*
> *are they shining just for me?*
> *The stars are in your eyes, dear,*
> *is that darkness I can see?*
>
> *The stars are in your eyes, dear –*
> *are they burning just for me?*
> *Are those tears of joy, darling,*
> *or of sadness I can see?*

The audience was full that night. He had never seen the auditorium brimful to capacity before and it was quite something. He stood up close to the microphone, with his right hand wrapped loosely around the chrome stand, and could scarcely believe that all of these people had come to hear *him* sing. He had the luxury of time, with more than an hour to fill with his songs of love and heartbreak until the evening drew to a close. He had heard all of the singers on stage before him from backstage and had even asked the management to make Henry Cliff and Laurie O'Riordan two of the opening acts that night. They had all been strong performers, with Henry the undoubted highlight, but Christoph knew that he was a class apart. He was being paid fifteen dollars for the performance and had bought a new charcoal-grey double-breasted suit for the occasion.

He could not make out individual faces in the dimmed light of the auditorium, just highlights of features here and there against the dark. Anne and Leo were sitting up in the front row of the dress circle, but he could not look up to where they were sitting without being dazzled by the light. König had not been able to make it to the biggest night of Christoph's career so far, but had sent a bottle of the finest French champagne to his dressing room.

His voice was on fine form. It soared up and swooped down low like the bird in flight he had joked about. The theatre was very hot due to the up-swell of people that filled the theatre that night. The air was dry despite the night being cool and damp outside, with the last remnants of a rainstorm that had come in from the Atlantic lingering on in a fine and persistent drizzle.

Christoph sipped from a glass of water placed on a stool beside him and struggled to stifle a tickle in his throat between numbers. When he sang, his voice was as powerful as ever, but when he rested between songs or said a few words to the audience by way of an introduction to the next number, he could hear that his breathing in and out dragged in his throat slightly and his speaking voice was getting husky. He did not want another chest infection, not when things were going so well.

He ended his first performance at the top of the bill with an upbeat number that had a jazzy, free-form piano accompaniment, 'It Couldn't Happen to a Nicer Girl'.

> *It couldn't happen to a nicer girl,*
> *This town's got her spinning in a whirl,*
> *Oh boy! Hugo, Henry and Miguel,*

They couldn't happen to a nicer girl.
Manhattan's got her spinning like a top
Where will it take her? Where will she stop ...?

His hour or so in the spotlight ended on a high and he had the audience laughing at the dizzy girl about town in his song. He did not tell them who the lyricist and composer were for this final number. They were one and the same person – Rittersmann the Romantic. It was his first ever composition and he was quite pleased with it. It was a very long way, a continent apart, from Schumann and Schubert, but this crowd did not want to hear those kinds of songs.

Backstage in his dressing room with Anne and Leo, he received visitor after visitor, coming to offer him words of congratulation or small bouquets of flowers. He signed their programmes and took the time to ask them a little about themselves. They all told him that they loved his singing voice and his accent.

By eleven o'clock, he was fit to drop and little Leo the lion cub was asleep on his mother's lap. It was three hours past his bedtime.

That spring, Christoph began to hear Fritz Kuhn's name around the neighbourhood. Kuhn had been appointed head of the successor organisation to the Friends of New Germany, the German-American Bund, in March and it seemed that he was a man in a hurry. He had apparently come over from Germany in the late 1920s, via Mexico of all places. He had earned an Iron Cross in the World War and Christoph knew all too well that for every hero – no, for every *survivor* – of the war there was a great rotting pile of corpses. He had seen it all with his own eyes and knew that there were no heroes, not of the sort that crowds cheered and waved flags at when they finally came back home, the hollowed-out shells of men.

Hitler had personally appointed Kuhn as the head of the Bund and he was certainly no hero. That summer he began to orchestrate an aggressive counter-offensive against the American Jewish Congress's campaign to boycott imported German goods and German-owned businesses across the United States. The *New York Post* carried a story on the Bund and showed a picture of Kuhn, who had the muscled hands and thickset neck and head of a butcher or a labourer. He looked like a man who could take, and give, a good punch without thinking too much about it. He had become a naturalised citizen of the United States in 1934. It seemed the Führer believed it favourable that an American citizen should lead the Bund, as if this would make the organisation somehow more palatable to the American public.

The Bund was now by far the largest and most organised of the surviving Nazi organisations in the United States and established two training camps: Camp Siegfried in Yaphank, New York, and Camp Nordlund in Sussex County, New Jersey. Later in 1936, Kuhn and around fifty of his fellow Bund members went to Germany by ship to try and meet with the Führer. They reached Berlin just as the Summer Olympics were about to get under way in the capital of the Third Reich. By all accounts, Kuhn's hoped-for warm reception by Hitler was more of a cold shoulder. Hitler, presumably, had other things on his mind. Yet when Kuhn returned to New York he was calling himself the American Führer.

PART III:
BUND

CHAPTER TWENTY

April 1938

There had been rioting on the streets of Yorkville. In the six-storey Yorkville Casino at 210 East Eighty-Sixth Street, where Matthias had met with the other members of Teutonia years earlier, a terrible fight had broken out between a group of American-Jewish veterans of the World War and around two thousand members of the German-American Bund. The Bund members had gathered at the casino to celebrate the Führer's forty-ninth birthday and his annexation of Austria. They wore swastikas on their upper left arms and chanted Hitler's name with incantatory voices, while the Jewish veterans had scattered themselves in twos and threes amongst this throng of American Nazis waiting for the right moment to strike. The veterans were outnumbered thirty-five to one and stood no chance.

News of the fight spread like wildfire through Yorkville that evening. Christoph had been to Yorkville Casino occasionally to watch German-language films that were screened there, and as soon as he heard from a neighbour what was happening only a little distance from the apartment, he ran the six blocks north to watch from across the street as the battered and bloodied veterans stumbled out onto East Eighty-Sixth Street, pursued by grey-shirted supporters of Hitler's regime, scenting blood like dogs.

Christoph was suddenly caught up in the large crowd of protestors outside the casino, who were waving placards with slogans such as 'Mankind Should Not Be Crucified on the Swastika'. As soon as he understood exactly what was happening, Christoph shouted as loudly as his lungs and throat would let him: 'Down with Hitler!', 'Shame on you, shame on you!', and, 'Assholes! *Ihr seid alle Arschlöcher!* You're all *assholes.*' He was boiling with rage but could only shout at the hooligans spilling down the street in front of him. Next time. Next time he would get closer to the action and use his fists against the Nazi swine if he had to. The bastards had to be stopped from spreading their poison, their hatred, their violence.

The police seemed completely ineffective against such large numbers of men fighting, brawling, shouting and blocking the road outside the casino. The New York City Police Department had obviously sent far too few officers up to the riot. The surging, seething crowd did what it wanted and the police lined up along its margins trying to prevent its spread. It was a policy of containment rather than direct intervention. The Jewish veterans hid in doorways where they could, trying to avoid further punishment. Christoph saw blood on the sidewalk and even a stray tooth.

He found it incomprehensible that this violence was happening in New York. He had not seen so much as a bar-room brawl in the almost eight years that he had been in the city. Perhaps this absence of violence on the Upper East Side had something to do with the after-effects of the Prohibition movement, at least in the first year or two after his arrival, before the authorities had more or less given up on the idea, or perhaps he had simply been in the wrong part of the city to see such aggression. Whatever the case, Berlin had been far worse. There he had seen a number of street battles, daylight robberies, even a knife fight once. That open, unabashed violence came, he believed, from desperation, from the poverty and shame that had hung like a pall over Berliners since the World War and it had led to Hitler's election.

Christoph stood and watched the casino riot lose its momentum, burn itself out in a last few grunt-mouthed scuffles and half-hearted punches and kicks, before the crowd of American Nazis dispersed and the police moved back further down the surrounding streets. It was almost ten o'clock at night. They seemed to have arrested no one. The anti-Nazi protesters gradually left the scene and made their way home, singly or in small groups, placards resting on their shoulders like crosses. Their protest had had little effect: the Bund members had celebrated the Führer's birthday and had the added pleasure of beating to a pulp the American Jewish veterans.

Christoph had shouted his protest. What else could he have done? He felt powerless in the face of so many supporters of the Reich. He could only decry what they stood for. He was comforted by the certainty that, despite the unpleasantness of what he had just witnessed, Kuhn could never in the end win enough support to pose any serious threat. There would be no American Hitler: the country was, at its very heart, far too optimistic for that.

*

Mae, a delightful little girl with a full head of golden ringlets, was born in the spring of 1936 and was now almost two years old. The apartment was getting too small for their growing family. Leo and Mae shared the only bedroom,

177

their small beds pushed side by side, with their wooden toys scattered across the remaining floor space in the bedroom. Leo was a gentle boy and kind to his sister, but was already five years old and would soon want his own room. Having sold their double bed to a newly married couple down the hall a while ago, Christoph and Anne now slept on a foldaway bed in the sitting-room, which they stowed away each day. Miriam's letters were still secreted away in their box in the obscurity of the loft space above their bed.

Christoph had begun searching for a new apartment in Yorkville, but was surprised at how much rents had increased since he had moved seven years ago. Even though his singing career was finally bringing him the financial rewards for which he had long hoped, a two-room apartment in the better area of Yorkville with a sitting-room, bedroom, kitchenette and bathroom was now at the upper end of his budget. And he was now a well-known singer! If only they knew where he had to live and what sacrifices he had made to stand in the spotlight and entertain his audience. Putting on a show meant exactly that; he looked immaculate up on stage, but pressed his shirts on the kitchenette's sideboard. His audience probably thought he was the sort of man to have a valet, but Anne was his only manservant. In truth, she had no reason to complain as they did an equal share of the household chores and he was a caring father.

'I won't be disappointed if we can't afford something nicer,' Anne said when they were discussing the situation one morning.

'If I could just get another show each week at Jackson's and the Palace gave me top of the bill *every* Saturday night, things would be fine. But the Palace likes to vary things,' he pronounced it 'wary', 'and the music hall doesn't have enough of an audience to make it worthwhile to pay me the fee I charge twice a week.'

'You're too good for the music hall,' Anne said. 'I wish you'd stop singing there. I don't like the audience; they're too loud. They don't shut up when you're singing.'

'It's work, and I need work,' he replied. 'König's found me nothing new in years.'

'Is he still acting as your agent?' Anne asked. 'I had no idea.'

'I'm still on his books, but he seems to believe that since I am top of the bill at the Palace, offers of work would easily come my way. It hasn't really happened like that.'

'At least you've had regular work for a long time now, people have got to know you and how good a singer you are,' Anne said proudly.

'I know you're right, but I wish I could find more work and earn a little more money. Then we could rent exactly the kind of apartment you want.'

'And I'm sure we will one day, even if it's not right now. We've got a roof over our heads and that's something. People have fared a lot worse over the last ten years. When Mae goes to school I can look for a job again, which will help.'

By the end of June they had found a two-bedroom apartment just within Christoph's careful budget on East Eighty-Third Street. It was run-down but it had high windows that flooded the apartment with a light that illuminated the dirt that had been swept into the corners and the cracks between the floorboards. After eight buckets of soapy water had been used to clean the floors and the walls, it bathed their new home in the dazzling colours of high summer.

They did not have many possessions, just their fold-up bed, the children's beds and toys, pots and pans, kitchen utensils, clothes, and the sundry stuff that every family accumulates. Some of the furniture belonged to their landlord and would be left behind. It was just a morning's work to pack everything into boxes and dismantle the beds to be rebuilt in their new home. Christoph wrapped the wooden box containing Miriam's letters in an old pullover and buried it at the bottom of a cardboard box containing the possessions he had shipped over in the trunk from his old life: a few books; some souvenirs of his childhood; an ammonite that he had found on the Baltic coast; his singing certificate from the conservatoire. Looking at these things for the first time in a long time, he felt that old familiar tide of homesickness rise up again and struggled to suppress it.

They borrowed a rickety old baker's delivery van from a friend of Henry Cliff's and Christoph loaded up and drove their belongings over to their new apartment in mid-July, under the oppressive heat of Manhattan in the crucible of the summer; humidity hanging in the air and wetting every living thing that moved.

He spent the whole day moving their belongings and placing them around the apartment, while Anne took the children for a picnic in Central Park and a trip to the zoo. He had wanted them out of the way so that he could get the move done as efficiently as possible, and so that he could find somewhere safe to put Miriam's letters. His shirt was wet after carrying a vanload of things up the two flights of stairs to the apartment, but by lunchtime it was done. He spent the afternoon trying to put everything in its place, although he knew that Anne would want to move things around to make the place her own. He rebuilt the children's beds and put them in the larger of the two bedrooms and placed the foldaway bed in the slightly smaller room facing the street below. Here there was no loft-space above any of the rooms or, at least, no hatch through which access could be gained from the apartment to any such space. Christoph simply left the box of Miriam's letters wrapped tightly in his old pullover in the cardboard box. He buried it at the bottom of a built-in cupboard in the main room, beneath a tightly packed pile of other odds and ends not needed on a daily basis. It would have to do for now until he could find somewhere safer for the letters.

The sudden blessing of space: no more sleeping in the living room. Christoph was pleased with his day's hard work and knew that the apartment was the perfect place for his family. It was so good to do practical things that raised a sweat. Singing, although a physical act, comes as much from the head as from the body. When he was doing practical things, immersed in physical labour, he had no time to worry, no time to think for more than a fleeting second or two about Miriam and Eva.

Anne had promised not to be back with the children before seven o'clock, after handing their herring-importer landlord the keys to the old apartment. At just after five o'clock Christoph put the small dining table under the windows in the main room, which would serve as a living room, dining room and playroom for the children, and sat at the table looking down at the street. People were making their way home from work, teeming along the sidewalk and darting aside like crabs if they were in danger of colliding head-on with a pedestrian going in the opposite direction.

He wondered why he craved fame as a singer if he had no feeling for these people; they meant little more to him than the crabs on the seashore of Long Island, but these scuttling creatures were his audience, his public.

It was no wonder that they preferred popular romantic numbers to the *Lieder* by Schumann and Schubert that told of heartbreak and doomed love. Watching their lives being played out below him, he could see precious little romance down there. The Palace and Jackson's Music Hall were the places to which they came to escape their lives, not to have their lives reflected back at them. His voice and the upbeat, humorous, swooning songs that he sang were a release from their humdrum realities, shuttling to and from work and hunkering down at night in the quieter corners of this great city.

Christoph had moved apartment but his past had come with him in the back of the baker's van. That inescapable box of Miriam's letters, now buried deep in the cupboard in his new home, and the photograph of Eva – he tried to call her Eva, and not 'my daughter' when he thought about her these days – were heavier to carry than any oak table, any solid mahogany chest of drawers. He wanted to forget about them, but even now he could not bring himself to destroy the letters or throw them away. They weighed down on him and he knew that they would continue to weigh down on him until he did something about them.

He had over an hour until Anne and the children would be coming home for the first time as a family to their new apartment. He searched in the unpacked boxes until he found some writing paper and his old fountain pen. He sat at the table overlooking East Eighty-Third Street, bathed in the soft sunlight of a summer's evening.

296 East 83rd Street
New York, New York

Lothringerstrasse 37
Wuppertal-Elberfeld
Germany

17th July 1938

Dear Miriam,

You will have noticed from the address at the top of this letter that I have moved apartment again. I wanted to send you my new address so that you did not send letters in vain to my old apartment. I do not think that the landlord there would think to forward them on to me.

I hope that things are not too hard for you and that you still have your work at the tailor's shop. How is little Eva? I trust that she is well and being a good girl. I look at her photograph often.

~~I am sorry that I did not tell you in one of my previous letters, but my wife and I had a girl, Mae, in 1936 and having a daughter has made me think about Eva more and more. They are quite different from little boys and not how you would expect: bolder and more headstrong, it seems to me. They know who they are more quickly. Having Mae has reminded me every day that I have not been there for Eva.~~

How are your parents, how are Abraham and Isy and Hedwig? Your family, your brothers and sisters and parents, were always so kind to me. I have been thinking often about dear Ida lately, too. ~~I have been over here for so long, but have not forgotten. How could I forget?~~

Please write again before too long to let me know that you and Eva are alive and well, despite things over there. You would be surprised, but Hitler has quite some support amongst the German population of New York. I am ashamed of them. Those that call themselves 'German', the children and grandchildren of German immigrants who have never even been to what they so proudly call their Fatherland.

I am sending you $20 and will try to send you more when I can.

Yours, as ever,
C

The light out on the street had grown hazy and the crowds of pedestrians on the sidewalk had reduced to a trickle of passers-by, making their way to the diners and restaurants on Madison Avenue or home after finishing work later than the masses. Christoph searched in vain for an envelope, and when he couldn't find one, he folded the letter carefully and put it in his jacket pocket to send the next day.

'Daddy's been busy,' Anne said to Leo and Mae when they arrived at the apartment. She was carrying the little one in her arms and Leo had climbed the stairs ahead of her. 'Look how much he's done!'

'It's been hot work,' Christoph replied. 'The only reason you don't see me dripping with sweat is because I've been sitting down at the table sorting one or two things out for the last hour or so. I had the window open and the summer breeze cooled my hot head.' He laughed and tickled Mae under the chin. She made her big eyes at him and Leo, who had not seen his Papa all day, hugged his legs.

'Well, children, this is our new home. Isn't it *big*?' Anne said. Leo ran off to inspect his and Mae's bedroom, with his sister close behind him, and came back looking triumphant.

'I like it. I like it very much,' he said.

'I'm glad you do, darling,' Anne said. 'We hoped you would. We knew you'd be happy here.'

CHAPTER TWENTY-ONE

The sun beat down relentlessly on New York that summer. It chased its own shadows into culverts and drains and a bleached white light fell on the city. The last rainfall had been weeks earlier and the only memory of the life-giving water that the parks and gardens of the five boroughs so desperately needed was a clinging humidity that hung in the air like a curse.

Christoph noticed that his voice was particularly powerful when there was moisture in the air, sucked up by the parched atmosphere from the ocean out beyond the East River. His voice flourished where others suffered in the cloying heat. His repertoire had to evolve constantly, to keep up with ever-changing 'popular' tastes, and he rehearsed more than a dozen new songs that were current hits on the radio. He did not sing from his classical repertoire any longer, at least not in public. He kept the Liszt and the Schumann for himself, for Anne and the children, although they seemed to have little affinity for *Lieder*. While his profile as an entertainer continued to grow and he was even occasionally recognised out on the street, he felt himself a long way adrift from what he had wanted to be as a singer when he was at the conservatoire. He was classically trained, for God's sake, not a crooner of popular hits.

His mother had written to him to say that his father was

ill, suffering from a cancer that she did not specify. She begged him not to worry and reminded him that Hermann – she always called him 'Hermi' – was almost seventy-five years old, still as strong as an ox and in good spirits. She told him that he did not need to consider coming home to see his father, leaving his family behind with all of the upheaval that this would cause, unless he heard from her that he had taken a sudden turn for the worse. Christoph wondered how sudden the news of any deterioration in his father's health would be when it finally reached him in New York, given the terrible slowness of the postal service between Germany and the United States. He did not want it to be too late.

He could picture his father now, sitting in the armchair by the window of the living room overlooking the garden on the Weinberg, pipe in hand, with his strong jaw and gentle good humour. He would have received the news of his illness with stoicism and a joke or two at his own expense. He was not a man to let his guard down and show you that he was afraid or upset. He was of the old school and Christoph had always thought of his stoicism and sense of humour as somehow very English. His father had always loved all things English, before and after the World War, and it was he who had encouraged Christoph to learn the language. He had gone to America not to escape his father, but because his father had made his escape possible.

Christoph kept the news from Anne, knowing that it would be another reason for her to want them to go to Germany to see his family. He wrote back to his mother to say how concerned he was to hear about his father's illness. He waited every day for another letter but nothing came and he hoped that this silence meant that his father was putting up a quiet, dignified fight; one that he was slowly winning.

The key to the postbox in the new lobby hung on a chain around Christoph's neck like a talisman to ward off evil.

Mae was an exceptionally strong-minded little girl. If her blonde ringlets reflected her sunny personality, then the sunshine that she shone onto those around her was broken on some days by squalls of temper and floods of tears if she did not get her way. Leo had a much more placid, even temperament and tried to comfort his sister, with little obvious effect, when her cheerful smile and bright blue eyes were eclipsed by thunderous, beetled brows and a mouth set for a storm. Christoph loved this unpredictability in his daughter and wondered whether Eva was the same: sweetness and *Sturm und Drang* in one beautiful little girl. Of course, Eva was seven years old now, almost five years older than Mae, so any extremes in her temperament might have evened out a little.

Christoph would be forty in a year's time. When he thought about his life in America it almost mirrored the American dream that he had heard so much about. He had arrived with very little except his voice and had found, if not exactly great fame, then at least some success in his singing career, earning enough money to keep a roof over his head and to put food on the table. His voice was described by those who knew their popular singers as one of the finest tenors in all of New York City, and he had built a family, with a loving wife and two children whom he adored. He was grateful beyond words for all of this, but what he did not have was peace; he could never unwind, and often tossed and turned in bed at night. His mind throbbed and hummed with the rhythms of the city and, as the saying went, the city never slept. He often found himself watching, as if in a dream, the dawn light slowly fill the street below the apartment, the street-cleaners come and go and the first workers trudge off east or west to their long days of labour in shops, offices or factories.

When he could not sleep, he looked at the sheet music for new songs and read poetry and novels, or simply stared out of the window if he was too tired to concentrate. Sometimes he tiptoed into the children's bedroom and, for a minute or two, watched them sleep peacefully and deeply. He was careful not to wake them or to disturb Anne when he climbed out of bed, and often his family had no idea that he had been up since before dawn on nights when his mind would not let him rest.

When Christoph saw the newsreels at the local movie theatre, he could not believe what he was seeing. He had not lost his bunk-mate Hans on the Front so that Hitler could be up on stage barking and screaming at the German people. The man was becoming ever more hysterical in his speeches and was clearly mad. It was as if the whole of Germany had been brainwashed.

American audiences now often booed Hitler when he was shown orating on screen, while the German crowds were cheering at the tops of their lungs and waving Nazi flags, under a collective hypnosis brought on by the thrall that their leader held them in. There were pictures of women fainting in the front of the crowd at Nuremberg as if they were in the presence of the Messiah. Christoph's mind, his whole body, recoiled as if he had been asked to swallow poison. He never wanted to go back home again. He hoped that his father would get well so that he did not have to return to Wuppertal. He had received no further letter from his mother asking him to go home.

'Do you still think of it as home?' Anne asked him out of the blue one day. 'Germany, I mean.'

'It's very sad and doesn't make me proud, but I can't think of it in that way any longer. It's not a country I recognise; it's nothing like it was when I left.'

'Well, the country's still the country; it's the people who've changed,' she replied. 'I'm sure it's still a beautiful place.'

'What's a country without people you can like or trust? It's nowhere worth being,' he said.

'Will you ever take us there to visit?'

'I might do if they ever get rid of Hitler. I wouldn't want you to see Germany as it is now. And I wouldn't want Leo and Mae to see it like that.'

'It would be nice to meet your parents before they're gone, to visit your sister and her little boy,' Anne said sadly. 'Surely you miss them? Leo and Mae should see their grandparents, their aunt and uncle and cousin.'

'It'll have to wait until after all of this is over, if it ever is,' he said. 'I don't think they would expect us to go back there with the way things are.'

'Even so, it's a shame we've never met them,' Anne replied.

'And if I don't sing, I don't earn,' he continued. 'What are we going to live on if I'm away from New York for a couple of months?'

'We'll find a way if we have to,' she said. 'Perhaps my parents would help us a little.'

'I don't want to take their money. Perhaps it's time that I asked the Palace and Jackson's Music Hall for a pay rise, so that we can actually save some money again. My fees have stayed the same for far too long and raising two children's not cheap in this city. If only König would pull his finger out and find me some new openings ...'

Christoph went to see König in early August: it was the first time he had spoken to him face-to-face for many months. He had called his office two or three times since they had last seen each other, to discuss his fees and one or two other things, but was surprised to see how much older König looked when he walked into his office and sat down on the chair in front of his desk. He looked like a septuagenarian, with rheumy, red-rimmed eyes and skin as wrinkled as an old peasant's after too many years in the sun, even though he was not yet sixty. In spite of this, his perfect set of cosmetic teeth still gleamed in his head.

He picked up the telephone when Christoph had sat down and called his secretary, who was at her desk just outside his office door.

'Janine, can you make us two coffees, please?' he asked. Christoph wondered why he had not simply got up from his chair and asked her this in person.

'So, how've you been keeping?' König said when he had put the receiver down.

'Oh well, you know, the little ones are keeping us busy and I've been doing a lot of new songs at the Palace, less so at Jackson's.'

'Sorry I haven't been in touch much this year,' König said. 'I haven't heard of any new openings for tenors of your type. The Met were looking for a new one to replace Salvatore Bergamo, but they got someone straight from Milan. And you don't do opera,' he added, as if Christoph was not aware of this fact.

'Still, if you *do* hear of anything, anything at all. Children are expensive …' Christoph began, stopping as Janine walked into the room with the coffee tray. König took a sip of coffee from his cup then leaned forward conspiratorially across his desk and said in a whisper:

'And I've had other things on my mind,' as if he had not heard what Christoph had just said.

'Other things …?'

'I left my wife in February and moved in with my mistress, Sophie. She's twenty years younger than me and she's just had our *baby son.*'

'My God! Many congratulations! I don't know what to say.' Christoph was appalled that a man of König's age had become a father again, and tried to hide his shock and discomfort. König's two other children were adults with their own families, so far as he knew.

'Yes, it's quite something, a man of my age,' König winked at him. 'We're not getting much sleep.'

'I know what that feels like only too well,' Christoph replied. 'But they're worth it, aren't they?'

'He's my first son, that's quite something,' König repeated himself.

Christoph left König's office with the bitter taste of coffee and disappointment in his mouth and little hope of finding more work through him. The matter had barely been discussed, so eager had his agent been to tell him the story of his mistress and son. König had confided in him as if they were old friends and Christoph was embarrassed that the man thought of him in that way. They hardly knew each other personally, after all. As far as he had been able to tell, König had never really been listening on the occasions that

Christoph had tried to tell him about his own life and family.

Christoph realised that König's mind was on other things: he had his percentages, his cut, coming in from the weekly fees of the fifty or so performers on his books and had little need to find any of them more work.

Rumours on the streets of Yorkville blew down the sidewalks like litter in the wind. The word was that Fritz Kuhn was building quite an army of trained supporters at his two camps in New Jersey and upstate New York. No one knew the true extent of his forces, but he was reported to strut around and bark orders at his entourage and just about anyone else that he met. It seemed that this little Führer was confident of making some political impact in America.

On the last Saturday of August, the American-Jewish veterans held a rally in Central Park to demonstrate against the Bund. Wearing their regimental berets, military badges and campaign medals from the World War, the veterans paraded up and down the Mall, holding up placards and carrying banners. Christoph had heard about the rally and headed down to the park on the morning, leaving Anne and the children behind. Judging by the casino riot, this protest could quickly turn bloody.

It was a swelteringly hot day and most of the proud veterans were marching in their shirtsleeves, lifting their banners and placards high above their heads. Crowds had gathered along the route of the march; mostly supporters of the veterans' anti-Nazi cause. There seemed to be no voices of dissent here, no followers of the Führer or of his pale *Doppelgänger* Fritz Kuhn to spoil the mood of celebratory defiance.

Christoph clapped and cheered along with the crowd, happy to be part of the rally and to show his support for the American Jews who had fought so bravely for their mighty nation. He had been on the other side during the World War; he had been their bitter enemy at the Front. How strange life was. What tricks time and space play on you.

Suddenly a lone shout. Then more shouting: *Heil Hitler! Heil Hitler! Heil Hitler!* The voices were coming from the direction of the fountain. The sections of the crowd nearest to the fountain turned as one to see who was shouting this atrocity. A pale-blond man in a brown shirt had been lifted up onto the shoulders of two other men in brown shirts. He was raising his right arm in the Hitler salute each time that he shouted his name.

Having pushed through to the front of the crowd, Christoph saw a densely packed mass of men covering the entire circular area of paving that enclosed the fountain, and in their distinctive brown clothing he could tell they were supporters of the Bund. They were waiting for the veterans to reach the end of the Mall. This time they were the ones who were outnumbered, but they looked younger and stronger than most of the veterans.

There was a surge of angry shouts from both sides as the veterans and Bund members came together at the end of the Mall. The veterans had nowhere else to go, unless they turned heel and retraced their steps. There were perhaps eighty Bund boys and two hundred veterans, but the outcome of the confrontation was by no means certain. Individual scuffles broke out: one-on-one at first but inevitably banners and placards were discarded and the two sides collided in a mass of brawling, a riot of punches thrown and taken. On impulse and without thinking, Christoph charged forward with others in the crowd. He ran at the first brown-shirted man he could see; a big fellow who was half turned away from him, grappling with a bald-headed veteran whose beret had slipped off and who was being trampled underfoot.

'You stupid, bigoted little shit!' Christoph shouted, delirious with anger. The man turned to see where this insult was coming from and Christoph threw a punch with his bunched left fist at the man's snout-like nose, full-square in the face and as hard as he could. The man looked startled for a split second and then threw both hands up towards his face to protect himself. Too late: his legs buckled beneath him.

Christoph had thrown a punch and bloodied the nose of a Nazi supporter. As the fighting and brawling, the shouting and the curses ebbed and flowed around him, Christoph retreated back into the crowd of spectators and then slipped away from the Mall and out of Central Park itself, heading home.

He felt inordinately proud of himself for days afterwards, but told no one.

CHAPTER TWENTY-TWO

The news from Europe was all bleak. It seemed that the situation in Germany could well escalate and that it might even lead to war, if Hitler's aggression was not curbed. Christoph took Anne to the movie theatre once a week to watch the newsreels, as he knew that she was keen to learn as much as possible about what was going on in his homeland. She had always been so curious about the world and about current affairs, but she rarely had time to read the newspapers nowadays because Mae was still so little and demanded so much of her time. Christoph wanted Anne to see what was unfolding in the country that her parents had also once called home. He suspected that she still did not quite understand why he was so concerned about the situation in Germany – it was, after all, half a world away.

C. Rittersmann
296 East 83rd Street
New York, New York

20th November 1938

Dear Christoph,

We have been living through terrible events here. On the night of the 9th November, it was as if some sort of local apocalypse had been visited on the towns and cities of Germany. Stormtroopers were sent by Hitler to those places throughout Germany where there are Jewish citizens to smash their shop windows. They are calling it 'Kristallnacht' and not only were shops badly damaged, but perfectly innocent people beaten and synagogue after synagogue razed to the ground.

Both of my parents, as I might have told you before, have died of old age over the last three years and are buried in the cemetery on the Weinberg where we buried Ida. It may sound strange but I am grateful that they are not alive to witness these events.

Eva woke up when she heard the shouting down on the street and wanted to know what was going on. She was very scared by the echo of the stormtroopers' feet beating down on the road and the sound of breaking glass. When she went to the window, she saw the orange-red light of a large fire at the end of our street. I have not told her what was burning. She begged me to allow her to sleep the rest of the night in my bed.

She was still looking out as the storm troopers beat up a man almost directly beneath our window for no good reason (can there ever be a good one?). He was simply trying to stop them from smashing the front of his shop. The whole scene played out under the harsh light of the street lamps and I had to pull Eva away from the window. I have not yet managed to get her to sleep in her own bed again.

You are far, far better off where you are — if only we could have been there with you. We might have been your family. Why did you have to start another one?

Yours, as ever,
Miriam

198

Christoph sat in his armchair by the window reading the letter, which he had retrieved that morning from the locked postbox down in the lobby. Anne was out with the children in Central Park; the wintry sky was a glutinous grey and threatening rain. He noticed that his hands were trembling slightly again. Letters from Miriam always seemed to have that effect on him. He had asked himself the same question that she asked, apparently rhetorically, at the end of her letter and he had no easy answers. But he knew now that he had Anne and the children that he could not leave them, or be without them. Still, what was Eva, if not his family, his flesh and blood?

Anne had forgotten her keys and rang the doorbell, bringing him back to his present after the horrifying reality Miriam described. He quickly stuffed the letter into his jacket pocket as Mae came running up the stairs, launching herself at his legs as he opened the apartment door. She was now two-and-a-half years old and, wrapped in her heavy winter coat against the freezing air, almost bowled him over as she ran against his legs and hugged them tight.

'Little one!' he breathed into her golden hair as he bent down to kiss her on the top of her head. Her hair had that matchless scent of healthy, young life.

'My Papa!' she said in her sweetest voice, still clinging to him. She was in a happy mood.

Leo had developed a passion for trains and the two of them often went to Grand Central Station on Sunday mornings for an hour or two to look at the locomotives, those great hulks of iron and steam, while 'the girls' stayed indoors. There was nothing nicer to Christoph than to spend some time with his son. The world of entertainment: the stage, the fans, the applause, was a universe in which his fame was growing, but he knew it was all show and sensation. It was his family that gave his life shape and meaning and kept his feet firmly on the ground. A sweet word from Anne or from one of the children meant more to him than any amount of applause at the Palace Theatre.

He and Leo had a habit of standing near the gates to the platforms, sometimes nearer the higher-numbered tracks and sometimes nearer the lower-numbered ones, watching the locomotives fire up for their great journeys across the American continent or creep under their massive weight into the station and stop just short of the buffers. The fireman and the engineer would step off the footplate with their faces and hands blackened by soot, wiping away the worst of the dirt with their neckerchiefs, while the driver emerged still smart in his liveried uniform. Leo was transfixed by the whole spectacle of the arrival and departure of these trains.

'Papa, I want to be a train driver when I grow up,' he said. 'Can I be a train driver?'

'You'll have to work very hard at school and get good grades. You know, it's a very important job,' his father replied.

'I will, I will; I really want to be one,' Leo said in a high, excited voice and held his father's hand tight.

'Just imagine setting off from here in the cab of that great engine there. What an adventure! Think of all the prairies, all the landscapes you would cross. That one's going all the way to Portland, Oregon. I wonder what it's like there.'

'Can I go on a train one day, Papa, please can I actually go on a train?'

'You did go on one when you were little; you went to see

Grandma and Grandpa all the way in Ohio. Don't you remember that trip at all?'

'No, I don't remember going there,' Leo said in a disappointed voice. 'I only remember them visiting us here. Grandma had funny hair.'

'Well, we'll have to see about going back there so that you can travel by train again. Perhaps the driver would even let you look inside his cab.'

Christoph and Leo were at Grand Central one Sunday morning a couple of weeks before Christmas, at their usual position near the gates to the platforms. A light snow was falling outside, covering the city in a fine layer of whiteness. The snow was not yet heavy enough to impede the flow of the traffic on the streets or interrupt the rail system, and the great machines whistled, slowed, blew out vast clouds of steam and ground to shuddering, heaving halts as they reached the echoing terminus. Christoph had noticed a small clutch of five or six press reporters and photographers gathering near to Track Five and went over to ask them who they were expecting.

'Fritz Kuhn and his entourage from the German-American Bund,' one of the photographers said. He was wearing an Associated Press lapel badge. 'We had a wire saying that he had an important announcement to make when he arrives from upstate.'

'Why would you be interested in what that poisonous fool has to say?' Christoph asked angrily. 'He's a shit with nothing worthwhile to say to anyone.'

'Sir, we're just doing our job. We're not here to take sides,' another man stepped into the conversation, raising his hands to calm Christoph. Leo was agog and looking up to his father for reassurance. Christoph was too distracted by his confrontation with the press to notice the anxiety on his son's face.

'The likes of you reporting on the bigotry that comes out of that man's mouth is exactly what no one needs,' he said, even angrier now that the reporter had tried to calm him down with empty platitudes.

'It's a free country and Kuhn can say pretty much what he likes – and we can take photographs of him saying it and the reporters here can report on what he has to say,' the Associated Press photographer replied defensively, moving off towards the platform now that the gates had opened and the train could be seen approaching in the distance.

Christoph retreated with his son away from the platform entrance, standing beneath a high stone arch that divided the platforms from the concourse.

'Daddy, why're you so angry?' Leo asked in a tremulous voice.

'I'm not angry with those men, only about what they're doing. A bad man called Kuhn is about to arrive here and they want to tell the world about him. There's nothing for you to worry about, Leo.'

Still, Leo was afraid and would not let his father move more than a couple of feet away from him before reaching for his hand and holding on to it tightly. The black locomotive let out a shrieking whistle as it came into the platform, smoke and steam billowed up towards the great vaulted roof of the station. The noise was almost deafening, Leo let go of his father's hand and put his hands over his ears. The train's smartly dressed passengers began to disembark, coming out in ones and twos through the platform gates. The reporters and photographers gave no sign that they had spotted Kuhn and it was not until the very last straggle of passengers had made their way out through the gates that the man appeared, a small brown suitcase in one hand, wearing a sharp grey suit. He was accompanied by two flunkeys who looked like thugs: thickset types with heads that rose straight out of their shoulders and hands the size of sides of meat. He turned back to grin at them and said: 'Look, boys, I told you they would come.'

Christoph wanted to wipe that fatuous smirk straight off Kuhn's face, but stayed half hidden in the shadows under the arch. Kuhn came through the gate with the other two men lagging behind him and raised his arm in the Hitler salute. There was the long click of a camera's shutter and otherwise a stunned silence from the press men, before they stirred themselves out of their apparent reverie and gathered around Kuhn. It was all that Christoph could do to hold himself back; he did not want Leo to see him get into a fight. What was he going to do, in any case, against three men who were built like stormtroopers?

'Gennelmen,' Kuhn began; he still had a strong German accent. 'I asked you to come here because I have an announcement to make.'

'We're all ears,' one of the press men quipped. Kuhn looked at him sourly, while his henchmen seemed to be drawn upwards like marionettes by some invisible force and to expand their chests in a synchronised display of defiance.

'We're going to hold a rally on the twentieth of February next year at Madison Square Garden,' Kuhn continued. 'You'll see then, gennelmen, *exactly* what I've managed to achieve with the Bund.'

He talked on, his voice rising to a harsh, monotonous

shrillness, directing at the small group of men a vile diatribe full of jagged consonants. The press men stared down at their notebooks and struggled to keep up. Christoph could no longer listen to this bone-headed man's rhetoric and invective; he led his son from beneath the arch towards the station's main doors. Leo kept trying to turn around to look back at Kuhn and his men, and his father had to drag him by the hand to make Leo follow him.

'Why's that man shouting so much, Papa?' Leo asked.

'I'm not sure. I think maybe some men are born to speak and be heard, while others are born to shout because no one will listen. He's one of those shouters.'

Christoph and Leo did not go back to look at the trains together at Grand Central again. Something that had once been almost a weekly ritual and a great source of pleasure, giving them time just for themselves, had been ruined by the chance encounter with Kuhn.

The Palace Theatre had Christoph singing most Saturday evenings now unless it could attract a star from somewhere out of town to head the bill for one night only. Since he had had his family, Christoph found himself far less interested in finding fame and success as a singer. Although he was still in love with the act of singing itself, he had come to view the whole process of putting on make-up and a smart suit, climbing up the green room steps, walking through the wings and out onto the stage, as simply a way of earning a living. Christoph might not have been interested in fame, but a certain level of fame, at least locally in Manhattan, had nevertheless attached itself to him. There had, of course, been some reviews over the years, all of them positive, but more recently there had also been several articles in the New

York newspapers discussing Christoph not as a singer but as a man – telling readers that he had two young children, one boy and one girl, and a pretty wife; that he lived in Manhattan but came from Germany to seek his fortune, and other such banal stuff that could equally apply to many other men with a German background in Yorkville. It was all quite harmless, but it annoyed Christoph that the press presumed the public could possibly be interested in any aspect of his quiet, ordinary life away from the stage. Surely the only thing about him worth talking about was his voice.

He hoped more than anything that these reporters hadn't been able to find out about the darker parts of his past. He wondered where they got their facts from; they had never once interviewed him for any of these short articles. He sometimes suspected that the press must have been speaking to König: now *he* was a man who liked to use the telephone.

Chapter Twenty-Three

The carollers were heralding in Christmas Eve on the wireless and Christoph was proud that he had been able to buy the set for his family. The children looked at the heavy, fine-grained wooden box as if it was emanating magic and they were given strict instructions *never* to touch it. Anne had decorated the small fir tree that Christoph had bought at a Christmas market on the edge of Central Park with white candles, which she lit every night of Christmas.

Like all German families, they ate an early supper before they exchanged their Christmas presents on the night before Christmas, sitting peacefully around tables with their loved ones and friends. The rest of the city held its breath in anticipation of the presents and festivities to come in the morning, on Christmas Day.

Mae sat on her low wooden chair with a bib tucked firmly under her chin. She was learning how to use her little knife and fork with more control now and food did not fly from her plate quite as often as it once had done. Still, Anne sat beside her and helped her to cut up her meat and the steaming roast potatoes that she devoured so eagerly. The advent wreath that was suspended above the table gave off the fresh, oily scent of crushed pine needles and held four candles that threw dancing light and shadows over the walls. Just one electric bulb was switched on in the room, on the standard lamp in the corner. Otherwise, the only light came from the four advent candles and the candles on the tree.

'So did Santa Claus bring you the presents you wanted every year, when you were a child?' Anne asked Christoph.

'I was a good boy, just like our own little lion cub here,' he replied and laughed. 'Well perhaps not *quite* so good, but my parents always forgave me. They asked the *Weihnachtsmann*, Father Christmas, to bring me the things that I had wished for.'

'What about our own two?' Anne asked, smiling. 'D'you think that Father Christmas has brought them what they've wished for tonight?'

'I think so; they've been good this year. I hope they'll be happy with what they get.'

They talked as if the children were not sitting right next to them and Mae looked up at them with wide eyes, full of curiosity and delight, while Leo had a quizzical look on his face, as if he was suspicious about something. After supper they opened their presents one by one and Leo got a beautiful leather baseball glove and a perfectly stitched white baseball, gifts that he had been asking his father for repeatedly so that they could play together in the park. Mae was given a new doll by Father Christmas, with a gleaming white porcelain face and rosy cheeks, and seemed very happy with her present, which she immediately christened Annie after her mother.

Anne cooked a roast goose on Christmas Day, which they did not eat until almost four o'clock as the sun was beginning to set, after Christoph had taken the children on a long Christmas morning walk around the park. He could picture himself so clearly sitting at Christmas dinners as a child, and the mood of quiet celebration and family togetherness had been just the same. It was almost as if he was watching a scene from his own childhood. He hoped that Leo and Mae could feel that same strong sense of mystery and magic that he remembered.

'What are you thinking about?' Anne asked.

'Oh, nothing much: I'm just remembering Christmases as a child. It was actually a lot like this at home on the Weinberg.'

'Did you have goose like us?' Leo asked.

'Sometimes, and sometimes we had a type of fish called a carp and other times roast pig.'

'You mean roast *pork*,' his son replied. He was becoming more and more confident in English, and corrected Christoph at every opportunity.

'Yes, roast pork, delicious with apple sauce,' his father replied.

Christoph was sitting in his armchair reading a copy of the *New York Post* one day in early January 1939. There had been a railroad accident somewhere in rural, upstate New York and the story dominated the headlines. A photograph showed carriages on their sides and the walking wounded hobbling away from the scene. Christoph only bought the newspaper once or twice a week, as he preferred reading sheet music and novels to the news, which was always bad these days. He had been about to fold the paper and put it away when a photograph caught his eye. There, with Hitler, was Matthias Walter! He couldn't believe his eyes and looked closely again at the grainy image. Matthias had aged a little but it was him, as the headline and the story that ran underneath the photograph made clear:

WALTER WALTZES WITH THE FÜHRER

Herr Matthias Walter, former resident of Manhattan on East 89th Street, has been appointed by Hitler the court composer of the Nazi Party at a ceremony in Berlin. Herr Walter, who made his mark in the United States with his Empire Symphony, *a paean of love for his adoptive country, was sworn in last Saturday evening as the Reichskomponist (Reichs Composer) on a glittering occasion organised by the Nazi elite to celebrate Aryan music. Herr Walter, who returned from New York to Germany some years ago, appeared to enjoy the event, at one point even apparently joking with the Führer. Herr Walter used the evening to mark the world premiere of his short orchestral piece,* Muttersprache und Vaterland *(Mother-Tongue and Fatherland). This work has been adopted as the official composition for the 11th Party Congress, named the 'Rally of Peace', to be held at Nuremberg next September.*

There was no mention of Valentina and no sign of her in the photograph. Christoph wondered whether she and Matthias had stayed together and finally had a child, or whether she had not wanted to go back to Germany and all that it now stood for. He could not imagine Valentina having turned into an ardent supporter of the Nazi Party; she had always been too sensitive, too sensible, for that to have happened. But who could tell what she had become after months in the centre of the political storm, what the rage for glory and for blood might have done to her, particularly when her husband had become so close to the regime?

Matthias would be right at home as the court composer

to Hitler: he liked drama, pomp, ceremony, order. Despite his brilliance, he had a narrow imagination, Christoph had always thought, and would not mind being told what to do or how to think by a leader whose adulation by the population, whose splendour might shine a little on him too.

Christoph was invited to perform as the main act at the Palace Theatre on Monday nights in addition to his usual Saturday night hour. With his Wednesday night at Jackson's Music Hall, he was now giving three top-of-the-bill performances each week and he could feel, after a couple of months of this new regime, that his voice was beginning to become strained by overuse. For his three hours of singing in the two theatres each week, he practised for another fourteen or fifteen hours, as well as warming up before each performance. He took no holidays apart from a few days around Thanksgiving and a week over Christmas each year; he desperately needed a break from singing for a month or so to allow his voice to rest.

He had sent money to Miriam only infrequently and had enough saved in the bank account now to get his family through a few months if he did not work, but he was worried that if he told the Palace Theatre or Jackson's Music Hall he needed a rest from singing, they would find permanent replacements for him. Although he had become one of the stars of the little universes that the theatres represented, no one was irreplaceable.

A light tenor called Antonio Carrera, still only in his twenties, was making quite an impact at the Palace Theatre; he had joined the roster of new singers just a few months earlier and had already been taken on by the artistic director as a young talent to nurture. He had come from Sicily, from a small village outside Palermo, four or five years earlier, but his English was still quite broken. He had an early-evening slot every Monday night just before Christoph's performance and Christoph had taken him under his wing. They talked about famous tenors of the past and about the recordings that they had enjoyed listening to on the wireless.

Far from seeing Carrera as a threat, Christoph warmed to his enthusiasm and his honey-toned tenor voice. He had an excellent range and an almost flawless technique. He saw the younger man as a kind of understudy, as someone who could step in if he needed to take a break from singing at the Palace. When the time was right, perhaps later in the year, when his voice could no longer take the relentless programme of performance and practice that his relative success demanded, Christoph would suggest to the management of the theatre to give Carrera a chance to top the bill on Saturday nights for a couple of months. If offered the opportunity, Carrera would be sure to grab it; the only question was whether he would let go again. Christoph could not really see the management of the theatre replacing him permanently, as he had become such a favourite with the patrons of the Palace, but you could never be sure what the management was thinking. The artists, the talent, generally had little contact with them: it was their agents who dealt with the direction, and König was very rarely in touch with Christoph these days.

For a belated Christmas present, Leo had asked to see his father sing at the Palace Theatre. He had only once seen him up on stage, but would listen quietly now and then, with a beatific smile on his face, while his father practised at home in the apartment. Anne had found a childminder for Mae for the evening and it was the very first time that they left her at home to be looked after by someone else. Anne found it hard to relax sitting next to her son and shifted in her seat, peering at her wristwatch in the half-light of the auditorium and wondering whether Mae was soundly asleep in bed or giving her carer, who was a rather stout woman called Mrs Krumlitz, an evening of tantrums and tears.

Antonio Carrera sang first and his dark good looks had the audience entranced, even though only a few of them were able to understand the meaning of the words that came from his lips, as he sang his three ballads in his mother tongue. Still, his dark eyes spoke of a yearning for a lost love and for his homeland, and a pale-pink rose in the buttonhole of his dark suit jacket set the tone of delightful melancholy perfectly. Leo sat in his seat without moving, a little overawed by the performance and the hushed atmosphere of the auditorium. Carrera's songs soared up to the heights like hymns sung by an angel and carried Leo with them.

After the applause that had greeted Carrera's performance had died down, Christoph took to the stage. He was the refined, calm intellect to Carrera's wilder passions, but both men shared the same sense of romance and nostalgia in the way that they delivered their songs. The audience seemed to agree as one that the older man's voice was even more powerful than Carrera's. Christoph could detect the weaknesses in his voice, the fragility that he knew its overuse had caused, but the crowd only heard its rich timbre and range and how beautifully his songs filled the auditorium.

Before he sang his last number of the evening, Christoph introduced it by saying 'I would like to dedicate this final song to my young son, Leo and my lovely wife, Anne who are sitting somewhere in the audience.' There were sighs from the women in the crowd and a spontaneous round of applause rippled through the audience as the pianist played the opening chords of the piano accompaniment to 'The Boy with the Broken Heart' by Ira Rifkind.

Little Leo sat there, full of pride.

CHAPTER TWENTY-FOUR

February 1939

Christoph decided it was time to naturalise as an American citizen and he asked Henry and Laurie from the Palace to be his character witnesses. He could not imagine calling anywhere else home and, after almost nine years in New York, wanted to declare his allegiance to the country. He had never been one for filling out forms, but Anne went through the application with him and it was ready by the beginning of February. Becoming a citizen of the United States would represent a final break with Germany and with his own past. He wanted to show his new fellow countrymen that not all Germans were like Fritz Kuhn.

He had sent off the documents a week earlier and was waiting for news. The children were Americans because of Anne and he wanted to belong to the same nation as them. There was a renewed air of optimism and hope in New York and he was proud to call it his home city. New York was the city of all cities and he really could not see a reason to be anywhere else. His children spoke German to him at home, but spoke English as their mother tongue without a hint of an accent. There was nothing German about them, apart from their understanding of the language and the fact that their parents had German backgrounds. They would grow up as American as apple pie. On his naturalisation application, he had asked for his name to be known officially as "Chris Ritter". He thought that it had a good American ring to it. It sounded like the sort of name a baseball player might have, or an All-American track star. He would keep his birth name for his singing career, for the stage, but be known as Chris Ritter in everyday life. He had not been able to lose his accent, but hoped that it had softened over the years.

Anne still wanted to visit Germany to show the children where her parents came from, but Christoph was insistent that he would not go home while Hitler was in power. Anne had tried to persuade him that they should visit his family as soon as she heard that his father was ill, but he said again he did not want the children to see Germany as it was now. What could she do but keep on trying to talk him round?

The United States Immigration and Naturalization Service had asked for a copy of his birth certificate, but he had not brought it with him on the boat journey. So Christoph went to the German consulate right down Manhattan on Battery Place to request a duplicate copy.

After waiting for more than half an hour, a senior official reporting directly to the German consul interviewed Christoph. The new consul, rumour had it, was rather less fond of the Bund than his predecessor had been and saw the organisation only as an embarrassment. The interview went well and the birth certificate was provided without too much fuss. Christoph was about to leave when he paused for a second. He had a moment of clarity, a sudden idea of a way to help Miriam and Eva. The official, a clean-shaven man in his thirties with side-parted dark hair and a mild manner, seemed more than friendly and helpful. Christoph hoped that the change in command above him might somehow signal the possibility that the consulate could help him in what he was about to ask.

'A friend of mine is a Jewess and living in Germany. She has a young daughter. I'd like to know whether it's possible to get them a visa to leave Germany, if I can persuade the US authorities to grant them entry here.'

'From what I know of the matter, in *theory* it's certainly still possible for Jews to get exit visas out of Germany – in fact, it's actively encouraged that they leave – if they have the means to pay the exit taxes and buy their way out. But in practice it's almost impossible, especially for Jewish adults to get out now through official means because they simply can't find anywhere that will take them. Without a host country they can't get an exit visa. I know for a fact that in the last year more than two hundred and eighty thousand German and Austrian Jews have applied for immigration to the United States but the US has limited its immigration quota for all Austrians and Germans – not just Jews – to only twenty-seven thousand per year. You can see the difficulty here.'

'Only *one in ten* Germans and Austrians is getting a visa to immigrate here? Then it's pretty much a lost cause ...'

'The maximum number of immigration visas has already been awarded here now for German and Austrian adults in this twelve-month cycle. Your friend could try, but if I were you I would probably tell her to try somewhere else. I've heard that the Dominican Republic has just increased the quota of refugees that it will take in. I've also heard that a number of Jewish children are getting out to England through some sort of children's rescue mission, so you might want to mention that to your friend as well.'

Although perfectly friendly and polite, the young man

said all of this without any hint of emotion or sympathy. He could have been performing a stocktake of nuts and bolts. The situation was even more hopeless than Christoph had imagined and he saw that it would take a miracle to get Miriam and Eva out of Germany, at least to the United States. The numbers were so severely stacked against them and he bitterly regretted not having looked into their coming to the United States much earlier, when it still might have been possible.

*

There had been a coup at the Palace. The owners had sacked the artistic director and the performers had no idea what would happen to them. There were rumours that the theatre would close, and others that the management wanted to breathe new life into the venue by hiring in an entirely new roster of performers. For several weeks, the green room was in a state of panic and every one of the artists was worried about their career. In the end, after the appointment of a new artistic director, some of the less successful acts were axed, but Christoph, Henry and Laurie were all safe, as was the rising star from the south, Antonio Carrera.

For the first time Christoph realised that he had taken his rise up through the rank-and-file performers for granted and, despite the occasional moment of uncertainty when someone with Antonio's talents came along, had generally come to think of his position at the top of the bill as his for as long as he wanted it. He did not know how he would support the family when his savings ran out if the Palace no longer wanted him; Jackson's Music Hall paid him nowhere near enough to survive. He would have to give his voice a rest when things were more secure. He sang a new song that he had just added to his repertoire on his next night at the Palace Theatre:

> *I've got this city under my skin,*
> *I've got its pulse in my blood.*
> *New York's heart is my heart:*
> *We're almost next-of-kin,*
>
> *Each and every neighbourhood,*
> *I love each and every part.*
> *Each and every neighbourhood,*
> *Oh, tell me where to start ...*

Some of these schmaltzy songs made little sense, but the audience lapped them up. Their appetite for syrupy, nostalgic numbers and for romantic ballads was insatiable. He could not remember having sung *Lieder* at the theatre for at least a couple of years. It all seemed a very long way from his classical training at the conservatoire, when he had never heard songs quite like the ones that he now sang as if he had been singing them his whole life.

What would they be singing in the beer halls of Munich or Berlin now? They would be singing drinking songs and songs full of jingoism and rage. They would be shouting belligerently and raising their arms in the Hitler salute; clinking their steins of beer together and spilling the foaming brew over stained wooden table-tops. They would be praising the Führer to the skies and hunting Jews and homosexuals with the malignant fervour of their words. Songs can, after all, be weapons of aggression or defiance, as well as melodies of joy or sadness. Christoph only had to think of Matthias's *Empire Symphony* and what sentiments lay

219

behind it to know that was true.

During Christoph's time at the conservatoire in Berlin, he had seen the bitterness in people even then. Listening to conversations in beer halls or nightclubs in the city, all you heard was negative talk: what had happened to Germany in the war; criticism of the new republic; gloom about the worsening economy. Very few people had anything positive to say, even in the mid-1920s when he was a singing student and things were supposed to be better.

Kuhn was cut from that same cloth. He was one of those who thought that Germany had been unfairly treated, shamed in the eyes of the world at Versailles in 1919. The Bund's rally at Madison Square Garden was happening in just a few weeks' time and Kuhn was making a lot of noise about the event. Every few days, some article or other about the Bund appeared in the New York press. Christoph was determined to go to Madison Square Garden and make his voice heard alongside the other protesters who would surely be there. Kuhn was claiming that it would be the largest Fascist event outside Europe, which was of course a completely meaningless claim.

Christoph received news from home in a letter from his mother. His father's treatment, while not successful in curing the cancer, had at least given him hope of surviving the year. The longer-term prognosis was not good; Christoph would have to go home before it was too late.

The thought of what he might find there made him shudder; he imagined stormtroopers on every corner, Nazi flags fluttering in the breeze from every municipal building. His parents had always been so patriotic, but they must abhor all of that. His mother never mentioned anything about the regime in her letters, other than saying that 'times were very hard' for a lot of people. He wondered whether Miriam had ever considered trying to contact his parents to tell them about Eva, their granddaughter. They had hardly known Miriam at all, she was simply the younger sister of their daughter-in-law. They had perhaps only met her twice: once when they went to the Bernstein family's home for afternoon tea to discuss plans for the wedding; then at the wedding and afterwards at the reception in that old-fashioned hotel they had chosen. He would have to tell his mother and father about Eva face-to-face when he saw them; it was not something one could announce in a letter.

Miriam and his parents lived less than two kilometres from each other in Wuppertal, but they might as well have been in different worlds. Christoph remembered her small apartment above a tailor's shop, simply but carefully furnished and surprisingly full of light thanks to two large windows that overlooked Lothringerstrasse. Miriam had kept it spotlessly clean and, although she had very little money, there was always a vase of fresh flowers on the kitchen table. She had made it *gemütlich*, even though it was such a simple little place.

His parents' house, his childhood home, on the other hand, was a grand old villa up on the Weinberg. Since he and his sister had left home, Christoph's parents had rattled around the large old house, not knowing what to do with all of their rooms full of furniture but devoid of human life. Places are homes only when you have the people and the things that you love in them. The house on the Weinberg had been their home for most of their adult lives, but in their old age it would have become an alien place to them, with half of themselves, their two children, long gone.

Miriam had written another letter to Christoph, which

arrived in the middle of February. It had been some months since she had last written and there was something of the end of things, some finality, in the way that she wrote.

C. Rittersmann
296 East 83rd Street
New York, New York

1st February 1939

Dear Christoph,

I hope that all is well for you and your family in New York.

Things are ever darker here. Abraham has managed to take his family to Australia after almost a year in Holland and Isy has been arrested by the Gestapo. We do not know why. Rumours are circulating that my brother is in Dachau, but we have heard nothing from Isy in over a month. What is left of our family here in Wuppertal, Eva, Hedwig and I, are all frantic with worry. Before he was arrested, Isy was able to make some contacts in England and Eva is going to go there if things get too bad.

I have tried and tried again, but the authorities will not give me a visa to leave Germany because I cannot find a country that will take me – let alone the money. The family in England who will sponsor Eva and foster her would also take me, as a domestic, if only I could get there, but the British will not grant me entry and Eva must go alone, if she is to go. Without obtaining permission to immigrate somewhere, getting an exit visa to leave here is impossible. Our family's Christian friends in Wuppertal are trying to intervene on my behalf, but I

222

think that it is hopeless. Hedwig has also failed to obtain an exit visa because she has nowhere to go.

Eva will be eight years old in a few weeks and she is so curious about the world. She asks so many questions. She wants to know what the swastika flags on the public buildings mean and why there are men in uniform out on the street. I try to shield her from the truth as much as I can. She is asking who her father is more and more often. I do not know what to tell her. I don't know him any longer.

A child should have a father, particularly in these terrible times.

Miriam

Christoph had read the letter down in the lobby. He had not wanted to wait until he was back up in the apartment as Anne and Mae were still there.

Even though he read and re-read Miriam's news it was barely comprehensible and it left him feeling numb and appalled. The kind of numbness born of an overloading of indignation and pity. He bitterly regretted not having tried to get Miriam and Eva visas to leave Germany until it was too late to do so. How had her family deserved what was happening to them? He would stand up and shout his lungs out when Kuhn took to the podium at Madison Square Garden.

Her quiet accusation at the end of the letter hurt him. Thinking of Leo and little Mae who put so much trust in him, and of Eva's beautiful face in the photograph with her soulful almond-shaped eyes, he felt nothing but shame.

CHAPTER TWENTY-FIVE

20th February 1939, Madison Square Garden

There was a large crowd of protesters shouting outside the Madison Square Garden building on Eighth Avenue between Forty-Ninth and Fiftieth Streets, a roaring wave of placards and banners, and a heavy police presence surrounded the building. Fritz Kuhn's greatest moment, the pinnacle of his career as a Fascist, had been planned to coincide with Washington's birthday.

Somehow Christoph had managed to slip unchecked through the security cordon and past the men on the doors; he looked, after all, like a good German. A vast illuminated image of Washington, standing with his hand on his hip and dressed in his long-tailed military coat and breeches, dominated the stage in the distance. The venue was so full of Kuhn's supporters that Christoph could get nowhere near the front. He felt very vulnerable and exposed in the midst of so much love for the Führer, and of so much hate. He had not seen so many people in one place for a long time, not since Berlin. Now he stood quietly in the throng, watching the event unfold.

There was a great murmuring and sense of expectation in the arena. Christoph looked around and the faces of the men – they were almost all men – looked exactly like those you would find out on the street in any German town or city; there was nothing at all sinister or remarkable in the way they looked. Many of the men were speaking English to each other, not German. The Bund's *Ordnungsdienst*, the military arm of the organisation, was out in force and stood in uniformed rows at the foot of the podium, with drummers standing at the very front, beneath Washington's portrait. Men from the *Ordnungsdienst* were also scattered throughout the crowd to keep order, Christoph guessed, in case things turned violent. He wondered if there were other protestors like him there.

Suddenly there was a clattering roll of drums and a column of men from the *Ordnungsdienst*, holding flags bearing the stars and stripes and others emblazoned with the swastika, marched up the central aisle of the arena, while the crowds on either side raised their hands in the Hitler salute and chanted the Führer's name. It was spectacular and appalling.

Christoph did not know what to do but to follow suit, so as not to reveal himself too early. He raised his right arm up stiffly towards the podium, his fingers pointing accusingly to where Kuhn stood. He felt physically sick and kept his dry mouth clamped tightly shut: he could not say the Führer's name.

There was such a din in the echoing building and it became a roar when Kuhn moved up to the microphone and began to speak. Christoph wondered what it would be like to perform in front of such a vast crowd: he had heard someone say that there were at least twenty thousand people there. Even for someone with Kuhn's fatal mixture of arrogance and idiocy, it must be nerve-wracking to step onto that stage and face such a large crowd.

He still had a heavy accent and his Bavarian vowels, fed

through electric static, bounced off the ceiling and the walls of the arena, which was vaster than an airship hangar. In the noise – and because Kuhn was so far away despite the amplification of his voice – Christoph could not catch every word that he said.

'The Bund is fighting shoulder to shoulder with patriotic Americans to protect America from a race that is not the American race, that is not even a white race … the Jews are enemies of the United States,' he caught Kuhn saying at one point, to great cheers and chants of *Sieg Heil* from the crowd.

He wondered if there would be any protest. Everyone around him seemed to be a fervent supporter of the Bund and he could see no one who had the look of anything other than complete belief in Kuhn's barbaric vitriol. He thought of Eva and those wide, innocent eyes.

Kuhn kept calling President Roosevelt 'Frank D. Rosenfeld' and referring to his New Deal as the 'Jew Deal', to widespread laughter from the crowd. He whipped his audience into a frenzy of outrage and adulation with his hysterical repetition of these phrases, expanding on his theory of a cabal of Bolshevik-Jewish interest going to the very top of the American leadership.

Christoph was standing perhaps fifty yards away from the stage and Kuhn's podium, but he had a clear view and watched as a man suddenly broke free from the ranks of spectators at the front of the crowd and rushed the stage, trying to launch himself at Kuhn's legs and tackle him down. The man missed his target, having tripped on the lip of the stage, and lay sprawling at the base of the podium as several men from the *Ordnungsdienst* jumped on him, picked him up and threw him back into the crowd as if they were tossing a pebble into the ocean. The protests had begun.

Kuhn's booming voice echoed around Madison Square Garden, but now there were other voices that could be heard. At first it was difficult to pick them out from the general hubbub of the crowd, drowned as the voices of the audience were by the magnified, static hiss of Kuhn's rhetoric. Then someone near Christoph shouted loudly and clearly: 'Fuck off back to Germany, then!' as Kuhn was declaiming euphorically about the Fatherland. Another man, in the banked seats to Christoph's left on the far side of the arena, shouted: 'Go home! Nazi swine are not welcome in America.'

The effect of these voices of dissent was almost instantaneous. Men from the *Ordnungsdienst* swarmed through the crowd searching out the culprits, who had been rounded on in any case by the Bund's supporters standing closest to them. They pummelled the protestors with gloved fists and kicked them with booted feet until they lay in crumpled heaps on the concrete floor. Sparked by this brutal treatment of the dissenters who had dared to voice their opposition, fights between the anti-Nazis and the men from the *Ordnungsdienst* spread like wildfire through the crowd. There were shouts of pain and outrage as the protesters revealed themselves and were meted out heavy beatings. All the while, Kuhn's vivid, angry monologue echoed through the arena. The whole scene reminded Christoph of something out of Dante or Hieronymous Bosch. He saw blood pouring from a man's nose and another man with a badly split lip, as Kuhn expounded the virtues of a Jew-free America.

Christoph could not keep quiet any longer as Kuhn shrieked out his catchphrase, 'Jew Deal' again. He shouted out with his singer's lungs: 'You should be done for treason.' He had only recently learnt the word, and felt that it described Kuhn perfectly; he was a traitor to the values of his adopted country. Again, more loudly, 'You should be done for treason.'

He saw a fist, then nothing more.

He came to and could not understand where he was. There was a stinging ache around his right eye and when he put his hand up to it and looked at his fingers, they were red. He had somehow staggered outside the arena before collapsing, or else had been carried there unconscious, and was sitting on the sidewalk under a lamppost. The protesters were still in full voice less than twenty feet from where he was sitting on the cold paving slabs.

Christoph hauled himself up with the help of the lamppost and tried to dust off his overcoat and suit trousers. He noticed that the seam had split on his thigh and his coat sleeve had a rip in it. He felt like a down-and-out.

His right eye was closing and the flesh around it was throbbing and hot. Christoph wiped it with his coat sleeve as he made his way over to the line of protesters outside Madison Square Garden. He still felt very unsteady on his feet and could not for the life of him remember how he had got outside the venue. He guessed that one of the Bund's supporters had hit him and that the *Ordnungsdienst* had thrown him outside.

FASCISTS GO HOME! one placard said; another *NAZI SWINE NOT WELCOME IN NY*. He joined the ranks of protesters and shouted his anger at the impervious brick walls of the building, while inside Kuhn shouted out his anger at the entire world.

Christoph wanted to stay until the early evening when the rally was scheduled to end and when Kuhn, the *Ordnungsdienst* and the audience would be streaming out of the building under a heavy police guard to be heckled and jeered at by the protesters outside, but he was desperate to relieve himself and walked off across the West Side to look for a public lavatory. After he had found one, he could not summon the will to go back to Madison Square Garden again. His head was hurting badly, his eye had closed up completely and he felt unwell.

He walked the two miles home across Manhattan and Anne gave a little shriek when she saw her husband in that state. Leo cried and hugged his father, asking what had happened, and Anne steered Mae into the bedroom that she shared with her brother so that she would not see her father's beaten face. Anne could not understand for the life of her why he had got himself involved in all that trouble.

She put Christoph to bed for the rest of the evening, telling the children to play quietly together in the sitting-room, and hurried off to the closest butcher's shop for some ice. He would not be singing next week, looking like that. After she had fed the children and put them to bed, she sat at the window in the sitting-room mending Christoph's suit trousers and overcoat, crying quietly to herself.

It was the first time that he had ever been hit. Christoph lay in bed with the bag of ice pressed against the right side of his face and could not sleep. The pain did not worry him; it would pass in a day or two and it had been worth it – he would certainly protest again. Seeing Anne and the children upset, however, kept him from getting to sleep and he lay there for hours, the ice slowly melting into water that leaked from the bag onto his pillow, waiting for Anne to come to bed. You always paid with your private life when you tried to do something out in the world.

In the morning, after having slept only for a few fitful hours, Christoph went to the bathroom and looked in the mirror above the sink; the swelling had certainly gone down, but there was now a deep purple and green bruise around his eye, fading to yellow at its edges. He could open his right eye almost as wide as his left and his vision seemed unaffected by the Nazi punch. He would have to wait until the swelling and the bruising had gone almost completely before he could perform in public again. A little make-up would cover the last stains of bruising and the audience were, in any case, ten feet away at their closest; it was more that he could not let the artistic director and the management at the Palace see him like this. He was meant to be Rittersmann the Romantic, not Rittersmann the Rioter. He felt strangely pleased with himself, however; almost a feeling of elation.

'How are you feeling this morning, darling?' Anne asked, coming in behind him as he was still looking at himself in the mirror, turning his head with her hand so that he faced her.

'Oh, a little sore. I'm sorry I've upset you, Anne, but I had to make a stand,' he said.

'You could've gotten yourself hurt. I mean seriously hurt.'

'But I didn't. I'm all right,' he replied. 'I'll just have to tell the Palace and Jackson's Music Hall that I'm unwell, that I've got flu or something, and start singing again next Saturday night. I'll look fine by then.'

'I thought you were going over to Madison Square Garden just to watch the event there, nothing more?'

'What the man was saying was so unforgivable that I couldn't just shut up and say nothing.'

'But you have the children to think about,' Anne said.

'I know I do. It is for them that I protested,' Christoph replied.

Christoph spent the week leading up to Saturday night rehearsing some new songs and helping Anne to look after Mae while Leo was at school. The first signs of spring were already to be seen in Central Park when he took his daughter for a walk; new shoots of life were pushing their way up from the ground and green buds decorated the trees, which would soon unfurl themselves into leaves.

CHAPTER TWENTY-SIX

May 1939

After months of silence, Christoph found another letter from Miriam in the postbox down in the lobby. He was on his way out to see König for the first time in almost ten months, and stopped for a coffee in a diner on Madison Avenue to read it. The traffic was heavy that morning, with trucks rumbling uptown and motorcars backed up and hooting their horns in frustration.

The waitress spilled a drop of coffee from her pot onto the corner of the letter that Christoph had opened and flattened out on the table in front of him. He could not stop himself from asking whether she had lost the proper use of her hands.

C. Rittersmann
296 East 83rd Street
New York, New York

18th May 1939

Dear Christoph,

    I turned thirty-two years old today. Eva brought me a cup of coffee in bed and a flower that she had picked on the way home from school yesterday afternoon.

Eva is my only family here now to wish me happy birthday, Hedwig was unable to find work and left Wuppertal for Berlin almost two months ago, to see if she could find employment there. It had got so bad that she could barely afford to feed herself and she took any kind of work she could find in Berlin, however menial. Non-Jewish friends of hers in Wuppertal gave her some money to travel and to survive in her first weeks in the capital. I have not heard from her for at least a fortnight now.

Isy was released from Dachau after the intervention of his German friends from the Christian community in Wuppertal, and has managed to get himself illegally across the border to Dornach in German-speaking Switzerland. The tailor's shop has kept open and kept me on, but who knows for how long?

So, it is just Eva and me now, hanging on as the beatings out on the streets, the deportations and restrictions on the lives of those who have the misfortune to have been born Jewish continue, and get worse and worse. How long we can stay together I do not know.

Yours,
Miriam

Christoph left the diner and went out onto Madison Avenue, raising the collar of his coat against the fine drizzle that seemed to hang in the air, wetting everything. It was only when the waitress came running after him that he realised he had forgotten to pay, so distracted and disturbed was he by what Miriam had written. The waitress accepted his apology and a generous tip before retreating inside out of the weather.

234

*

König was all smiles; it seemed that life with his young mistress and child was suiting him. A radio executive from one of the big New York City networks had seen Christoph perform at the Palace and had approached König to have him audition for a weekly show on one of the network's stations. Christoph neither recognised the name of the station nor the show. In fact, he found it hard to concentrate on what König was saying: he kept thinking about Miriam's letter and what was happening in Germany. Surely, if it was still possible, she would send Eva to safety in England before it was too late to do so, even if Miriam herself could not get out? He felt so bad even to think that Miriam might find herself stuck in a country where her life was at risk.

'Mr Rittersmann,' König said, his teeth glittering in a puzzled smile, 'I was saying that it's a very good break for you, this radio show.'

'Ah, yes sorry, perhaps it is,' Christoph replied. 'But, to be honest, my voice is getting tired and I've been feeling for quite a while that I need to give it a complete rest for a month or two. I was hoping to do that later this year.'

'But if you don't sing, you don't earn,' König said. 'How're you going to get by?'

'I have some savings that would last us a couple of months, maybe a little longer at a push.'

'And do you really think the Palace would have you back if you told them that you needed to take an extended holiday to rest your voice? Do you know how many singers I have on my books who can't find work?' König's tone had become quietly hectoring; the weekly fee from the radio station must be high.

'I think I'll have to take that risk,' Christoph answered, losing patience a little with König's sharpness. He did not trust the man any longer to want what was best for him, only what was best for himself. He told König that he would audition for the radio show but was not sure that he would take up the offer, if successful. It all depended on his voice.

Christoph heard that Kuhn was under investigation by the New York tax authorities for embezzling money from the Bund. While the Bund's members viewed their leader's powers as absolute and inviolable, the New York district attorney had other ideas and was gearing up for a prosecution. It gave Christoph a great deal of pleasure to think that what might topple the American Führer and get his poisonous views out of the public domain was a simple fraud investigation. He could not imagine that the Bund would continue in any effective form without Kuhn's bigot's zeal and dark ardour.

Since Madison Square Garden, there had been regular reports on the Bund's activities in the popular New York press, focusing chiefly on the violence and disorder that it seemed to leave in its wake wherever it held speeches or parades. Kuhn was described as a figure of hate to most right-thinking Americans and his constant craving for publicity appeared only to fuel that hatred. Christoph knew more than ever that the United States would never be fertile ground for the fascism that was blighting his homeland. Americans liked their way of life far too much to let that happen.

In early June, Christoph's naturalisation card arrived. He looked older in the photograph than he saw himself –

heavier set around the jawline. There he was, an American citizen with a new name: Christopher J. Ritter. He had invented the initial entirely, as he did not possess a middle name. He was as American as apple strudel, he joked with Anne, and showed Leo the card, as they were now fellow countrymen.

'You look funny. You don't look like my Papa,' his son said.

'I look a little serious, don't I?' Christoph replied. 'Going to the photographer, I must have forgotten to smile. I think the flash bulb blinded me a little.'

'You look like a very respectable American citizen in your smart jacket and tie,' Anne said fondly, kissing him on the cheek. 'You're finally one of us!'

Christoph still had his German passport and was now a citizen of two worlds, the old and the new. He knew without the shadow of a doubt which one he would rather belong to. He put his old passport in the box at the bottom of the cupboard in the main room, and kept the new one proudly in his wallet, carrying it at all times in the breast pocket of his jacket. He was a resident of New York and a citizen of the United States and never in the farthest reaches of his imagination would he have pictured that future for himself when he was a child.

The audition for the radio show took place in the second week of June, in a cramped booth in a studio on Rockefeller Plaza, right next to Radio City Music Hall. The show's producer and editor were both there and it turned out to be called 'The Singer and the Song', a popular twice-weekly show of light numbers: show tunes, ballads, theatrical pieces. They wanted to hear how his voice sounded through a microphone, through the static fizz of reproduction, more than how it sounded in and of itself. They seemed to like it chiefly because its timbre meant that it could be mixed for broadcast with an accompanying backing band without too much trouble. They complimented him on his voice, not on his singing.

The producer was a southerner, judging by the gentle twang of his accent and his pale summer suit. He took Christoph on a tour of the studios after the audition, showing him around the vast complex of corridors and cubicles and sound rooms. Red lights glowed above sound-proofed doors behind which broadcasts were under way and a general hush sealed the building in a world of its own. It was strange, but Christoph had never thought about how the radio waves reached his wireless set and about the whole complex, alchemical process of their production.

The producer told Christoph they would let his agent know within the week whether they wanted to take him for the show, and accompanied Christoph to the front door of the building. It was a shock to the senses to leave the dark hush of the studios behind and to walk out of that door into the glare and hustle of Midtown Manhattan on a midweek lunchtime. The whole world seemed to be out on the streets in the shimmering heat of summer.

Christoph hardly ever bumped into people he knew on the street when he was more than a block or two away from home; the odds of that happening were far too slim. As he was walking uptown away from the studios, however, he saw Henry Cliff coming towards him, his head bowed under a black homburg hat, looking down at the pavement as he walked. He did not see Christoph, but walked briskly past in the oncoming crowd. Christoph was certain that he must be hurrying, late as usual, to an audition for the same show. What else would he be doing in the neighbourhood? Work for singers was always scarce and it was inevitable that they would have to compete against each other sometimes for the same jobs. If one of the singers from the Palace actually found more work, the others would offer their congratulations and carry on looking and auditioning. It was a question of professional survival, not of friendship.

After only a few days, Christoph received a note asking him to call König. He did so from a new telephone booth that had been installed on the corner. The news was that he had been offered a once-weekly hour-long starring role, starting in September when the new season of the show began, with the other night belonging to a South American tenor whom he had never heard of. He wondered whether he should tell Henry or let him find out in his own time. He tried his best to sound pleased, as the money would be good for the family, but he was more worried than ever about the impact on his voice.

'Papa's famous! He's going to be on the radio!' Leo said, echoing the words of his mother when they heard the news.

'Well, I'm not famous *quite* yet,' his father replied with a laugh. Mae smiled and danced gleefully around the living-room, without really understanding what the news meant and why her mother and brother were so pleased.

'Perhaps we'll be able to move to a house somewhere a little out of the city one day,' Anne said.

'I'm sure we can sometime; let's see how the show goes first,' he said, 'and how my voice holds up.'

The following Saturday night at the Palace began awkwardly, as Christoph did not know whether he should tell his fellow acts about the radio show or keep quiet, and felt uncomfortable not mentioning the news when asked how he was. They all seemed to be keen to speak to him that evening in the green room as they waited to go on.

After he had sung as the last performer of the night, getting loud applause and cheers, Christoph made his way back to the green room, thinking that he would just take off his stage make-up and put on his overcoat and head home through the warm night. When he opened the green room door, however, all of that evening's acts and the artistic director were standing there with smiles on their faces. There was a cake on the table in the corner with a lighted candle on it. They must be thinking that it was his birthday.

'Congratulations,' Mia Salgado the mezzo soprano said, and gave him a kiss on the cheek.

'We heard the news,' the artistic director added, passing Christoph a glass of water to soothe his vocal cords with one hand and a glass of sparkling wine with the other.

'How do you know?' Christoph asked a little dumbfounded.

'Mr König called the management,' the artistic director said. 'He was asking for a pay rise for you. They said they'd have to get back to him on that.'

Everyone in the room laughed, but the mood was jolly and good-natured, people seemed genuinely pleased for him rather than envious. Only Henry was a little quiet and spoke just briefly to Christoph, offering him a few words of congratulation, even though they were good friends and usually would have a lot to talk about.

It was after eleven o'clock in the evening when he got home and it was unusually quiet; the wireless, which Anne was fond of listening to in the evenings after the children had gone to bed, was silent. The children were fast asleep when he looked in on them, and Anne was not in the living-room or the kitchen. He went into their bedroom to take off his jacket and hang it up in the wardrobe, before pouring himself a drink, and found her sitting on the end of their bed, her eyes red from crying and her hands trembling. She was holding a letter and the wooden box of Miriam's letters was lying open on the counterpane beside her.

'Leo was looking for his spinning top in your cupboard, and he found this box,' she said.

'Have you read them all?' was the only thing that Christoph could think of saying. He was blank with shock.

'I said goodnight to Leo at eight,' she replied, sobbing. 'I've been sitting here since, reading through them over and over again. Why didn't you tell me? Why didn't you *tell* me?' she repeated, her voice louder now and the pale skin on her throat and cheeks flushing pink.

'I'm so sorry. It all happened long before we met, Anne. It's another lifetime ago to me.' He could feel the blood draining out of his cheeks.

'But they're still with you here in these letters,' Anne's voice rose angrily. 'They're still with you.'

'I hid the letters and never thought anyone would find them,' Christoph replied feebly, the fight quite gone out of him.

'You have a daughter that you've never *once* had the guts to tell me about and she's in *danger*,' Anne continued as if she had not heard what he had said, her voice still raised in incredulity and anger.

'I didn't tell you about her and that was wrong,' Christoph said, now kneeling down in front of her and trying to clasp her hands. Anne pushed his hands away then

241

slapped him hard on the right cheek, before bursting into tears again. He leapt up aghast, his face stinging from the slap, and sat down hard on the chair by the bedroom door.

'I've wanted to tell you about Eva so many times; it's been eating away at me,' he said, on the verge of tears himself. 'But the longer I didn't tell you the more convinced I became that you would leave me if you ever found out. I'm so sorry, so sorry.'

'Leave you? *Leave* you? Not everything's always about you,' she replied, angrily. 'I've been sitting here reading the letters and still can't believe that you were already a father when we met. I thought that I'd given you at least *that*.'

'I was a father, but not a parent,' Christoph replied.

'She's beautiful,' Anne said, indicating the photograph of Eva that was lying next to the box on the counterpane, separate from the sheaf of letters. 'Poor, poor girl. You sing about love and devotion and abandon your *child*? How could you DO that?'

'I didn't abandon her – she wasn't even born when I came over here.'

'That poor woman is trying to cope all on her own,' Anne said, deeply angry and moved.

'But Miriam didn't tell me that she was pregnant until after I left Wuppertal,' he tried to reason with her.

'Even so, even so,' Anne replied. 'I've never once been ashamed of you, but now …' Her voice petered out into sobs again.

Leo had been woken by the raised voices and came into their bedroom to see what was happening and why his parents were arguing. His little worried face stopped Anne from crying and she spoke softly to him.

'Everything's all right,' she said. 'Please go back to bed, Leo.'

'Why are you sad, Mummy?' he asked.

'I'm not sad, darling. Really, everything's fine,' she reassured him again.

That night, Christoph slept on the sofa and he tossed and turned all night with regret, and with relief that Anne finally knew. The children did not realise that he had been banished from their parents' bedroom, although they both sensed a chill between them for the first time. It was Anne and Christoph's only serious argument in seven years: their marriage shifted on its axis that night in an indefinable way, and neither of them had the words to describe how it had changed.

PART IV:
EUROPA

CHAPTER TWENTY-SEVEN

Early July 1939

The Nazi government had ordered a change of name for the *Albert Ballin*, because the ship had been named after a Jew. As the sun beat down on her deck, Christoph found himself looking back at the receding skyline of Manhattan from the stern of *Hansa*. It was not quite the same ship that he had arrived on nine years earlier: it had also been lengthened by fifty feet in 1934.

Anne had taken the children to stay with her parents in Ohio for the summer. She had told Christoph that he risked losing her if he did not go back to Germany to help his daughter and to see his sick father. Christoph had been living in a state of terrible agitation for weeks now and had hardly slept; he had never known Anne to be so angry or so determined. He had asked the Palace and Jackson's Music Hall for a two-month sabbatical and, to his surprise, both venues had agreed. It was the first time that he had left Manhattan in years and he was glad to be getting out of the city, although any feeling of relief or escape was cancelled out by the fear of where he was going and what he would find there.

The captain of the ship was a music-lover and, learning that a successful German-born singer was on board his vessel, he had awarded him a higher-class cabin in return for him singing on a couple of evenings in the ballroom after dinner. Although Christoph was going back to where he came from – he refused to call it home – much better off than he had left it, he had chosen the same simple style of cabin that he inhabited on his outbound journey, deep in the bowels of the ship, hearing the low reverberation of the engines thrumming through his sleeping quarters all night. He was therefore grateful for the free upgrade to a first-class cabin. His savings would be severely tested over the next couple of months.

Each morning of the week-long crossing, he spent several hours walking up and down the uppermost deck of the vast ship, trying to quell his fears. He had always got on well with his father, and was not concerned about the distance that they might feel on seeing each other again after all this time, although he was worried about the state of health that he would find him in. His mother would be overjoyed to see him and he would be a boy again in her presence.

But should he tell them about Eva, when his father's illness gave them so much to worry about as it was? Miriam would be proud and strong and any anger that she might once have felt towards him would have long since subsided into resentment, at worst. When he tried to force his mind to picture seeing Eva for the first time, talking to her in her mother's little apartment or perhaps taking her for a walk around the park, it would not cooperate. It went blank and he could not conjure up any images of such an encounter: all he felt was guilt and a fluttering sense of shame in the pit of his stomach.

How would he explain to Eva who he was? How would he explain his complete absence from her life? Pacing up and down that sunlit deck, he felt more than ever that the whole thing was impossible. If it were not for Anne's insistence and intervention, he would be at home in his apartment in Manhattan with his family around him. But he was forgetting, he was forgetting: she had taken the children with her to Ohio and things were far, far from happy at home. He had to try to help save his daughter from an uncertain future if he wanted to save his marriage. More than that, even without Anne's ultimatum and whatever shape the revelation about his daughter had left his marriage in, he now saw it clearly as his undeniable *duty* to do all that he could to try to help her as the Nazi stranglehold tightened its grip on the Jews of Germany. He had to do what he could to help Miriam, to ease her situation, even if getting her and Eva to America was impossible now. He just had no idea what he could actually do for them now, and he felt deeply ashamed of himself for not acting sooner.

These thoughts went round and round chasing their own tails, and at some moments during that lonely voyage he felt close to a despair that threatened to overwhelm him. He kept thinking of Hans' shattered face on the Front and what he had had to witness when still so young. He did not want Eva, or any of his children, ever to have to suffer or to learn what man was capable of. He wanted to get away from the world. He wanted to be back on the stage.

Christoph sang when he could not sleep. The cabin next to his was empty and he had noticed that the ship was far emptier than it had been on his outward voyage. It seemed that fewer people wanted to go to Germany than had wanted to leave it in 1930. Many of his fellow passengers back then had been emigrants looking for a better life.

He sang for the captain on the last two nights of the

crossing. He did not bring a dinner jacket and the ship's purser had to borrow one for him from a senior member of the crew so that he could sit in proper fashion at the captain's table before the performance. The captain was from Warnemünde on the Baltic coast. Christoph had not failed to notice the *Gösch*, the marine jack with its black swastika in a white roundel on a bed of blood red that fluttered from the stern of the ship, but signs of the Nazi regime were not as obvious on board as he had feared. Kapitän Becker, however, was a great hulk of a man with a poisonous allegiance to the Party. Christoph had the displeasure of sitting directly opposite him across the long table, as the guest of honour. The man shovelled the *hors d'œuvre* into his mouth with all the delicacy of a bear eating a salmon.

'Herr Rittersmann, you were not tempted to leave our American friends and come home sooner? I heard that you've been in New York for a long time.'

'I have a wife and children there,' Christoph replied. 'I'm only going back to Wuppertal, where I grew up, to visit my sick father and my mother for a month or so. Then I'm returning home to New York again.'

'You no longer think of Germany as your home, as your *Vaterland*?' Kapitän Becker asked suspiciously.

'I've been in America for a long time,' Christoph said, trying to bring the conversation to a close.

The captain went on eating and turned to the woman on his left, who Christoph had gathered was from Berlin. It appeared that her husband was something big in armaments, as he was sitting to Christoph's right and talking to his other neighbour in a strong Berlin accent about the manufacturing of anti-aircraft guns for the possible war that was on everyone's lips.

For a moment Christoph had no one to talk to and sat there in silence, looking at the elegantly dressed guests sitting around the captain's table. They were all German: there was not a single foreigner amongst them. It was a shock after the lively diversity of New York to be surrounded only by his stolid countrymen again. He had nothing in common with them any more, apart from a shared language.

He sang half a dozen songs after dinner on the last two nights of the voyage, standing in front of a microphone on a low stage at one end of the ballroom. On the first night, the assembled dinner guests did not know who he was and many of them were seated at their tables so that they had their backs to him. Some did not even have the courtesy to stop their flabby mouths from talking as he sang, so that he felt nothing more than a generator of incidental noise in a corner of the vast room. It was a humbling experience and it made Christoph miss the warm acclaim of the audience at the Palace Theatre acutely, and detest his fellow passengers even more.

Kapitän Becker barely thanked him when Christoph took his seat at the table again for coffee. Perhaps the captain did not like *Lieder* and preferred something a little more modern instead; perhaps he was disappointed that Christoph had subdued the tone of the evening with the melancholy of his songs; perhaps he was simply a philistine and not really a music-lover after all. The men sucked on cigars in a fug of smoke and the women looked on, yawning discreetly into perfumed handkerchiefs: it was already nearly midnight.

*

The weather turned on the last full day of the crossing as they came up the north coast of France after stopping at Cherbourg to let off some passengers. The sea became rough and the ship rolled in the heavy swell.

Christoph lay in his bed that last night of the voyage and could not sleep. He still felt angry about the lukewarm response that had greeted his first performance, even though the second night had gone slightly better and he had added two or three modern numbers to his song list. They were popular American songs and his accompanist, who was German, had had to sightread the scores as he was not familiar with them.

Christoph tossed and turned in his bed. He missed Anne and the children beyond words. The motion of the ship was unsettling his stomach and he vomited into the lavatory two or three times during the night. It felt, in some small way, like a revenge when he thought of Kapitän Becker and how he had watched him gorging himself on the very same food that Christoph was now vomiting up.

The sea was still rough in the early morning and Christoph felt washed out by his night of sleeplessness and nausea. He went up on deck, hoping that the fresh sea air would do him some good, and saw that the clouds that had crowded the sky the evening before had been scoured away by the wind. It was not yet six o'clock and the summer sun was coming up over the horizon. The margin of the sky just above the sea was turning from the deep blue-black of night to a pale blue tinged with orange-yellow.

There was a low, dark landmass to his right and he guessed that this was already the German coast. A shiver ran through him; perhaps it was just the chill of the early-morning air getting under his clothes. A shiver ran through him again and he knew that he was afraid. The distant silhouettes of scattered houses on the coast were now coming into view on the horizon, and the great ship began to slow. Soon it was making its way through channels between large boats and ships, anchored far out from the mouth of the river Elbe in deep water. Their vast hulks loomed black and cold grey in the morning light.

Announcements now came over loudspeakers that the *Hansa* would soon be docking and Christoph went down to his cabin to pack his case. The next leg of the journey would be by train from the river port into the city of Hamburg itself, then a change at the *Hauptbahnhof* onto another train destined for the south-west of the country and Wuppertal-Elberfeld. In total, the journey would take a further six hours.

As *Hansa* ground to a shuddering halt at the quayside, like a planet stopped mid-orbit, Christoph looked out through his porthole into the dazzling summer morning light. Down below, men were busying themselves on the quay, and soon passengers were disembarking down fenced walkways and luggage was being offloaded into great piles.

The crowd quickly gathered on the harbourside, a throng of passengers and white-liveried crew, and families who had come from the city centre to welcome their loved ones. Amongst them moved men in mustard-brown uniforms and high, peaked caps. This was the first time Christoph had seen it but readily recognised the uniform from the newspapers in New York. He shuddered involuntarily: they were from the *Sturmabteilung*. They were Hitler's stormtroopers.

CHAPTER TWENTY-EIGHT

The black train rattled at high speed through the flat countryside of northern Germany. Christoph was sitting in a sweltering compartment with four other passengers: two elderly women chatting to each other about nothing much in particular in heavy Swabian accents, a man about his own age in a well-cut business suit who kept opening and closing his briefcase, and a young man with sharp features and pale blond hair who had so far not said a single word. Aside from the young man with blond hair, the others had all swapped pleasantries about the hot weather and complained of the hardness of the train's seats.

The nearer he got to his destination, the more apprehensive Christoph became. While he was looking forward to seeing his father and the rest of his family, seeing little Eva filled him with trepidation. He had promised to help her and he would do everything in his power to fulfil his promise. But he was driven by an overwhelming sense of having failed Eva; of having failed Anne, his children, himself.

He carried Eva's photograph in his breast pocket, not knowing exactly why. While for years he had tried to suppress any thought of her in his mind, he now longed to meet her, but he was afraid too, afraid that he would fall in love with her like he had with his other children and that he would not be able to leave her behind in Europe when it was time to go home to America. He was anxious that something might have already happened to her. He had not heard from Miriam for more than two months now. He didn't know how he would face Miriam, and look her in the eye.

The young man with pale blond hair turned with a thin-lipped smile to his fellow passengers as the train slowed towards Wuppertal-Elberfeld station and asked to see their identity papers. He did not tell them on whose authority he was asking, but they all knew by the black leather trench coat folded carefully on his lap and the small Nazi insignia on his lapel that he must work for the Gestapo. While the two old ladies muttered complaints under their breath and fumbled in their handbags, Christoph had the presence of mind to pull out his German passport from his breast pocket and leave his American one where it was.

The man looked carefully at the document and then handed it back to Christoph without a word. He could not have been more than thirty, yet his power over them because of whom he worked for gave him a complete sense of assurance and control. His eyes were cold and vacant and disturbed Christoph greatly. His was the face of a brutal new Germany.

As Christoph got off the train, the smartly dressed businessman from his compartment who had been opening and closing his briefcase, as if searching for something or nervously filling his time, got off the carriage behind him. Christoph had only taken a few steps along the platform when he heard a loud cry of protest and turned to see the man being arrested by two plain-clothed men. They were standing to either side of the dark-haired man and had firmly taken hold of him by both arms. The man continued to shout and protest in a loud voice in a language that Christoph could not quite catch: it could have been Russian or Hungarian or Czech. It could have been Yiddish. It was certainly something from the east. They pulled the man along the platform towards the stationmaster's office. His heels were off the ground and he was almost being carried – dragged – along by them. His voice had risen to a shrill shriek now, and everyone on the station went about his or her own business with heads down and eyes to the ground, as if nothing at all untoward was happening. Christoph left the station with heart pounding and palms sweating. He wished more than anything that he had not come.

Christoph had decided to walk from the railway station through his home town and up the Weinberg. He had his coat draped over his arm and the top buttons of his shirt undone. It was late afternoon and still very warm. There were swastikas flying from the flagpoles outside the *Rathaus*, the old town hall building in the Barmen district of the town.

The sky was an almost lapis blue with not a cloud in sight; only swifts darted from eaves to eaves in the upper part of the town. Christoph hardly recognised himself as the man whose eyes had last looked at these very same streets and buildings nine years earlier. Although the fabric of the town had remained the same, with only a few new buildings having sprung up here and there, this new, severe style had changed the soul of the place profoundly. Wuppertal was an alien place to him now. Yet there was his childhood home up ahead, standing proudly in its large garden on the hill. Christoph squinted into the sunshine to take a good look at it again. It was so large, so solid that it represented a refuge against the madness of the times, something that could never be destroyed or where any harm could come. Wuppertal might be alien to him, but that house with its memories of love and childhood happiness was still home. Christoph had never realised until that moment that you could have more than one home.

His mother opened and closed her mouth when she unlocked the heavy front door to him, but no words came out. Her hair was almost completely grey now, with only a few strands of her once blonde hair that had been a lustrous golden colour showing through here and there. Her face was heavily lined from the strain of looking after his father over the last few years. She couldn't bring herself to speak, but tears did come and she cried with joy and surprise as he hugged her; he had not told them that he was coming. '*Mein Sohn,*' was all that she could say after some moments as she led him into the house, 'My son.'

His father seemed to have shrunk in on himself. Where Christoph remembered a great bear of a man, in the old leather armchair by the fireplace sat a husk, a hollowed-out shell of that once proud figure, a man who had been able to chop logs out at the back of the house for half a day while barely breaking sweat. He began to get up from his armchair when he saw his son, but Christoph told him to stay seated and leaned over his chair, embracing him where he sat. His body was frail and fragile; Christoph worried about crushing him in his embrace. The skin on his face was almost translucent, pulled shiny and taught over pronounced cheekbones and hollow cheeks.

'When did you arrive?' his father asked, his voice sounding as if he had just emerged from a deep sleep.

'Just now, Father. I wanted to surprise you. I've been worried about my old man.'

'It is a *wonderful* surprise,' his father said. 'Your last letter must have been a month or so ago and your mother and I suspected, from something that you wrote there, that you might come home soon.'

'Now here I am,' Christoph said, 'and it's so good to see you both, in spite of things …'

'You've grown up while you've been away. I still think of you as a boy and how you were before you left – a young man with big dreams. Now you look like you've got only worries. Let me take a good look at you,' his father said, and smiled his gentle smile before taking a sip of water.

'I've been worrying a lot about you, Father. How are you feeling?'

His mother went off to make them all a pot of coffee and to prepare some cake and biscuits.

'I'm old and ill. I'm not the young man I used to be, that's for sure,' his father said and chuckled gently. His chest rattled, Christoph noticed, when he laughed.

'You're the strongest man I've ever met, Father, and you're still here. What have the doctors said?'

'That I have perhaps a year.'

Christoph slept in his childhood bed in his childhood bedroom. His toes touched the wooden end of the bed and his head knocked against the headboard whenever he moved, forcing him to sleep in the foetal position. Or, rather, he did not sleep but lay there curled up for most of the night before falling into a deep sleep as dawn crept over the horizon.

His mother had kept his room exactly as he had left it, as a shrine to their lost son who had abandoned his old life to find a new one. His new life had first been at the Front, then at the conservatoire in Berlin and then, as a final act of separation, in New York. Now here he was, back in that old life as a dislocated guest. He felt completely out of place in that bedroom up under the eaves, yet knew every nook and cranny, every object on the mantelpiece and every book on the bookshelf, intimately.

He had talked to his mother a little about what was happening in Germany before he went up to bed, while his father slumbered in his chair. It was clear to him that she had not grasped the magnitude of the situation. She kept referring to the Führer as 'Herr Hitler', as if he was the friendly local butcher or baker. She spoke of him with no hint of reverence, but certainly with no loathing or fear either. It was as if, cocooned in the quiet safety of that old house, the last six years since Hitler had come to power had simply passed her by without troubling her. But then, in fairness, she had had other things on her mind – a sick husband and a grandchild living locally, a boy on whom she doted. The political life in Munich and Berlin was of no interest to her, so long as they left her family alone. Those flags and parades in town were all far too much for good taste, but nothing like that ever happened up there on the Weinberg.

The next morning, Christoph went looking for Miriam and little Eva, even before paying a visit to his sister and nephew. His stomach lurched when he thought about what he was doing. It was a spectacular summer's day: birds were singing in the parched trees and the sun shone out of a cloudless sky, flooding the hillside with light. He knew his way from the Weinberg down to her apartment on Lothringerstrasse without having to think about where he was going. Everything was so low-rise, so settled into itself with age compared to the upward thrust of Manhattan. It was as if he were walking through a town in Grimms' fairy tales. He had never realised how small Wuppertal was.

He had woken late, eaten a hurried breakfast, and had not told his parents where he was going. Although he had not left the house until after eleven, his father had still been resting upstairs. His mother had busied herself refilling his coffee cup and clearing away his used bowl, plate and cutlery, and had talked about this and that; she was so happy to have him home again. She thought that she knew why he had come back to Wuppertal: to see his sick father again. To have her family all together in one place again had been a long-held dream for her. Her daughter and grandson would be coming over in the late afternoon for tea.

Several businesses on Lothringerstrasse were boarded up, and on the rough boards nailed to the window-frames swastikas and Stars of David had been clumsily painted, with slogans running unevenly underneath them: *JUDEN RAUS* and *KAUFT NICHT BEI JUDEN*. It had never been anything other than a working-class street full of small shops, businesses and cramped apartments, but its complete disintegration and the hate-fuelled words of the anti-Jewish slogans were such a shock that all Christoph could do was to sit down on the kerb and stare at the row of buildings that he had once passed with barely a second look. He knew before he went up to the apartment that he would find no one there.

A few passers-by glanced at him sitting on the kerb, but the road was otherwise quiet: it was a Sunday and church bells were ringing out across the town. Some men in blue overalls walked past and a uniformed policeman was standing outside a shop in the distance with its shutters down, talking to a man in rolled-up shirtsleeves who could be its owner. It all looked harmless enough, apart from the awful graffiti and those empty premises.

There was a fallen-over bicycle in the entrance hall through the open wooden double doors to Miriam's building, the front door of the tailor's shop to the left had been boarded up and one of its windows was smashed. Christoph climbed the stone steps up to the third floor where Miriam's apartment was, his heart in his mouth, and met no one on the way. A baby was crying somewhere in one of the apartments further down the landing.

At first, he was not sure that he had the right apartment, as all of the doors to the apartments on this floor had been newly painted a uniform, dull brown colour, but then he recalled from somewhere deep in his memory that hers had indeed been No. 22, Lothringerstrasse 37. He knocked gently on the door and waited: there was no response. He knocked again, harder, still nothing. He pushed the door with both hands and to his surprise it swung open, revealing a completely bare room. A ladder was standing against one wall and a tin of paint was in the middle of the floor. The whole apartment was being redecorated. Christoph walked into the second, larger room, which was all that there was of the apartment. Miriam's and Eva's home had been completely gutted; there was not a trace of them here: no lost hair-clip, no dropped postcard, no coin that had fallen into a gap between the bare floorboards. The walls had been stripped back to bare plaster. He could see no evidence at all that anyone had lived there.

'What are you doing here?' a man's brusque voice asked. Christoph turned round to see one of the men in blue overalls standing behind him in the first room, his hands on his hips.

'I'm looking for the woman and her daughter who lived here until recently. What's your business here?'

'We've been decorating some empty flats in this block and others nearby for the landlord. They've been recently vacated.'

'What happened to the people who lived in them?' Christoph asked.

'Deported east, so I heard,' the older man replied. 'Best place for them.'

Christoph went towards the man to hit him, he was suddenly so angry, but the workman had already turned and begun to run down the first flight of stairs before Christoph could reach him from the other room.

'The girl who lived here was my *DAUGHTER*, you shit,' he shouted down the echoing stairwell after him.

'Then you're a Jew-lover,' the man shouted back up at him as his hobnail boots clattered down the last stone steps towards the street.

When Christoph got out onto Lothringerstrasse, still shaking with anger, he saw the workman at the other end of the street, talking animatedly to the policeman who was still standing where Christoph had seen him a quarter of an hour earlier. They both had their backs turned to him.

Christoph turned sharp left and walked as quickly as he could across town and up the Weinberg towards home.

CHAPTER TWENTY-NINE

He had not sung for three days, not since the journey on the *Hansa*. He hadn't even practised scales or warmed up his vocal cords. It was as if he had forgotten how to breathe. The phrase 'Jew-lover' went round and round in his head. There was nothing at all to sing about. Although he had been happy to see his sister and nephew again after all this time – he had not recognised the boy, who was now thirteen – he had not been able to concentrate and had barely said a word. He had slept fitfully again that night.

He was praying that the workman was wrong about Miriam being sent east and even more wrong about Eva. Miriam's parents were dead and he knew no one he could ask about what had happened to them.

The worst thing was that he could not talk to his mother. Although she remembered Ida with sadness and sympathy, for her young life which had ended so early and the bitter sorrow it had meant for her son, she knew nothing about his affair with Miriam and his illegitimate daughter, Eva. She asked him endless questions about Anne and Leo and Mae, so desperate was she to get to know them through his words. She could have no inkling that she had had another grandchild much closer to home all along.

Christoph wrote a letter to Anne, imploring her again to forgive him, and walked down into town to the post office to send it care of her parents' address in Columbus. The postmaster wore a stiff black uniform and the postage stamps bore either Hitler's brooding profile in purple facing left, or swastikas encircled by laurel wreaths. He remembered the postmaster in Manhattan and all he could think was that the man had been right all along: he had certainly been right about this bloody country.

He was missing the children a great deal. He was usually at home with them all day, or waiting for Leo when he came home from school. Anne's anger would surely have burnt itself out by now. He missed hearing their voices and having Anne beside him at night. He had rarely felt this alone. He was almost a stranger to his parents and they had problems enough of their own. He didn't want to burden them further with any of his.

He decided to go over to the synagogue, on a quiet, sloping street right in the heart of the old town. Perhaps the rabbi, if there still was a rabbi, would be able to tell him whom he could ask about Miriam and Eva, or he might even know something himself. This was the only lead that Christoph could think of that might get him nearer the truth. Even though he was unsure whether he wanted to know what that truth would be.

He walked to the fine old central library on Kolpingstrasse in Elberfeld, which was almost deserted except for a few bitter-looking men sitting on hard chairs reading copies of the *Völkischer Beobachter*. He asked reception where he could find a recent telephone directory for Wuppertal-Elberfeld. Once he had located last year's copy, which had been misplaced on the shelves in a long row of other telephone directories, he flicked through its endless, thin pages until he found the synagogue's telephone number and the rabbi's name and address: Dr Schreiber,

Genügsamkeitstrasse 5. Frugality Street. What a name for a street in a town where the Depression had sucked out the lifeblood before the Nazis got their hands on its citizens.

It was a long walk but he had nothing else to do. His parents were not expecting him back home before supper-time and, in any case, he was already beginning to suffocate in his childhood home: the silence punctuated only by his poor father's coughing as he sat the whole day in his armchair, and the grandfather clock's loud ticking in the hall, its chiming the hours, while his mother busied herself in the kitchen. He needed the busyness of the world beyond that house's sleepy existence far too much to be able to stay there for long.

He got to Genügsamkeitstrasse at around noon and saw immediately that he would not find the rabbi there. There was a large gap between two buildings on either side of where the synagogue had once stood. The fine, old, stone-built temple where he and Ida had sworn their marriage vows was no longer there, a hoarding lined the pavement and the vacant lot was shielded from public view. He had read in the New York newspapers that synagogues had been razed in towns and cities across Germany over the last year, but had not seen any reports that it had happened in his own home town. He wondered whether it was the synagogue that had been on fire, the building Miriam had referred to in one of her last, horrifying letters and from whose destruction she had wanted to shield Eva.

He went up to the high hoarding and tried to peer through the cracks to see what was behind it. The authorities had certainly boarded up the site well, but he could see a huge pile of blackened bricks, fallen masonry and charred timbers. Weeds had sprung up in the rubble here and there. The street was very quiet, even though it was a weekday, and there was no one around to ask when all of this had happened, although looking at those tall weeds it had been some time ago. He did not need to ask who had been behind this brutal act of vandalism. If they were doing this to Jewish-owned buildings across Germany, what were they doing to the Jews themselves?

He could not believe that Miriam and Eva were still in Wuppertal. They had to have gone, either willingly or unwillingly. Miriam's having mentioned England in her letters gave him the hope that at least Eva had got there. He shuddered to think where Miriam might be now, or what she might be going through. He walked slowly back across town under the oppressive midday sun and could think of nowhere else to go but back to the library.

The only other newspaper on offer apart from the *Völkischer Beobachter* was the *Westdeutsche Zeitung* and Christoph sat with the old, bitter men in the library looking through copies from recent weeks without really knowing what he was looking for. The papers had certainly changed their tone since he had last read them. The news stories were exclamatory and shockingly one-dimensional, lacking a nuanced and balanced reportage. Every feature on the National Socialist regime portrayed it in an unalloyed golden light. Then a stroke of luck: tucked away at the bottom of a page from the paper of the twelfth of June was a two-column piece on the Jews of Wuppertal.

Even though the article was full of barely veiled ridicule and scorn, it gave Christoph two vital facts: a train taking Jewish children to England had left Wuppertal for the Dutch coast on June 1st and another train, taking Jews to the Polish border, had left exactly one week later. Had Eva been on the first train or the second one? Had Miriam been on the second train? He had no way of knowing, but he just *had* to find out when the most recent trains had left, bringing Jewish children from Wuppertal to the safety of England, and whether Eva had been on one of them.

He could not go in opposite directions or be in two places at once. Sitting in the oppressive silence of that library he decided to follow his instincts. He would take a train into Holland and a ferry from the Hook of Holland across the Channel to England. There would surely be some sort of agency in London that could tell him whether Eva Bernstein from Wuppertal had come over on a train and, if so, where she was. He hoped against hope that if he found Eva he would find Miriam safely with her, but given what she had written about exit visas he feared this was far from how things would turn out. What harm exactly would it do the Nazi bastards to allow Miriam to leave their rotten country and for the English to let her in? He could feel a flush of anger rising in his neck and face again and the blood pulsing in his veins.

Christoph decided that he would board the *Hansa* at Southampton when it stopped there on its way from Hamburg, and make it back to New York by the time he had promised Anne he would return. He could not wait to get out of Germany; he could not wait to cross the border into Holland, even though he had always found the Dutch to be a rather dour sort. He would, in any case, only be there for a few hours.

His parents were sure to be upset that he was leaving so soon, but he could not stay. His mother believed that he had come home only because his father was so ill and she would simply not be able to understand why he was going again after only a few days. He suspected that his father knew that there must be other reasons for him to visit after all this time, reasons to do with his singing career, perhaps, but if he had any suspicions he had said nothing.

What could he tell them? Perhaps that he had been invited, at short notice, to sing at some prestigious theatre in London's world-famous West End. Perhaps that one of the children was unwell and that he had to get back home to New York. He did not know what they would sooner believe or hear. He did not like having to lie to them, his own parents, but he could not tell them about Eva. They must never know about Eva. It was far too late to tell them about her now.

On his way back up to the house, on impulse, he took a right-hand turn off the Weinbergstrasse and followed the small road that skirted around the hill to the gates of the Jewish cemetery. He had not been back there since Ida was buried. The gates were not locked and he walked along the gravel paths and between the gravestones, which to his relief were still intact; they had not thought to come up here yet. The cemetery was small, as the Jewish population of Wuppertal had always been low compared to other German towns and cities.

Ida's gravestone was simply done in dark granite. There was her name in Hebrew and Roman letters and her year and place of birth and death: *'Iddy' Rittersmann/Lódz, Poland 1899 – Wuppertal-Elberfeld 1929*. He could scarcely believe that she had ever been his wife; those brief months of happiness seemed to him to be scenes from someone else's life.

She had already been dead for a decade, while he had

gone on living. So much *life* had happened to him, and here was only death and silence in the unflinching late-afternoon sunshine. On either side of Ida's grave there were two, much more recent burials: a stone for her father, Leiser, and another for her mother, Perla. Both Jews from Poland who had died, as Miriam had told him in her letters, of old age in 1935 and 1937.

He searched for some smooth, round pebbles in the unkempt grass and along the paths near the graves and lovingly placed one stone on each of their graves, to show that he had been there and that he had not forgotten them. Ida's and Miriam's parents had been kind to him and Ida would have been a devoted wife; she would have given him children, they would have grown old together, if she had lived. How different life would have been.

He took Eva's photograph out of his breast pocket and looked at it again, closely, for the first time in days. She had so much of Miriam's family in her eyes, in her dark eyebrows and the symmetrical frame of her face, and so little obvious sign of him. Three generations of the Bernstein family had lived in his home town and two had died here. Where was she, and how would he find her?

Christoph left the cemetery and the shade of its tall cypress trees. He was walking up the Weinberg towards home, still deep in thought about Ida, Eva and the Bernsteins, when he became aware of the bending figure of an elderly woman pulling at straggling weeds along the base of the hedge that lined the roadside of one of the Weinbergstrasse's largest villas. When he looked up towards the façade of the house visible above the high hedge, he recognised Matthias's childhood home. The frail figure stood up from her work, pushing with both of her hands at the small of her back as she did so, and turned at the sound of his footsteps slowly nearing in the stillness of the deserted road. She wore gold-rimmed glasses high up on the bridge of her nose and her white hair was held in a tight bun, pulled back severely from her forehead. It was Matthias's mother.

He hoped that she would not recognise him and was about to step past her on the wide pavement without any greeting, when something sparked in her eyes. Perhaps she remembered him from his visits when he and Matthias were both still students? Or she recognised his face from one of the posters advertising his small concerts in the town hall more than a decade ago?

'Herr Rittersmann! It *is* Christoph Rittersmann, isn't it?' she exclaimed, the glass in her oval spectacles glittering in the sunshine.

'Yes, that's me,' he replied, hesitating for a split second before he answered her. It had occurred to him that he could simply say 'no', flatly denying who he was, and walk on past her, but something in him, some pride or sense of defiance, made him stop and face her.

'You went to America like my dear Matthias, didn't you?'

'I still live there, Frau Walter. I'm just here visiting my parents.'

'Did you hear Matthias's latest news? It's such an honour, the Professor and I can barely believe it.'

'I haven't been in touch with him at all for years now. We lost contact even before he came back home to Germany.'

'He's left his music behind completely, despite being a favourite composer of the Führer's, and has been appointed the Gauleiter of the Ostmark. The Gauleiter of the *whole* of

272

the Ostmark! Such an honour! We're all so incredibly proud of him.'

'Gauleiter ... of the Ostmark? And he accepted this "honour", as you call it? Then he's an even greater shit than he ever was, Frau Walter, and he can rot in hell!'

With that, Christoph pushed past Frau Walter, continuing up the steep Weinbergstrasse, without a backward glance. Their exchange had taken barely thirty seconds and he knew, he *knew*, that he had to get out of this godforsaken place as soon as possible.

At home, he ate his supper with his parents in abject silence, still reeling at the horrifying news of Matthias. His father barely finished half his plate of meat and vegetables, his mother encouraging his father's every meagre mouthful, and when they were all done with their food Christoph went up to his bedroom to pack his small bag. He turned in early for the night as he had a long journey to face the next day.

He woke at dawn feeling that he had hardly slept, stretching himself awake in that hot room, his bedclothes thrown off during the night of restless dreams. Thoughts of what Matthias had become and of the journey ahead jostled with each other as he lay there.

He would tell his parents that he was leaving straight after breakfast.

Chapter Thirty

The train left Wuppertal-Elberfeld station just before noon and snaked its way westwards across the flat German countryside towards the Dutch border. He did not know when, or if, he would see his parents, or even Germany, again. Christoph's departure had something definitive about it this time. They both said goodbye to him as if for the last time. There was a great sadness weighing on him; he was sure that he would not see his father again. There were silent tears from his mother when he told them he was leaving – he was leaving so soon. His father sat mute with a haunted look in his eyes. Christoph felt that he knew he would not be seeing his son again.

As soon as he left the oppressive silence and gloom of his old home, a weight lifted from his shoulders and he remembered his purpose with vigour and hope: Eva. He no longer shied away from the conflicting emotions he felt when he thought of his daughter. He wanted to find her so that he could help her, so that she might know him, for however brief a time. He was even prepared to take her back to America with him, to make her part of his cherished family there, if that was what she wanted and he could get the necessary paperwork in place. But he was getting too far ahead of himself …

He presented his German passport when the train

shuddered to a halt at the Dutch border, letting off a series of whistles and great clouds of steam. From then on he would use his United States passport; he would make himself American. Things were far too precipitous between the two nations for him to be travelling to England with any degree of anonymity as a German.

How many Germans were leaving, had already left, their homeland recently? Jews were getting out where they still could, but there must be thousands of others who had seen what had happened to the country over the last six years, who had seen what was coming, and wanted to leave. The National Socialist rhetoric, the newspaper articles, did not mention the Germans with a conscience and clear sight who were abandoning their homeland. Or, if they were mentioned at all, they were demonised as traitors to their nation, as Bolshevik conspirators, or enemies of the Third Reich. No good German would leave.

Well, he had left and did not imagine that he would be going back. There was a commotion in the next carriage, raised voices and what sounded like the thump of falling luggage, while the train was still stationary at the border, and word quickly spread amongst the passengers that the Gestapo had arrested three Jewish adults, two men and a woman, who had been trying to cross the border without exit visas.

As the train sped on again across the dead flat land, a landscape becalmed, the story became more elaborate: three Jews were travelling on forged Dutch identity papers but were German Jews from Frankfurt; they had been trying to get to London to tell Chamberlain not to sign any new peace accord with Hitler; they were saboteurs working against the Nazi regime and had been pulled off the train to face a possible firing squad.

Thus the terrible cruelty of Germany followed the passengers on that train even into Holland and it was not until they were nearing the Hook of Holland that Christoph began to settle back into his seat and to relax. He was not sure how frequently the ferry left for the east of England and he would have to find an inn or guest house to stay in for the night. He would go to the port straight off the train, but guessed that the ferry left in the early morning each day.

When Christoph stepped onto Dutch soil, or rather onto the station platform at Hook of Holland Haven, the stop nearest the centre of the town and the ferry terminal, he felt free for the first time since leaving New York. The train carried on towards the Strand station, the very end of the line nearest the beach, before beginning its journey back through Holland towards the German border. Many of his fellow passengers were German or Dutch holidaymakers who had come for a few days or a week on the coast, to take the sea air and to dip their toes in the North Sea, which was ice-cold even in the heat of July.

The harbourmaster's office told him that the ferry to Harwich departed at eight o'clock in the morning each day. Christoph walked to the small town looking for somewhere to spend the night. There was not much to the town: a few streets with low buildings and locals going about their late-afternoon business. The smell of the sea was everywhere; that air filled with oxygen, salt and the scent of life from the deep. He found an inn called De Hems and asked to see the one room that was available. Although it was very simple and sparsely furnished, it was clean and would do for the night. The innkeeper was a thin man of great height, who stooped as he led Christoph through the doorways of his establishment.

'Just passing through?' he asked in a heavily accented but perfect English. All of the Dutch people that Christoph had ever met had seemed to have an excellent command of other peoples' languages.

'I'm on my way to England, to London,' Christoph replied.

'You're English?' the tall man asked.

'No, American. I'm from New York.'

'What's your name?'

'My name's Christopher J. Ritter,' Christoph said. 'Chris Ritter.'

'Well, welcome to De Hems, Mr Ritter. I trust you will find your short stay with us comfortable.'

'I have to leave very early tomorrow morning on the eight o'clock boat,' Christoph replied.

After the innkeeper had asked him to sign the Moroccan leather-bound guest-book that lay in some state on the humble front desk, Christoph felt familiar enough with him to ask what he had seen passing through his town over recent months.

'Have you seen anything unusual on the railway recently, any special trains that don't normally come here?'

'There have been trains with only children on them,' the man readily replied, much to Christoph's surprise. 'They come through at night and I've heard that the children get onto specially chartered ferries at the Nieuwe Waterweg.'

Christoph felt his pulse racing and could picture Eva stepping off the train and standing on the pier before getting onto the boat, as if it was happening now, right in front of him. 'When did the last train arrive?' he asked.

'Must be about three weeks ago now, but I've probably slept through the arrival of one or two of them since then.'

'Three weeks ago would be about right,' Christoph said, half to himself.

'Why all of these questions about those trains?' the innkeeper asked, a slight suspicion creeping into his voice now.

'I'm looking for a girl who I think was on one of those trains.'

'The boats with the children all head over to England, where you're going,' the man said.

'I'm going there to try to find the girl,' Christoph replied. 'She's my daughter.'

The man nodded from the other side of the desk, but said nothing.

Christoph ate dinner alone at a simple wooden table set with a single place-setting, his food brought to him by the tall man's silent wife. He noticed that she hesitated slightly when she put the plate of ham, eggs and potatoes in front of him. At first he could not understand why, but then he realised; she thought he was a Jew. Perhaps she was wondering whether her husband had misunderstood him when he had heard Christoph ordering the ham.

'It looks delicious,' he said to reassure her, and she smiled silently back at him, nodded and made her way back to the kitchen.

He had not been to England before, other than docking at Southampton, and could not wait to get off this damned continent to that island, which was one step nearer to home. Not being able to speak to Anne and the children was choking him; he was suffocating in his loneliness.

Depending on how things went in England, he would see if he could transfer his ticket home to another ship on the Hamburg-America Line and sail from Southampton in August, three or four weeks earlier than he had planned. Perhaps he – *they* – would go straight over to Columbus from New York to surprise Anne before she was due back in Manhattan with the children.

But he was getting way too far ahead of himself again: he could not go home without any news of Eva but had not come close to finding her yet. He didn't even know with any certainty that she had gone over to England on one of those trains. He realised that he was staking everything on this one gamble, and that it just had to pay off. He hoped against hope that the English were as organised as he thought they were, and that they would be able to find her for him if she was there.

After supper he went for a walk out to the harbour. It was almost nine o'clock but still perfectly light and warm. The waters of the Nieuwe Waterweg were as flat as a mirror and all boat traffic had ceased for the night. Married, well-worn husbands and wives walked in comfortable silence side by side, young couples giggled hand-in-hand, solitary figures strolled along in their shirtsleeves, all making their way along the paths of the inlet out towards the open sea, taking in the last of the summer light. Birds had flown to their roosts in the treetops or in the eaves of the town's buildings, and bats flitted in the approaching dusk.

It was a scene of utter serenity, and it was impossible for Christoph to reconcile this reality with that other reality; train-loads of young lives that had passed through only recently, torn away from their families and the homes that they loved. Walking out towards the sea, it seemed impossible to Christoph for such hatred and cruelty to be taking place only one country away, while life continued uninterrupted over here. It was low tide and he went far out onto the sandy beach towards the water's edge. The sea was far livelier than the waters of the Nieuwe Waterweg and powerful waves broke on the rocks that lined the beach, sending spray up into the air. It would be a rough crossing in the morning if the sea stayed this choppy.

England beckoned on the other side of the Channel, through the fading light. The Tower of London, marching guardsmen in scarlet uniforms and tall beaver-fur hats, the King in his golden coach: he only knew the England that tourists came to visit, and nothing more. What had Eva understood about her new destination? What had she thought as the train sped on relentlessly through the landscape? How had she consoled herself as the train took her further and further away from her mother with each passing second? He kept on having to remind himself that his daughter was only eight years old; what was she supposed to know, what was she supposed to think or feel when faced with all of this but *fear*?

He woke early and gathered his things together before going downstairs to drink a cup of coffee. The innkeeper's wife poured him his coffee, her husband being nowhere to be seen, perhaps still tucked up in his bed. Again, she nodded and smiled but said nothing. The coffee was bitter and strong. Christoph sat in a chair by the window watching the morning light play over the street, and over the walls of the building across the way. When he rose to leave, having paid her husband for his room and board the night before, she uttered her first and last words to Christoph. Her strong Dutch accent lingered as she gently said: 'Good luck in finding your daughter. Good luck.'

The kindness of her words stayed with him during the crossing to England, as the boat ploughed on through the valleys and hills of the rolling, swelling sea, and the sky shone under an immense sun.

CHAPTER THIRTY-ONE

The coast of England rose as a dark mass above the blue of the sea in the late-afternoon light. Before long they were docking in Harwich and Christoph presented his American passport to one of the immigration officers when he stepped off the boat. The sun that had accompanied him on his journey since the early morning was still shining, lower in the sky now, above the green coast of England. There was the familiar hustle and bustle of the offloading of passengers and goods in the port.

The railway station was right next to the ferry terminal and he asked the man at the ticket office, who had a thickset, flattened, whiskered face like a walrus, for a one-way ticket to London. When he came to pay he realised that he did not have any English currency, only the dollar bills and Reichsmarks in his pocket.

'I'm sorry,' he said, 'but I don't have the fare in British pounds. I've just come from abroad. Would you take it in American dollars?'

'I can't do that I'm afraid, sir,' the man replied.

'No money exchange is open at this hour, I suppose?'

'There's an exchange and two or three banks in town,' the ticket man said. 'You will have to catch your train after they've opened again tomorrow morning. It's a Sunday, sir.'

'Are you sure there's really nothing you can do?' Christoph asked again.

'I'm sorry, sir. You'll have to pay in sterling in the morning.'

'Can I speak to your manager?'

'I *am* the manager,' the man replied from behind the glass, his whiskers twitching in irritation.

It was an exceptionally fine evening and Christoph wandered through the handsome, well-kept town, the sound of seagulls in the air and salt on the breeze, looking for somewhere to stay. Lorries and goods vehicles rumbled through the streets away from the port and the whole town had something of the feeling of being in transit about it.

Mrs Baxter's Guest House, as it proudly announced itself on a faded board tacked onto a stake driven into the stunted grass of the lawn, was a pebble-dashed villa on the seafront. The notice in one of the windows facing the road advertised that rooms were available. Mrs Baxter herself was out, the man with a paunch who answered the door said. He was her husband and was looking after the guests while she was at bingo. Christoph did not dare ask what 'bingo' was; it sounded like some kind of exotic dance.

'I have no English money on me and have to go to one of the banks in town tomorrow before I can pay. Will that be all right?' he said.

'Do you have anything of value that you could leave with us in the morning as a deposit?' Mr. Baxter replied.

'I have my father's Swiss wristwatch. It's a Rolex: he gave it to me when I turned twenty-one. It's made from silver, and quite valuable.'

'Then that'll be fine,' the man said.

The room was small but tidy and comfortable. Mr Baxter had promised that his wife would be back before too long and would bring him up his meal by nine o'clock. Christoph sat on the wooden dining chair that his hosts had placed incongruously by the window of the bedroom, overlooking the sea. The tide was right in and powerful little waves were breaking on the rocks on the other side of the railings that lined the front. He felt a surge of sudden hope again; he couldn't explain why, but he was sure that Eva was in England. He took her photograph out of his breast pocket and placed it carefully on the window-sill. She looked back at him with her dark eyes. She really did have the most open and honest gaze, and he shrank a little under it.

While waiting for his food he got up from the chair and paced up and down the boarded floor of the small room. As if without meaning to, he found himself singing for the first time in more than a week. At first he was not sure of his voice; it did not sound like the instrument that was as much a part of him as his breathing or his soul. It sounded lower somehow, as if his range was moving towards that of a bass. There was some slight loss of flexibility in the vocal cords. Not having sung, nor practised his scales for weeks had tightened his voice-box, but after almost an hour's warming up he felt that he could reach the higher notes of the tenor's range comfortably once more. He did not know what he was singing at first, he was simply ascending and descending the scales and humming snatches of song. Gradually, the melody of the *Erlkönig* insinuated itself into his mind and the words seemed to him to be truths about his own life:

> *Who rides so late through the night so wild?*
> *It is a father with his child …*

The scene suddenly meant more to him than it had ever done before when he had sung the *Lied*. The man riding on his horse through the storm with his child in his arms does not realise that it is far too late, the child is already dead. That would not, could not, be the case here: Eva was somewhere safely in England. He just had to find her, to see her standing in front of him to be sure.

Miriam's fate was unknowable to him and he feared the worst. She certainly could not have stayed in Wuppertal, having seen with his own eyes what was going on there. Had she managed to evade deportation eastwards on the trains that he had read about in the newspaper? Perhaps she had gone to non-Jewish friends in other towns who could help her and give her somewhere to stay for a while. But she had never mentioned any friends in other towns to him when they had been together.

In the morning, after sorting out English currency at one of the banks in town, retrieving his watch and paying the Baxters, he took the next available train bound for London. He arrived into the cavernous terminus of Liverpool Street Station without knowing where he was. The echoing space was alive with announcements that he could barely hear, drowned out as they were by the din of other passengers rushing to catch their trains on time.

He had no idea where to start his search. How did you find one small child in a vast city, or a country that you were visiting for the first time? One thing he did know was that the English, like the Germans, were a highly organised nation; they liked institutions, bureaucracy, ministries, officialdom. There must be somebody that had taken official charge of the refugees when they arrived here.

He went looking for a taxi, switching his case from one hand to the other as it was getting heavy. The sun was beating down on the tarmac of the road and men walked past with their hats in their hands; it was too hot to wear them. He had overheard someone on the train saying that it was one of the warmest summers in England since records began.

He asked the driver of the cab to take him to the 'ministry of the interior', and the man looked puzzled for a moment.

'You mean the Home Office,' he asked, 'for things going on in this country?'

'I think so,' Christoph replied.

London passed by in a blur of crowds and streets and buildings; nowhere near as high as New York, nor as electrifying as Berlin, but somehow conveying an impression of the city's scale, from wherever you happened to be in it.

As they were crawling through the traffic, the driver pointed out Trafalgar Square to him. He had seen it on a postcard before but had never imagined himself actually being there. It was a stately, wide-open space with the four great sculptures of lions lying benignly at the foot of a tall column with a figure standing on top of it. The whole thing was somehow smaller and less massive than Christoph had pictured it. Suddenly, the cab veered left and then sharp right before speeding through a maze of streets and along a wide boulevard. Before he knew it, the car was drawing up in front of an impressive white building.

'This is the Home Office, sir,' the driver told him.

Christoph was completely unprepared: he had no idea what he was going to say; no phrases of explanation or elaboration in his head.

The grey-haired lady at the reception desk was dressed in

tweed and looked rather severe, but smiled when he introduced himself.

'My name is Christopher Ritter,' he said, putting on his best American accent, 'and I'm trying to trace my daughter.'

'Shouldn't you be trying at the American embassy?' she asked, kindly enough.

'The thing is, my daughter was born in Germany and has recently come to this country.'

'Did she come with her mother?' the lady asked.

'No, I think that she came on her own. I mean, she's a Jewish child and came on one of the transports of Jewish children from Germany, I believe.'

'Let me see who might be able to help you with this enquiry,' she said, before indicating a row of upholstered chairs to one side of the lobby where she invited Christoph to sit and wait for her to find the right person.

She turned her back to him to reach for the telephone, and he saw from the movement of her right arm that she was dialling a number. She spoke with a hushed voice into the mouthpiece and he could not make out what she was saying. The newly polished black and white tiles of the lobby floor gleamed in the light. Before long, a young man was striding towards him across the lobby.

'Hello, I'm Peter Barrington, one of the juniors on the immigration desk. Been waiting here long, sir?' he asked, hand outstretched.

'No, not long,' Christoph replied, adding 'My name's Christopher Ritter,' while shaking the man's firm hand.

The man's hair was cut in a short back and sides and he had a set of very straight teeth. He spoke and looked like one of those English public-school types that Christoph had read about.

'My colleague over there tells me that you're an American, but that you're looking for your German-born daughter. Is that right?' The man, who could not have been more than twenty-five, looked at him with unblinking blue eyes, but his gaze had something genial and warm about it.

'That's correct,' Christoph replied, looking at the man unflinchingly in return. 'The mother of my daughter is a Jewess and, given what's been happening over there, I believe she sent our daughter to England on one of the transports of children a short while ago. I live in America and wasn't there to know exactly what happened.'

'How can the Home Office be of assistance exactly?' the younger man asked, still focusing his eyes on Christoph, but with his head turned very slightly to one side now to try to catch what the lady on the reception desk was saying to one of his colleagues.

'I'm hoping that you might be able to tell me where my daughter, Eva Bernstein, is.' Christoph noticed that his voice was rising in pitch and fought with himself to continue evenly and neutrally: he did not want to plead or to sound desperate. 'She's just eight years old and comes from Wuppertal-Elberfeld in the west of the country.'

'We'll certainly do our best to try to help. I've not heard of these transports of Jewish children that you mention, but will see what I can find out over the next couple of days.'

'Yes, thank you so much,' Christoph replied.

'And do you have a photograph of your daughter for my file?'

'I only have this one and it's very precious to me,' he said, taking Eva's photograph out of his breast pocket. 'I'm carrying it on me wherever I go until I find her. If I leave it with you, is there a photographer at the ministry who could

289

take a copy and you could then give me back the original?'

'You have a lovely-looking daughter, Mr Ritter,' the man from the Home Office said, holding Eva's photograph and looking down closely at it. 'Let's not worry about the photograph. I know her name, and yours. Would you mind writing them down for me on this piece of paper? Here's a pen. Why is her surname different?'

'Her mother and I never married. In fact, I was already living in America when she was born, I have never met her.'

'In that case, do you think that you could get her mother to write a letter, I'll give you our full address in a moment, and send it to me by airmail this week, so that I have something in writing from her that you are indeed the girl's father?' Christoph could sense a new note of resistance in the young man's voice. 'I'm sure you'll understand that in situations like this there are certain protocols we have to follow.'

'That would be impossible,' Christoph replied. 'I was in Germany only very recently and went to Wuppertal-Elberfeld where she and my daughter lived. I could find no trace at all of either of them; their apartment was empty and they were gone. I have no way of finding my daughter's mother. Believe me, if I knew how to I would have found her already. All I have is a box of letters she sent over the years, but they're in New York.'

'I see. If your daughter is in England and I manage to locate her, would you at least be willing to sign an affidavit that you are her next-of-kin, just so that we have something for our files?'

'Of course, I'd be happy to do so,' Christoph replied. 'I'll do whatever it takes to find my daughter.'

'I'll talk to my head of section, but in theory that should

work,' Barrington said. 'Would you like to come back on, say, Thursday morning at ten o'clock and I'll tell you what I've managed to find out?'

He looked at Christoph as if he was now slightly unsure of what to do, but his eyes were still friendly and warm and Christoph believed that he would help him if he could.

CHAPTER THIRTY-TWO

He was not in London as a tourist. He had time to kill until Thursday, but was not interested in taking in a myriad of sights. He had little appetite for exploring the vast urban sprawl that spread in every direction outwards from the four walls of his small hotel room on the Tottenham Court Road.

This life in limbo was no life. His loneliness without Anne and the children, the sucking vacuum of their absence that went with him wherever he went, was like a physical presence in the room. He just had to find Eva. She was the key to his being with his family again, the solution to the riddle of how to regain his life. But he knew that he was fooling himself when he thought like this; that this was all that his daughter meant to him, that she was only a means for him to bring about a rapprochement with Anne, a way to prove himself to her, to regain her trust. No, he wanted to find Eva to make sure that she was alive and well, to see her with his own eyes at least once in their lifetimes, above all to make her part of his life if only she would let him.

The city was heating up and August was around the corner. Talk of an impending war with Germany was everywhere on the streets. From newspaper advertising boards and cinemas broadcasting the latest Pathé news, to the mouths of millions of people across the metropolis. Words of war and aggression became a common language that bound the people together. Although Christoph hated his old country and what it stood for with a vehemence that was beyond words, it was still hard to hear the English talk with such sour passion and glee of 'blasting Jerry to smithereens' – an entirely new word to him, that 'smithereens', and he had never heard the Germans referred to as 'Jerry' before – and 'giving Fritz a good bashing'. He had seen it all before from the other side, half a lifetime ago, and knew full well what horrors such jingoism led to.

There would be no more appeasement; if Hitler's troops invaded Poland, Great Britain would be at war with Germany. Europe was on a knife-edge and the public's mood honed the blade ever keener. There seemed to be a mixture of fear and excitement out on the streets of London: fear in those who still held fresh memories of the World War, and excitement in those who believed that if Germany had not learnt its lessons back then, Great Britain would have to teach them again.

Christoph practised his American accent in his head before he said anything, and used all of the skills that he had learned as a performer, the inhabiting of roles, the mimicry of voice, to convince his listeners that he was indeed an American. In fact, he spoke to only a few people: the young man, almost still a boy, at the reception desk of the cheap hotel; the man selling newspapers from a kiosk on the corner of Oxford Street; the middle-aged woman who came to clean his room, and who wore a blue floral head-covering that reminded Christoph of a Sikh turban.

He went back to the Home Office, as arranged, on the Thursday morning. Peter Barrington was all smiles when he came down to meet him.

'The very good news is I can tell you that Eva Bernstein

from Wuppertal-Elberfeld entered the United Kingdom just the other day, on the twenty-sixth of July,' he said. 'She travelled alone, I mean only with the other children and the head of the train. There's no immigration record for her mother.'

Christoph's heart leapt with sheer joy and relief, before it quickly sank to the pit of his stomach. He remembered Miriam's last letter, sent on her birthday, saying that Eva was the only family left there for her. What a terribly bitter belated birthday present to have to send her daughter away not long after. He wondered where on earth they had been when he was in Wuppertal; he guessed that they must have been in hiding somewhere after all and had not been deported or sent away at that stage as the workman had suggested. He could hardly take it in that they had perhaps been in the same town all along when he was at home.

'The bad news is that I haven't yet found out where your daughter is,' Barrington continued. 'The foster families are arranged, it seems, by the Jewish relief agency that helped bring the children here in the first place, and those arrangements have nothing to do with us chaps here at the Home Office.'

'Where is that agency? Whom can I ask?' Christoph said excitedly, before adding: 'Thank you so much for telling me this, Mr Barrington.'

'I'm just pleased to have been able to help a little,' the younger man said. 'The agency is officially called the Jewish Refugees Committee.'

'And it's somewhere in London?'

'Yes, it's in South Kensington in Sumner Place. I've written down the address for you,' Barrington said, handing him a folded piece of paper. 'Our legal chaps have also prepared this short affidavit for you to sign, on the Home Office letterhead. Read through it now, sign it and I'll countersign it. You should take it with you when you go to the Jewish Refugees Committee: it might help.'

'I can't thank you enough for all you and your colleagues have done,' Christoph replied.

'Please, don't mention it, it was nothing, the very least we could do … so, you'll soon be heading to wherever she might have ended up in this green and pleasant land of ours? It will be quite something to meet your daughter for the first time.' Barrington smiled kindly.

'I cannot take it in yet,' Christoph said. 'It's too much for me to believe after all these years of wondering what she's like. Was there anything at all in the files about her mother, anything that could help me to find out where *she* is? Although we have been living apart for many years now, I don't want to leave Europe without knowing what's happened to her.'

'As I said, all we know is that Miriam Bernstein didn't come into this country. Although she is on your daughter's records as her next of kin with what I take is her home address in Wuppertal, a road called … um …' Barrington faltered, glancing down at the sheet of paper in his hand, 'um, *Lothringer-strasse*, if I've pronounced that correctly, the records unfortunately don't tell us what happened to her or where she is now.'

'Yes, that was their apartment,' Christoph said quietly. 'It's empty now. I was there. I read in the German newspapers that they've been deporting Jews east, to the Polish border. I'm afraid she may have had to go on one of the transports. Her parents came from Poland and I think that they've been deporting Polish-born Jews back to where they came from, and where the Nazis think they belong. Either that or to Dachau in the south of Germany.'

'What's there?' Barrington asked, the smile long gone from his face.

'Some kind of detention or labour camp,' Christoph replied. 'I think it's used for political enemies of the regime and Jews.'

Christoph decided to walk back to the hotel to gather his thoughts. Now that he was getting nearer to finding Eva, the old fears of how she would respond to him were surfacing again. What if she did not want to know him? Was an eight-year-old capable of deciding to reject a father who had been absent from her life? Christoph was afraid that Eva was quite old enough not to want to know him, as she really had never known him.

To see her, to make sure that she was safe, to get to know her and try to make her part of his life, however belatedly ... if he did all of that, at least he could return home to Anne and the children with his promise fulfilled, his past absolved, his head held high again. He *had* to try to be a father to Eva, if she would let him. He sighed: if only it was as simple as that. First he had to find her.

The Jewish Refugees Committee was located in a large office in one of a terrace of handsome white-fronted Georgian town houses in South Kensington. The area seemed to Christoph to have once been very grand, but was now faded, dusty and a little worn around the edges.

The neighbourhood was quiet, with few people out on the streets, and when the cab dropped him off outside the building Christoph was not certain that anyone would be in: he had not made an appointment. Sure enough, when he rang the bell marked 'JRC' no one answered the door and he walked off in the direction of South Kensington tube station without really knowing where he was going.

He was inexplicably nervous and his stomach felt unsettled; his legs seemed to walk him along with no involvement from his head. Would the people at the Jewish Refugees Committee simply give out Eva's address to him? He could not, after all, prove that he was her father.

He found himself on a road called the Old Brompton Road and went into a Lyons Coffee House to sit down and think for a while, and to use their conveniences. He ordered a black coffee from a pretty young waitress, who seemed to be an Italian, and sat there sipping his hot drink. He took in the life of the coffee house, the coming and going of the customers, the pretty waitress, and the traffic outside, for a good hour before he decided to try the Jewish Refugees Committee office again.

At first he could not recall how he had got from Sumner Place to the Lyons Coffee House, but then it was as if his legs did the remembering and twenty minutes later he found himself back in front of the Committee's offices. This time when he rang the second-floor bell, he heard feet on the stairs after a minute or two and a well-dressed woman of no more than thirty-five opened the door to him with a querying smile.

'Can I help you?' she asked.

'My name's Christopher Ritter,' he replied. 'My daughter came over on one of the transports of children some days ago and I'm trying to find her.'

'Do come in,' she said, opening the door wide and letting him into the hallway. She closed the door and led the way up the bare wooden stairs.

'You're one of the lucky adults who managed to get

papers to come here?' she asked, half turning to him as they reached the top of the stairs.

'I, I have been living in America,' he stumbled. 'I'm an American citizen; I'm not a Jew.'

'But still your daughter had to come here from Germany?' she asked, sounding slightly puzzled now.

'Her mother's a Polish-born Jewess and they lived together in Wuppertal-Elberfeld near the Ruhr, where Eva my daughter was born. I don't know what's happened to her mother.'

'Have you not been able to make contact with your wife?'

'I, ah, I went back to Germany the week before last,' he stumbled again, 'to look for them both, but could not find them.'

'Perhaps your daughter was already on her way to England?' the dark-haired young woman, who had introduced herself as Mrs Susannah Gold, said.

'No, I think they were in hiding somewhere. The Home Office has told me that my daughter only arrived here on the twenty-sixth of July.'

'What's your daughter's full name?'

'Her name's Eva Bernstein, B-E-R-N-S-T-E-I-N. She has her mother's surname. She's only eight years old.'

They had reached the large two-room office, flooded with daylight, of the Jewish Refugees Committee and, apart from two desks with telephones and a wall of files, what caught Christoph's eye were rows and rows of shallow boxes laid out on trestle tables that held what seemed to be small card files. Mrs Gold saw where Christoph was looking.

'There are nearly ten thousand Jewish children on those

cards; children we have been able to save by bringing them here,' she said.

'Can you find my daughter?' Christoph asked.

'If she came here, she will be on an identity card in our file.'

'What happens to the children once they get to England?'

'They're usually sent to the homes of the people who sponsored their coming here on the *Kindertransport*, mostly Jewish families, but by no means always. Sometimes they have to be sent to temporary accommodation, to children's homes or orphanages, anywhere that will take them and where they'll be safe. Even holiday camps that have been turned into temporary holding centres until somewhere longer-term can be found for them. This is because they may have been sponsored by people who can't actually give them a home themselves.'

'Wherever they are, it will have been an almost unimaginable shock for them,' Christoph said.

'Can you picture having to leave your parents behind, and often also brothers and sisters, then coming to a foreign country not knowing whether you will ever see your family again?' Mrs Gold replied.

The 'B' index cards were tightly packed together in their low boxes, and took up almost an entire trestle table of their own. Mrs Gold pushed back her dark hair as she leaned over the table and separated the cards with her fine fingers, looking for BERNSTEIN, Eva.

'There are actually three Eva Bernsteins: one from Prague, another from Berlin and …' she said, pulling out a postcard-sized identity card, '… here must be your daughter.'

There she was! Her clear-eyed, beautifully symmetrical face looked out at him from the photograph stapled to the card. She looked older than in the photograph he was carrying in his breast pocket; it must have been taken recently. And there was her home address: *Lothringerstrasse 37, W. Elberfeld*, and her date of birth: *24.2.31*. He could not believe that she was right there, looking at him from the card. He was speechless.

'That *is* your daughter, isn't it?' she asked.

'It is,' he said. 'It is.'

'Do I understand it correctly that you and her mother are not married? I don't mean to intrude, only to understand the situation,' she said.

'No, we're not married. I was already in New York when my daughter was born,' he replied.

'Then her mother is her sole legal guardian?'

'I believe so,' he said. 'I've not yet met my daughter. I've come here to do so. But I have this affidavit from the Home Office and they told me to give it to you.'

'I need to speak to the head of the Committee to ask him whether we can give out her foster family's address to you,' she said, not looking at the document that he had handed to her. 'You understand that there are procedures in place.'

'But I have made a promise to find her,' he said.

'These poor children have come over here in the most *terrible* of circumstances because their parents can no longer keep them safe. Their well-being is now the most important thing. Imagine how it would be for your daughter, having recently been severed from her mother, for you to arrive unannounced in her life.'

'I *have* to find her. *Please* do this for me,' he said, looking imploringly into her dark eyes.

'I'll explain the matter to the head of the Committee. He's back from Germany in two days' time,' she said, kindly but firmly.

'Please, I'm begging you,' he said, beginning to plead with her.

'I'll do everything I can to put your case strongly to Sir Herbert,' she said. 'Would you come back on Friday in the early afternoon, so that I have time to speak to him that morning?'

'Thank you, I will. Please, you're my only hope of finding her,' he said as he turned for the stairs.

Christoph spent two sleepless nights up under the eaves of the hotel in his oppressive room, sweating and turning in his damp sheets in the thick air. The weather was getting hotter and hotter now that August had arrived and the city moved as if in a torpor. The traffic ground up dust from the streets and the endless stream of pedestrians walked with heads bowed against the heat of the sun and the threat of war.

During the second half of that week, he paced the streets of the central parts of the city, going back to Trafalgar Square again, this time on foot, and walking along the Mall to the gates of Buckingham Palace, then up through Green Park to Piccadilly. The names of these places and roads became familiar to him, but he barely took in what he saw. Only the white monolith of Buckingham Palace seemed to lodge with any permanence in his brain; he was stirred by the romance of the British royal family who were emblems of a nation that might do something to stamp out Hitler.

The Royal Air Force was beginning to test barrage balloons over London. Clusters of these vast silver harbingers floated in the sky, tethered to the ground far beneath them by cables. Christoph knew what they were, what they meant, and understood that the authorities were testing their defences against a possible aerial attack on the city by the Luftwaffe.

One afternoon he stopped for a cooling drink at a public house called the Hope & Anchor near the Strand. The few drinkers propping up the bar fell silent and turned their heads to look at him like cows at pasture when he walked in. It was the first time that he had drunk alcohol since he had been in London and he found the beer to be unpleasantly warm. Although its sweet, malty taste suited him, it certainly did little to take the sweat off his brow.

As he sat there cradling his pint at a corner table on his own, the familiar nagging doubts came back again. What if the Committee refused to give him Eva's address – what then? The whole journey, the entire enterprise would have been in vain. He could not face going back to New York, to Anne and the children, with his tail between his legs and his promise broken. He was worried that he would be marooned in Europe by failure, and then by war.

CHAPTER THIRTY-THREE

August 1939

The train thundered out of Paddington Station on its way to the westernmost point of England. The Home Office affidavit had swung it in the end and Sir Herbert, the head of the Committee, had allowed Mrs Gold to give Christoph his daughter's address. Eva was living with Sidney and Helen Lewis in the town of Minehead, on the Somerset coast. Ever since Mrs Gold had told him three days ago where Eva was, there had been a knot of excitement and fear in the pit of his stomach that he could barely contain. He felt as if he was about to explode.

He had been told by the guard to change trains at Taunton and to take a local service north to Minehead. The sun accompanied him on his journey; whenever he looked out of the train window, there it was blazing away in a clear sky. He had no idea that England could be like this; it was almost as hot as a New York summer. He pulled the vent in the window open to let some air circulate and a speck of soot landed on the lapel of his jacket.

The lunchtime train to Penzance was quiet and there was only one other person in his compartment: a well-dressed woman of early middle age, sitting diagonally across from him on the other banquette, nearest to the carriage's sliding door. She was reading a newspaper and did not look at him. As the nameless stations came and went, passengers got off and on the train, and some joined their compartment, so that the two banquettes were more or less occupied as the journey progressed. The woman got off somewhere an hour or so out of London, and several stops before he reached Taunton Christoph found himself alone in the compartment. All the while his excitement and nervousness grew.

The landscape going past the train window was beautiful. Peter Barrington had used the phrase 'this green and pleasant land' and it was exactly that, despite the long summer heat having turned the crop fields a golden-brown. It was almost harvest time. He had lived in the city for far too long. When he got back home he would have to make some changes; perhaps with the money from the radio show, he would buy them a house somewhere out of New York, in the countryside. It was so good to see the fields, the trees; they were antidotes to all that asphalt, all that glass.

The train sped on towards the south-west and when it arrived at Taunton station Christoph alighted, carrying his brown leather valise. For a moment he stood there without knowing where to go. The stationmaster, who happened to be inspecting the raised flowerbeds that decorated the down-line platform, directed him up over the footbridge to a smaller platform from where the local services left.

He had more than half an hour to spare before the train to the coast was due to leave. He sat on a bench in the sunshine and tried to write a letter to Anne, but did not get very far.

Dearest,
I cannot tell you how much I miss you and the children …

It began, but he did not know what words to use to describe what they meant to him, and the depth of his loneliness at this particular moment, so far from home. He knew, in any case, that he would be home not long after the letter could possibly reach Anne. He wished more than anything that he could speak to her, but the best that he could hope for was to send a telegram to her parents' house in Columbus. He wondered whether the town of Minehead even had a telegraph office.

A small locomotive with only two brown-liveried carriages behind it came into the platform and the few passengers at Taunton who were heading north-west climbed on board. There seemed to be mostly pasture land in the north of the county and the fields rolled by full of once-lush grass that was beginning to turn from green to pale brown in the heat. They reached Minehead in no time, coming into the town and onto the seafront having descended from the high escarpment through a deep cutting. The small station building with its tiled roof looked almost like a country cottage.

He was not quite ready to find the Lewis family's house, Eva's new home, just yet. He walked down towards the sandy beach, carrying his bag in one hand, his thin summer overcoat in the other, and followed a groyne far out to the receding water's edge. This part of the beach was almost deserted, but there were groups of holidaymakers further down the sands, in the distance a dozen or so children were paddling in the shallow waves. She could be any one of them.

With furrowed brows, Christoph asked himself again and again what he could do for Miriam now. He racked his brains, standing out there on the sands, but could think of nothing at all. There was no one that he could turn to for help, either in England or in Germany. There was no agency over here, it seemed, and no institution over there that would help him to find a single missing Jewish adult amongst so many. The focus was now on the children, the next generation, and on saving their lives where they could still be saved. He could think of no clever stratagem, no solution that would enable him to find Miriam, or discover what had happened to her.

If he had taken Miriam with him to New York, if they had had Eva there together, Miriam would have been safe but would they have been happy? He didn't think so. He had not loved her the way he had loved Ida, or Anne. If by some miracle Eva had made it to the safety of England, he reassured himself, there might even be a chance, however small, that Miriam might also be safe somewhere; perhaps hiding with friends in Germany, or abroad in a country where the darkness of National Socialism had not yet reached. But he knew she didn't have a wide circle of friends, and he remembered the letter she had written: '*I have tried and tried again, but the authorities will not give me a visa to leave Germany because I cannot find a country that will take me – let alone the money.*'

So absorbed was Christoph in his thoughts that he did not notice the tide had turned and was now lapping at his ankles. He walked back to the low wall lining the beach and spread out his wet shoes and socks to dry them in the late-afternoon sunshine.

Eva's address was written in Mrs Gold's neat hand on a folded sheet of paper embossed with the Jewish Refugees Committee's letterhead: *c/o Mr & Mrs Sidney Lewis, The Old*

Rectory, 3 Furze Hill, Minehead, Somerset. It would not be getting dark until after nine, but he should start looking for the house before too long if he wanted to find Eva before she fell asleep.

It felt good to sit on the wall in the sunshine, to watch the waves breaking silently on the sand, and to see children, whole families, playing in the water. As his nervousness and anticipation grew, so his legs began to feel heavier and heavier, as if they were rooted to the wall and, perhaps because of the sunshine beating down on his head, he became convinced that he would not be able to stand when he tried to get up. After another half an hour or so of sitting in this stupor-like state, he heaved himself forward with an enormous effort of will, and placed both feet on the dry sand, brushing them off one by one and then putting on his half-dry shoes.

Families were going home for their evening meal or to their guest houses and small hotels for the night. There was no hint of the hostility with Germany here; none of the clamour evident in London. Here everything seemed to be going on as it always had been: buckets and spades, and a penny for an ice cream in a cone. But Eva's arrival here meant something; it was that first drop of rain, that first eddy of leaves heralding a storm in Europe.

Was there much of a Jewish population here in this coastal town on the edge of a rural county? Christoph very much doubted it. Eva would be doubly out of place: exiled by a nation that had threatened her with death to another that met her with incomprehension. He could only imagine how her new classmates might make fun of her with her German accent and her foreign manners, especially now when hostilities were high between the two nations.

A newspaper vendor selling the evening edition of a paper called the *Western Daily Press* was crying his wares along the front and Christoph asked him if he knew where Furze Hill was. The man had a world-weary look about him, as if he was used to being asked for help with directions around his town by the day-trippers and tourists who came to Minehead.

'It's a bit of a ways from here,' he said in a thick Somerset burr. 'One of the roads out towards Exmoor.'

'What's the easiest way to get there?' Christoph asked.

'Walk as far as you can along the front in that direction,' the man said, pointing to his right down the coast, 'and then carry straight on until you get to the edge of town. It'll be the second or third road on the left running steeply up towards the moor. It's about a twenty-minute walk from here.'

Christoph's legs still felt heavy as he walked along the road, with the sea on his right. The sea air was beginning to cool as the sun, still high above the horizon, started its slow descent towards the water. It was almost six o'clock. He inhaled deeply, great lungfuls of the sweet-salt taste of the air, as he walked along the front and began to feel calmer, more excited and less frightened about meeting his daughter; he was, after all, the adult and Eva the child. She would not, could not, reject him after he had come all this way to find her.

Christoph tried to work out how Eva might feel when seeing him for the first time. Shock, surely; incomprehension, surprise, perhaps even a little relief amidst all of this darkness, that she wasn't alone in the world, that there was still someone looking out for her. He had no clear plan of what would happen after he met her; what he would do if she rejected him, or what he would do if she wanted him to take her with him. He had no idea yet.

At first he thought that he must have walked too far then realised that he had not walked far enough; Furze Hill was not really in the town but a steep road that formed one of its very outer limits. Large old houses towered above the road with high gardens to their backs; the sorts of houses in which successful merchants might once have lived, in peaceful seclusion away from the life of the lower town proper. There was no one out on the street, no children playing marbles or jacks on the asphalt, or couples out for an evening stroll. He had noticed in London that the English liked to eat their evening meal early. Seagulls shrieked and wheeled away out towards the sea.

The Old Rectory was on a section of the road where it levelled out before climbing steeply once again, free of houses now, up to the moor itself. Exmoor hung there behind the houses with its massive green weight, its grass and clumps of heather and bracken dappled here and there by the shadows of evening clouds that had come in off the sea.

The Old Rectory was a large white house built, Christoph thought, in the early nineteenth century. He sat on a low wall across the road from the front door, out of breath from the climb; his heart was pounding in his chest and it did not slow as he sat there. There was a light on in the room behind the main front window with its curtains drawn and another in an open window on the first floor. He could see no movement in the windows and, although the road was very quiet, he could hear no one talking in the house. Perhaps they were somewhere at the back dining quietly together.

Suddenly, the sound of a young girl's voice; the bright cadence of a child's words, followed by a delightful laugh. He could not hear what she had said, but he knew that it was her. The sounds were coming from the garden to the left of the house, hidden behind a high wooden fence. Now a boy's voice joined in, older. He must be the couple's son.

A tennis ball flew in an arc above the line of the fence, from right to left and back again. There was more laughter and the sound of running feet. 'Catch it, catch it,' the boy shouted excitedly.

Their game continued for some minutes, Christoph still sitting in the evening sunshine on the wall opposite the house. Sometimes the girl spoke, but her voice was quieter than the boy's and he could not make out what she was saying behind the heavy wooden fence. The ball, a white moon describing an arc against the darkening blue of the sky, flew back and forth between them and their feet moved in staccato bursts of softened sound across the grass.

Christoph was tired from his journey and the repetitive rhythms of their game had an almost hypnotic effect on him. He no longer felt afraid, lulled as he was by the heat and the tranquillity. He had entered a dream world on the edge of that small English coastal town. What he had tried to picture for so long was about to become real.

A soft thud and a bounce and the ball had come over the high fence, rolling across the road almost to Christoph's feet. He got up from the wall and bent down to his left to pick it up from the gutter. There were footsteps on the stone steps a few seconds later, and the high wooden gate opened.

There she was! There she *was*. His stomach gave a great lurch. Eva stood there, first looking down at the road to search for the ball and only noticing him when she looked up because she could not find it. He thought that his heart would stop as he began to cross the road. He held out the ball towards her and then dropped it wordlessly into her cupped hands.

'Sank you, Mister,' she said and smiled as she turned back to the gate behind her.

EPILOGUE

Frau Miriam Bernstein,
Litzmannstadt Ghetto
Poland
10th December 1941

Dear Miriam,

As you will see by the envelope, if this letter reaches you, I am sending this letter care of the International Committee of the Red Cross. The wife of my childhood friend, Matthias Walter, whose name you will remember and who I can no longer call any sort of friend at all, did me one last favour by finding out through her husband where you had been sent.

I was appalled and truly sorry to learn that you had been sent east to Łódź. Although I cannot begin to imagine the conditions there, I do hope that somehow you are managing in the quiet, dignified way that you always had and that I will never forget.

I wanted to tell you, now that I have finally found you, that I went to England and met Eva. She is really the sweetest, loveliest little girl.

I am not sure that she knew what to make of me, and I cannot say that she recognised me as her father, but we have struck up at least an occasional correspondence. I have asked her if she would like to join me, my wife and our children here in New York, but she has settled into her school in England and is adamant that she wants to stay there with her foster family until this infernal War has finally ended and she can be reunited with you.

I pray that that day will come soon.
With my love and abiding friendship,
Christoph

ACKNOWLEDGEMENTS

I am deeply grateful to Maggie Traugott, Evangelia Avloniti, Rukhsana Yasmin and, above all, to my agent Sharon Galant from Zeitgeist Media Group Literary Agency, whose advice on this book during its long development has been insightful and always correct.

I would like to thank those archivists and historians whose research has helped me to gain greater insight into the situation for Jewish families in Wuppertal during the Third Reich, particularly Frau Michaela Herrfurth at the Stadtarchiv, Wuppertal.

I am indebted beyond words to my friend Dr Britta Olényi von Husen and her family for locating my great-grandparents' and my great-aunt's graves in the Jewish cemetery up on the Weinberg in Wuppertal.

Finally, I would like to thank my family for giving me their encouragement and support along the way.

This book is for Henry, my cherished son.

READING GROUP QUESTIONS

- What explains Christoph's inaction or, at best, his timid attempts to help Miriam and his daughter?

- Why does Christoph not tell anyone about Miriam and the baby? Is it possible to keep a secret of this magnitude?

- Christoph tries to be as good a father as he can be to Leo and Mae. Is his love for them a kind of compensation for his actions towards Miriam and Eva?

- Christoph's stage name 'Rittersmann the Romantic' sounds especially ironic for a man who doesn't take responsibility for his actions. Does Christoph see any contradiction in this?

- Why was Matthias a Nazi sympathiser? What happened to him in order to make him a supporter that didn't happen to Christoph?

- Why does Miriam pine for Christoph? Why is she not more angry with him? She seems to be at the mercy of both Christoph and her family, why is this?

- Were the anti-Nazi protests in America and beyond successful? What else could have been done at that time?

- In the final chapters, Christoph sails back to Germany and England, a few weeks before war breaks out, to find Eva. Can this journey be considered his catharsis? Is he shedding the guilt and inaction of an entire decade to take on more responsibility?

The Paradise Ghetto

A powerful story of hope, love, and imagination, set against the horrific backdrop of the Holocaust.

Two Jewish girls, Julia and Suzanne, are rounded up in Nazi-occupied Netherlands and transported to a ghetto together. Although their world views are wildly different – Julia is jaded and bitter, Suzanne naïve and optimistic – they become each other's closest confidants as they experience the horrors of the journey to 'The Paradise Ghetto'.

The young women use a precious smuggled notebook to write a story, each contributing to an imaginary world that takes them away from the horrors of their lives. As the story unfolds it becomes the way they communicate their feelings to each other and come to terms with their pasts. But there comes a point when reality can no longer be held at bay. If the girls' names end up on the lists of deportees to Auschwitz there will be no return. Is there a chance of escaping that fate – and at what cost?

For more information about **Richard Aronowitz**
and other **Accent Press** titles
please visit

<u>www.accentpress.co.uk</u>